DOUBLE JEOPARDY

MARIE GOODACRE

PROLOGUE

It was after three in the morning, cold and dark. Why was I walking through the streets of Leicester city centre on a Thursday morning in January? My head ached dully, as though I had taken a knock I couldn't quite remember. I pulled my coat collar higher to shield my ears from the biting wind. They were almost numb already, and my toes were freezing. Why were they so cold?

In fact, in this light, this doesn't look like my coat, I'm sure I had on my black coat. I feel like I've lost a few hours. There is frost on the ground already, which crackles beneath my feet, still some dirty snow covered in footsteps and rubbish piled up along the edges of the pavements and buildings. It's too cold to snow I think, what does that mean - it needs to be cold to snow!? I was clearly wrong as I was about to discover. I am feeling a little drowsy.

I had gone to an apartment at Queen Street Quarter to discuss the accounts at the Cathedral, as the Dean had raised some queries and anomalies the previous week. That was at eight in the evening. After the meeting ended around midnight, we ordered a takeaway. Now, I can't shake the feeling that they suspect me.

Ed was pointing the finger, but then he is the accountant. Who had been there? I remember that cocky young upstart, he seemed to be pointing the finger at me, only seen him once or twice, didn't even catch his name Nicky maybe? Some kind of tech-genius I am told, so maybe he is hiding or transferring money. Freddie Stokes, he was there, whiter than white, probably never even driven through an amber traffic light in his life, his wife Elenor, can't say the same about her, she is well known in a couple of the local bars, a lot of the regulars know her well, intimately indeed. Freddie turns a blind eye as she is a decent mother, earns a good wage and causes him no hassle. He bumped into her in Latvia 12 years ago on a business trip, he bought her home with him to visit and she never left, paid for her visas, her applications, her everything, she was pregnant within a month of setting foot in the Country and begging him to marry her before their first child Alise was born in the March of that year. There was a tall, athletic black male there I'd never seen before, they called him Kay, or maybe 'K', he took control of the meeting, writing the notes. He was able to control 'Nicky' with ease when he started to get a bit big for his boots. He had offered me a lift home, but I told him I'd already got an Uber on the way, so didn't want to put him out. I take my phone out of my pocket, it was off, strange, so I power it back up and I continued to walk, did I book the Uber? Why am I still in town?

I opened the Uber app and scrolled to my bookings. Yes, a pick-up had been scheduled for 00:15 outside Athena, just by Queen Street. Then I noticed a red line through the pick-up time. Cancelled 00:02. Who cancelled that? It couldn't have been me it was the only way I had to get home.

I'd already turned Kay down at about 11pm and he hadn't mentioned it again. I was hoping things may get a bit clearer, but they are becoming more blurred. My brother was there, like peas in a pod, well looks wise, he is a little slimmer than me and we called him 'spot' as a kid, as he had a birthmark on his shoulder and that would tell us apart when we were small. There have always been issues between us, but generally stayed amicable. Our wives are friends.

There are still a few dwindlers from the clubs that are closing down, as I walked by the clock tower, I didn't really know where I was going, drunk kids, throwing up in the gutter I never did that, never found that appealing. I've always been a glass of wine with a meal and a whisky coffee before bed kind of man. Old before my time is what my friends always say.

I decided to leave the main road and head down a few side streets, hoping to get away from it all and gather my thoughts.
The snow is starting to fall again. I'm on Guildhall Lane, close to the entrance of the Museum, it's a bit grisly in there, the old cells with the prisoner in, I haven't been there for a while, and I might take the Ewan there. It's like I'm on auto-pilot. I can't remember where I have walked.

The street is cobbled and makes it uneasy to walk on especially with it being a bit icy, I didn't want to go over on my ankle. The street is quite narrow, I could probably touch both walls if I stretched out far enough. There is a distant hum of music still and chatter of people, nothing distinguishable now.

Where is my bag? Damn have I left it at the apartment? Or did someone hit me over the head and steal it, that would account for my headache?

These side streets are particularly dark at this time of year, the street lights are out, the Christmas lights have been put away. But I tread them knowingly, this has been my home town for many years. But the place has changed, and not for the better. Over the last 5 or so years there has been a noticeable decline, whatever time it is there are groups of swarthy looking males hanging around streets, watching, following people, especially young women. Knife carrying, drug using, drug dealing young men hanging around. The shops have slowly closed down, leaving Turkish Barbers, Vape Shops , takeaways and the odd High Street Store which has managed to make it through this far. I mean, who doesn't like a nice M&S jumper at Christmas, right?

The Highcross feels safer, but the city centre itself doesn't anymore, not even for a six-foot well-built man. It is unsettling when people surround you, speaking in words you do not understand. It makes me feel uneasy and on edge.

The side streets are quiet now. I can neither hear nor see any of the revellers.

As I begin to walk along Guildhall Lane towards the Cathedral and Richard The Third Museum, I wonder what I am doing. I still have to get home, no buses at this time of night, so I decide to book another Uber.

Our family have always had a connection with Churches and Cathedrals, our Mum, Lynda, cleaned at the Cathedral, what is formally called the Cathedral Church of St Martin, for over 15 years. Now my brother, our wives, and I all have some involvement there.

As I reach for my phone, I hear cracking behind me, as though someone is treading down the Lane on the frost. I turn around, no-one there, the snow is falling a little heavier now. I enter into St Martins East quickening my step, the cobbles are quite slippery with the icyness and the new thin white layer of snow, my feet sometimes glide rather than step. Maybe that's it, did I fall and hit my head somewhere? I again hear footsteps and a quick glance around I see no-one. If I can just make it into the gardens it's a bit brighter, I can either book an Uber or walk to Jubilee Square where there is a taxi rank. I'm sure I hear someone's heavy breathing but there is no-one around, is it in my head. I hear a noise like someone rapping the knocker on the heavy wooden door

I've just passed. I hear breathing all of a sudden, the steps get louder and I'm grabbed around the neck as I've half turned to see what's approaching, all I see is a ski mask, that's the last thing I see.

That's the last thing I will ever see. I offered my phone and my wallet. The wallet fell, it was grey, and it shouldn't have been grey. My phone was ringing, it was my wife. Then I felt something hard hit the side of my head, and a moment later the cold, soft snow pressed against my cheek. Somehow, I managed to scramble up and stumbled blindly around a corner.

, I can't see a lot, the Cathedral, I've got the keys haven't I? I fumble in my suit pocket, yes, let me get in there for safety. I smell the familiar smell, I'm in the Cathedral though I can't really see, then a sharp pain in my chest, am I having a heart attack? I stumble, I then feel a warmth running down my neck and chest, I feel the flagstones against my head and then I feel no more and then I feel no more.

The darkness has come.

Time, for me, has gone.

The snow still fell

CHAPTER 1

The Cathedral lay in silence, broken only by the click, flap, and echo of the cleaner's worn shoes. She walked more slowly than usual. On her way in, she had noticed that the metal gates at the Vaughan Porch entrance were not locked. They were closed, and no one would have known unless they had tried to pull or turn a key to open them.

This is what she had done, put the large key in and tried to turn it but it wouldn't. Instead, she opened them; the wooden door was locked.

Whoever locked up last night must have forgotten or was in a hurry to get out of the snow. She would have words with Derek when he arrived shortly. That must be it; it was too early for other staff to have arrived to open up for Morning Prayer. It was only just a little after seven o'clock.

She thought no more of it as she entered through the main public entrance. There was not much cleaning to do that morning; she had finished most of it the night before.

The air was cold; it carried the faint scent of polish and candle wax. The light slanted in through the stained-glass window in shards of red and blue, softening the edges of the nave.

As she walked further in, there was another smell, unfamiliar, metallic. The scream shattered the silence.

The snow was still falling at seven thirty-five when a call came into the Leicestershire Police switchboard reporting a body at the Cathedral. The call taker had struggled to make much sense of the caller, Susan Callaghan, the cleaner who had made the report.

Derek, who had taken over the call, was no more coherent and struggled with his own surname, possibly Maghee.

A response call-sign had been dispatched to the scene and reported back immediately that they required supervisory and an on-call DI, as there was indeed a dead body inside the nave of the Cathedral with a head injury. Ambulances were called as a matter of procedure; there was no doubt, however, he was deceased.

DS Katie Lounds stepped out of the drizzle and into Euston Street Police Station. The air inside was warm, tinged with stale coffee and the faint tang of disinfectant. Voices drifted down the corridor, low and purposeful.

She tugged her jacket straight and ran a hand through her short, dark hair, dampened by the rain. First impressions mattered. She had learned that long ago in the classroom, and the lesson had never left her: if you let them see the cracks, they would pull until you broke.

The moment she entered the room, a voice said, 'Lounds, we are thin on the ground. Uniform have two scene preservations and a jumper on the roof of the Lee Circle Carpark threatening all sorts. You're going to have to take those two and head down to the Cathedral, body, suspicious. I'll come down initially and then leave it with you.'

DS Katie Lounds had only just joined the Murder Team. She had only just moved to Leicestershire. She had been in Yorkshire for many years. She had needed some space, a change of scenery, just in the same way she did years before when she ended her teaching career and became a cop.

DI Grahame Keene, despite his name, didn't seem very keen well, not on her. He'd been the DI on this team for many years, but was now job-sharing with DI Rook. Too many years, if his lacklustre attitude was anything to go by, and something told her he wasn't a fan of women in rank either.

Katie had been a DI in West Yorkshire, but with no sideways move available, she had to accept a step down, taking orders and direction instead of giving them. Still, she told herself, it made life a little easier.

DI Keene, though, may not make it easier. He was a big man, solid, not muscle but solid, with a ruddy complexion and a tweed-style suit and a light blue shirt that looked like it was trying to escape his ample stomach, which was visible where the buttons stretched. He must be in his late fifties, she thought, but hadn't aged well. His hair was sparse, and the dye-job was poor.

It was not usual for a DS to be doing the groundwork, but needs must. With no staff and a murder to deal with, it was all hands on deck, as they say. Katie also liked to be hands-on; she believed she should never ask someone on the team to do something she wouldn't do herself.

'Those two,' who were DC Jane Reeves and DC Alan Briggs, went in one car. Keene took his own. Katie hadn't been introduced to Reeves yet, though only having been here a couple of weeks she had already had a run-in or three with Briggs. Keene had told her he wasn't easy. He'd been a DC for eighteen years and had been trying for DS and failed. He said that Briggs had expected when DS Marshall moved on, he would get the role, but instead, she had been transferred in, and he wasn't happy and wasn't about to let her think he was.

Katie went to the board to get the keys to a pool car, probably a ten-year-old Corsa or similar, but as so often in police stations, they were either out or waiting for collection for repair. No point looking around for some keys, so she grabbed her own from her desk and went back out into the rain in the car park.

Katie jumped back into her red Honda Civic and made her way into the city.

By the time DS Lounds arrived, uniformed officers had cordoned off the south entrance, Vaughan Porch. She had arrived about ten minutes after the others. She had not driven into the city centre in rush hour, with all the pedestrianised areas before. She ended up just leaving her car on Jubilee Square and walking. She ducked under the tape, her boots clicking against centuries-worn stone, and let her eyes adjust. It was cold. She removed her heavy coat, which was soaked, leaving her quite cold, and laid it on some pews, a cathedral full of police officers, and she shouldn't have to worry about her property.

A man lay sprawled across the flagstones, head tilted unnaturally against a carved step. Blood had soaked into the cracks of the stone, stark against the pale floor. A heavy silver candlestick rested inches from his outstretched hand. Why leave a piece of evidence like that?

Katie stopped a pace short. She was not the type to flinch, but something about the incongruity of it, the violence in a sacred place, made her swallow hard. The large, mostly empty building echoed with the sound of shoes on flagstones and wooden floors, and the low hum of voices coming from different parts of the Cathedral.

'ID found in his wallet,' a constable said quietly, passing her a clear evidence bag. Inside, a driver's licence bore the name Edward Blake.

Katie studied it, her green eyes narrowing. The face was ordinary, unremarkable, yet something about the neat haircut and the crisply pressed shirt suggested a man who cared about appearances.

They seemed to match up, the face on the licence and the distorted, bloodied face in front of her. Maybe a little chubbier now, but the licence was issued eight years ago, and we've all put on a little weight, she thought, especially through lockdown.

'I've PNC'd him, Sarge. His last address is in Knighton, as per his licence. He runs an accountancy business. The only record we have is that he reported a break-in at the business premises last year. He's insured on a blue BMW. I've checked around the area but can't see one.'

'Thank you, PC Elliott,' she said, looking at his epaulettes. 'It's James. Thank you, James. Time of discovery?' she asked.

'Seven-fifteen. Cleaner found him. Place was locked overnight. No sign of forced entry, but the metal gates over the door were unlocked.'

'Did the call not come in until seven thirty-five?'

'Yes, Sarge. The cleaner, Ms Callaghan, found him first. Then another member of staff, Derek wait, let me get this right Mkhize came in. They were both in shock. They saw the body and two ledgers lying nearby. They panicked. Susan insisted on making a cup of tea before she was calm enough to call the police, said she'd had a wobble. They're over there now, making tea for the boss.'

The officer gestured ahead to where seats were lined in front of the altar. A white lady in her fifties, looking very pale indeed, wearing a pinny and a brown dress, and an older black gentleman were standing, handing tea and cake, of course cake, to DI Keene.

Katie crouched, her cords brushing against the stone, and took in the scene carefully. No footprints in the blood. No sign of a struggle beyond the impact wound. Someone had come prepared. A matted bloody mess on the side of his head, but that didn't make sense. With all that blood pooling, Katie suspected when he was rolled, they would find further injuries.

She rose, brushing her hands together. 'Secure the entry points. I want a full log of everyone with keys to this place. And someone get me background on Edward Blake family, business, criminal history, please.'

Her voice carried, steady, clipped. Authority without needing to raise it.

'Katie, dear,' DC Briggs stepped forward, tugging at his tie to loosen it. Tall, broad, with a smirk that never seemed to leave his face, a bit creepy and a bit familiar, having only been on shift with her twice. She estimated him around fifty-five. He had quite a dominating personality, she had determined, watching him around colleagues. 'Looks open-and-shut. Lover's quarrel after a night out, robbery gone wrong, take your pick. Won't take long to put this one to bed.'

Katie glanced at him. 'We'll see. Nothing about this is open-and-shut.'

Katie was not sure about Briggs. He was confident, too confident, overbearing, but others seemed to like and respect him.

She turned back to the body, clenched her teeth. She was meticulous, always had been, and something here felt off. The cathedral, the candlestick, the stillness of the victim's expression all unsettled her.

It wasn't just murder. It was personal.

Katie scribbled her first notes into her book; she still liked her pocket book, unlike most officers who now used a mobile phone to take their notes neat, precise, almost artistic handwriting she always relied on when her thoughts threatened to scatter.

Behind her, the voices of her team hummed, but she tuned them out. She doubted herself often enough, but at a scene like this, instinct mattered. And her instinct told her this was only the beginning.

Katie spotted something and crouched down again, ignoring the creak in her knees. She wasn't the youngest officer in the room, but detail was detail, no matter how small. Blood had pooled neatly beneath the torso no spatters where you'd expect from a bludgeoning, or a stabbing. Which meant…

'He was moved,' she said quietly. 'At some point, but no bloody drag marks.'

A shadow fell over her shoulder. DI Grahame Keene, built like a worn-out bull, leaned in with a grunt. 'Body's a body, Lounds. Don't start with theories before we've even bagged him.' Had she said it that loud?

Katie kept her face neutral. She'd been on his team less than a month, and he still spoke to her like she was a trainee, even though she had once been the same rank as he. 'Just an observation, sir.'

He gave her a look that said drop it.

Another officer was already snapping photographs. DC Reeves stood further back. She was comforting Susan and Derek and sipping on her own cup of tea. She caught Katie's eye and gave a small shrug. She wasn't about to back her against Keene. Not yet.

Katie made her way over to where Susan and Derek were seated, still visibly shaking. 'Is it usual for the outer gates to be unlocked in the morning?'

'It is,' said Susan. 'I was about to have a go at Derek, assuming he'd forgotten to lock them last night, but then I found that there, I mean him,' she said, flicking her head over to the right where Blake lay, tears in her eyes.

'I locked up properly, ma'am. Always do. The good Lord's property's my priority.'

'Are there many sets of keys to the gates and doors?' she asked Derek.

'Oh yes, ma'am. Cleaners, vergers, choirmasters, charity leaders, the office staff, and there are a few spare sets in the office.'

They both looked terrified.

A voice broke the tension.

'Shall I get the CCTV from the square, Sarge?'

Katie looked up. The young female detective constable with dark hair tied back and a sharp expression was waiting by the entrance.

'Jane Reeves,' Briggs said casually. 'Eager one, that.'

Katie gave a nod. 'Yes, good idea. Pull everything you can. If no one already has, can you and one of your uniform colleagues have a walk around the perimeter, just see if there are any other potential crime scenes, in case it didn't take place here?'

'Yes, of course.'

'Come on, Katie, dear,' said a sneering Briggs. 'Don't start getting on your high horse on your first murder. He's in here, he's got a smashed-in head, and there's a candlestick about three feet away covered in blood.'

Katie raised her eyebrows. Reeves met her gaze, gave the faintest smile, and slipped out. A thread of connection, small but real.

'Derek, it was mentioned that when the body was found there were two church ledgers near him and the candlestick. When I arrived, there was just the candlestick.'

'Err, yes, sorry, ma'am. I had no idea why many of the accountants' books would be out in the nave. I didn't think it was linked, so I picked them up. They are on the pulpit, or did Susan? One of us did. I'm sorry; I don't remember.'

Katie gestured over to the constable called James and asked him to bag the ledgers, which he did.

'We will need to take both of your fingerprints for elimination. There are a lot of people who would have touched things around this scene, and we need to work quickly to rule out those who aren't involved.'

CHAPTER 2

Katie approached the body one last time and knelt down alongside. Something wasn't right. Despite Keene and Briggs knocking her, she was sure he wasn't killed here. But why break into a Cathedral to leave a body here? It's a lot more risky than leaving him where he was. Was there a message, a double cross, what was the killer suggesting?

She closed the notebook with a snap.

'Let's find out who wanted Mr Blake dead.'

Katie walked out of the Cathedral. The snowy rain had stopped, giving her time to get back to her car and stay dry. Some uniformed officers remained on scene. Reeves and Briggs had headed back already. A PC Parsons, to whom she had not been introduced, was remaining to direct SOCO and the Pathologist when they arrived. He, in turn, had been briefed by DI Keene. Her intention was to attend the brief and return to the Cathedral when SOCO were there.

The drive from the city should have taken seven or eight minutes, but the weather, a road closure, and an accident on Welford Road turned that journey into almost twenty.

The Major Crimes Unit's briefing room was already full. Laptops were open, jackets slung over chairs, and the quiet buzz of professionals waiting for orders filled the air. Katie paused in the doorway, feeling the familiar prickle of being an outsider. Half a dozen heads turned. Some nodded. Others offered flat, unreadable stares. She scanned the room for a seat among the uniformed and CID officers that filled it. DI Keene had seconded some extra personnel to assist in the initial stages.

Then a man rose from the front row, broad-shouldered, neatly pressed suit, the kind of presence that drew attention. His smile was practiced but disarming.

'Detective Sergeant Katie Lounds, is it?' His voice was smooth, Midlands lilt. 'Welcome to Leicester. DI Rook.'

They shook hands. His grip was firm, confident. He seemed more amiable than Keene. 'Not supposed to be in today, but called in on a rest day.'

Katie managed a polite smile. 'Good to meet you, Sir. Sorry I'm late.'

'You're not.' He gestured to the front. 'Shall we?'

Katie looked at him, bemused. 'You've been at the scene all morning, have all the notes. I thought it would be a good way to introduce you to the full team if you took the briefing.'

Katie stumbled over her words. She hadn't prepared for this. She had thought she would be briefed by the DI, but she knew she couldn't look weak and had to face it head-on. 'Of course.'

Katie walked to the board where photographs were already pinned: a man's body on stone flagging, taped-off pews, the vast shadows of the cathedral looming overhead. The crime scene stills were clinical, but the sheer wrongness of death in such a sacred place bled through them.

Katie drew in a breath. 'Male deceased. Found at seven-fifteen this morning by a cleaner, forty-seven, well dressed. ID suggests he's Edward Blake, but we'll confirm. Cause of death appears to be blunt force trauma, but the pooling of blood around the torso may reveal something else once the Pathologist and SOCO attend. The body was found inside Leicester Cathedral, in the nave.'

A murmur rippled around the room. One of the constables, barely older than a student, muttered something about sacrilege.

Katie let the silence stretch until it settled. Then she continued, 'this case will attract attention: press, public, and' she glanced at Briggs, who watched her steadily, 'internal. We do this by the book. No leaks, no shortcuts. One last thing: everyone we speak to who had access to the cathedral artifacts and ledgers, we need to get elimination prints from them, please.'

She saw a flicker in his eyes. Challenge? Amusement? Hard to tell.

Questions began. Alibis. Forensics. CCTV. Katie answered what she could, scribbled notes where she couldn't. She was meticulous, cautious with details, determined not to stumble. Every constable and detective in the room was weighing her authority against the man beside her, who had offered her the floor. She felt like it was a challenge to see if she would step up, rather than someone trying to undermine or show her up. She didn't feel like Rook would become an adversary, unlike Briggs or Keene.

Tasks were allocated. Officers had already been to Edward's address, the address on his licence. The occupants were a Mr and Mrs Babar, who said there was no one there called Blake. They had been renting the house for over three months, and the landlord was not Blake. They were tasked to go to his business address in Oadby.

When the briefing ended, chatter rose. Files closed, chairs scraped. Katie gathered her notes, conscious of the room emptying around her until only Keene lingered.

'Good briefing,' he said lightly. 'You've got a steady hand.'

'Thank you.'

'But.' He leaned a fraction closer, voice pitched for her alone. 'These people don't warm quickly. I've worked with them for a long time. If you want their trust, you'll need more than neat notes.'

Katie met his gaze. Green eyes cool, even though inside she felt the faint tug of doubt. 'I'm not here to win popularity contests, Sir. I'm here to solve murders.'

Keene smiled again, the kind of smile that didn't reach the eyes. 'Of course.'

By mid-afternoon, Katie was back at the Cathedral. Rain beaded on the ancient stone, sliding down gargoyles and weathered statues. Police tape fluttered in the breeze.

Inside, the vast nave was silent, save for the echo of her footsteps. Forensics were still at work. The place smelled of polish, candle wax, and something metallic beneath the faint residue of blood.

She stood where Blake had lain. Pews stretched away, the stained glass dim in the January afternoon gloom. A sacred place defiled.

'Sergeant.' A voice behind her. Dr Evans, the pathologist, lifting his mask. 'Time of death is roughly between three and six a.m. Blunt force, yes, but when we've moved him, he has a stab wound to the torso.' That explained the pooling blood.

Katie nodded, absorbing details. 'Anything to suggest positioning? Message?'

Evans hesitated. 'That… doesn't fit with blunt trauma. Or stabbing. Not personal enough.'

Senior SOCO Sebastian Bench approached her. She had met him once before, last week at a stabbing in a nightclub. 'As you probably suspected, Katie, he wasn't initially attacked in here, though probably was killed here. No blood spatter.'

'But he wasn't dragged in here either. No drag marks, no blood smears.' Katie noticed that the bloodied candlestick had already been bagged. That seemed too convenient. Why leave it there? Was it a red herring? If he hadn't been killed here, the killer wouldn't have come in to get a candlestick, kill him, then bring the body in and leave the weapon behind.

She stared at the stone flags, seeing it in her mind's eye: a man struck down, then posed. A puzzle piece she couldn't yet place.

Outside, the press had gathered, vultures with cameras. Katie ignored the shouts of questions as she crossed to her car. Sliding behind the wheel, she let herself breathe for a moment.

She loved the quiet of her car. A little box of stillness between the storm of the job. But today something felt… off.

Her hands paused on the steering wheel. The seat was closer to the dash than she ever left it.

A small thing. Trivial, maybe. She stared for a long time, the unease crawling up her spine.

She adjusted the seat, started the engine, and told herself it was nothing.

But the feeling followed her all the way back to the station. She tried to convince herself that she hadn't accidentally knocked the car seat forward when she pulled it to get her briefcase from the back seat.

Back in her temporary office, Katie began typing her initial report. The steady rhythm of the keys helped her relax. Facts, details, evidence; those were what she trusted far more than people.

A knock came at the door. Reeves, tall and dry-humoured, leaned in. 'Settling in, then?'

'Trying to,' Katie replied, with a faint smile.

'Briggs can be a lot. Don't underestimate him.'

Katie looked up from the screen. 'I don't underestimate anyone, Jane. Learned that the hard way.'

For now, Blake was her focus.

Tasks were in hand, enquiries into Edward Blake underway. Locating his address and next of kin foremost in everyone's mind. When you got to know a victim, it was easier to ID the killer. She hoped that would be the case here too. There would be a scene left on the Cathedral and surrounding streets overnight as there was still SOCO work to be done; the falling darkness impeded.

DI Rook popped his head around the door. 'Good job, Katie. Impromptu briefing, thought I'd see if you would jump in. Keene not happy I'd asked you to do it, but he is rarely happy, unless he has a greasy cake in his hand. Late shift's doing their enquiries. Go home, get some rest, and I'll see you bright and early.'

'Thanks, boss.'

'Call me Duncan when there aren't any troops about.'

Katie got back into her car and drove back to her house that she was renting in a little village outside Great Glen.

She got out of her car, walked across the muddy path to the front door, and let herself in.

Katie had decided when she moved she didn't want to be in the hustle and bustle of a town. She wanted some peace, far enough away from work but in easy travelling distance. This was ideal. She had found a little two-bed (well, one and a half) barn conversion on a farm. Quiet, no passing traffic, no random door knockers. It was a modern rebuild, made to look vintage but with all the mod cons. She had loved it the moment she saw it, and said yes to renting immediately.

It had an open-plan kitchen and living room. The Aga kept the whole of the ground floor warm, even when the weather dipped below zero as it had the last couple of weeks.

It had minimal furniture provided, and a cream palette. Katie had bought a lot of her own stuff to personalise it. She had only been there a couple of months but made it feel like home.

She put her bag down, took her coat off, and hung it by the door. She removed her walking boots, put her mobile on the lounge table, and walked into the kitchen.

Monty strolled in from the bedroom into the kitchen to greet her. He was her four-year-old longhaired tortoiseshell cat. She had only recently started letting him out when she was home, but she still wasn't comfortable with him being outside while she was at work, so the litter tray remained. She had asked the landlady about fitting a cat flap but had yet to hear back.

'Hello, boy,' she whispered as he jogged up to her and started rubbing his orange and brown fur around her legs. 'I know, I know, hold on, which flavour tonight, beef or tuna?' He head-butted the blue pack. 'Tuna it is then.'

It was getting late. She was very tired, so picked a Chinese ready meal out of the fridge, popped it into the microwave, and went off to the toilet to get changed.

It was only eight thirty, but she was tired and decided to put on her pyjamas. She heard a ping as she came out of the bathroom. She didn't think the seven minutes for the food was up and then noticed her phone flashing on the table. Unknown number.

She frowned and opened the message.

A photograph. Grainy, blurred by rain, but unmistakable. Her. Leaving the Cathedral a few hours earlier.

Her pulse hammered. The phone slipped slightly in her grip. Someone had been there. Watching. Close enough to capture her in frame.

Katie closed the message, locked her phone, and forced her hands to be still.

Not now. Not yet. She would deal with it later; she was too hungry. But she knew now that she hadn't accidentally knocked the car seat forward.

CHAPTER 3

Katie was awoken by her phone alarm. It was 07:30. She should already have been up. She felt like a zombie. Quite appropriate, seeing as that was the song title of her alarm.

First things first, she fed Monty, gave him a few more strokes, and kissed him on the head while making herself a travel mug of coffee to wake up. 'I'll leave you some extra chicken, baby. Mummy doesn't know when she'll be home tonight.'

The A6 was busy at this time. She wished she had reset her alarm and been on her way about half an hour earlier, but it was what it was. Traffic crawled as she reached Asda and up to the Racecourse Roundabout. The sky was a dull grey-white, looking like it was going to snow again.

At the roundabout, she made a quick decision: straight on or left. She chose straight on. As she passed the petrol station on London Road, she wondered if she had made the right choice. Fighting the traffic up to Victoria Park, she took a left at the roundabout and headed up towards the station, passing The Range and making a mental note to pop in for some picture frames on her way home.

She pulled into the station thirty-five minutes later. It should have taken twenty. She was still early, but wanted an even earlier start. There was no dedicated staff parking, so she reversed into a space at the far end of the car park.

She made her way into the changing rooms, hung up her coat, and put her bag into her locker. She changed out of her walking boots into her flats and made her way up the stairs into the offices of the station.

The briefing room was set up as an incident room now, with photos and evidence on boards and a timeline developing.

Jane Reeves was already at her desk, and Briggs was at the water machine, eyeing her up. Katie sat down with her coffee and flicked through the pages of her pocketbook. White male, forty-seven, identified by driving licence as Edward Blake. Blunt force trauma to the back of the head, stab wound to the torso. Not killed in the Cathedral, it appeared, but moved there and posed. Where had he been killed? Why? By whom? There was little information gleaned so far about Edward Blake, an accountant whose address had been occupied by an Asian family for three months, who had never heard of him.

'Sarge.' DC Reeves approached, notebook in hand, expression steady but guarded. She was younger than Katie by at least a decade and had the habit of standing as if braced for impact.

'Neighbours at Edward's licence address confirm he lived there until about six months ago, when he just upped and left. They said his wife, Pam, disappeared too.'

'Post mortem is to be done this afternoon. They've confirmed what we know about the injuries: head wound and stab to the torso. One of each, but the rest will be done later.'

'Oh, Sarge. SOCO email has just come through. Now the snow has started to melt, someone has reported an area of blood staining on some cobblestones on St Martins East, a walkway not too far from the Cathedral. Uniform have been sent, as well as SOCO.'

'Don't know if it's a coincidence, but a missing person report was made in the early hours of this morning. Uniform weren't sent; they were all too busy. An adult male, a man by the name of Michael Blake, was reported missing by his wife. No idea if he's related to Edward.'

Katie's pen paused over the page. 'Missing?'

'Yes. She said he hadn't come home by midnight. She called him but got no answer. She contacted the station around four a.m., worried. Logged it as a domestic concern a fully grown man doesn't have to tell his wife where he is, and it wasn't as if he had a habit of going off for a day or two. But unusual for his phone to be off.'

Katie clicked her pen shut. Too quick to worry?

'If she hasn't been spoken to in person yet, bring her in carefully. I'll speak with her,' she said.

'No press, not yet. And I want every camera near that Cathedral pulled, every keyholder for the place accounted for.'

Reeves nodded, already on her phone. Reliable, she thought. Unshowy but thorough. She preferred her to Briggs, who was leaning against the water cooler, hands in pockets.

'Easy job,' Briggs muttered as she passed him. 'Domestic, guaranteed. My money says the wife's got blood on her hands.'

Katie stopped. 'You've already decided that?'

'Wife reports him missing, body turns up a few hours later. Nine times out of ten, it's the spouse,' he shrugged. 'Saves us the legwork.'

Katie met his eyes, cool and steady. 'And one time out of ten, it isn't. That's why we do the work.'

She paused, then added, 'We have a dead Edward Blake, and she has a missing Michael Blake.'

'What's the wife's name?' asked Briggs.

'Helen. Helen Blake,' she responded. She momentarily noticed a flicker across Briggs's face.

'Ah, okay. The wife couldn't get that wrong and kill the wrong brother.'

'No, but someone else could,' thought Katie.

Rook had asked her and DC Brenton to attend the post mortem. The drive from the station to the infirmary was straightforward   five minutes. Parking was not easy. They had to go into the visitors' car park and pay, even in a police car. Brenton was driving. He navigated the queue and the barriers. They parked after zigzagging their way around the flat car park, no space to be found, and ended up in the multi-storey, collecting their ticket. They parked as close to the Windsor Building as possible and made their way through the white, disinfected clinical corridors. They had both spent many days and nights in these corridors as PCs on bedwatches with prisoners or victims of assaults, trying not to fall asleep as the lights dimmed.

The mortuary was quiet except for the low hum of the ventilation system. The fluorescent lights buzzed overhead, draining all colour from the room. Katie stood at the foot of the steel table, arms folded, notebook tucked under her elbow.

They had both already donned their gowns and wellies, but Brenton stood behind the glass in the viewing area. If he wanted a career in the murder team, he would have to learn to deal with dead bodies and the post mortem procedure, Katie thought. It's important to get down there, to look, and to ask questions, to have things explained in plain English instead of the medical speak the reports would quote.

Dr Malik, the pathologist on duty, pulled back his gloves with a snap. 'Cause of death is the stab wound. There was also blunt force trauma to the skull   single, decisive blow. No defensive wounds. He didn't see it coming, which would have disabled him enough to be an easy target to stab. The single deep stab wound to the torso is the cause of death.'

Katie nodded. That much she had expected. 'How was he stabbed?'

'From behind, with a good-length knife. It came all the way through. You couldn't see it when he was clothed, as the thick woolly coat disguised the knife entry point.'

Malik had already used the saw to remove the top of the skull and removed the brain. They had missed the Y incision into the body and the removal of the organs, much to Katie's annoyance. She was fascinated by the procedure.

'But,' Malik continued, glancing at his notes, 'there's a complication. His dental records don't match those of Edward Blake, unless, of course, Edward had some work done abroad, which is very likely nowadays.'

Katie frowned. Malik looked up, expression grave. 'Sorry to throw a spanner. You'd best see if he had any dental work done. We have some other checks to do, but we don't currently have access to his medical records. Computer says no   well, for the time being. Hopefully it will say yes later, when the techie has looked into the doctor's system. This deceased has had knee surgery many years ago.' Malik pointed out some damage to the inside of the right knee, and a small, faint scar, almost hidden in dark hair, to the skin just underneath the knee.

For a long moment, Katie just stared. Her pen rolled slowly between her fingers.

Less than half an hour after Katie returned to the station, Reeves knocked on her door to say Helen was in an interview room on the ground floor. Katie made her way downstairs and into the large room at the end of Corridor One.

Sat at the table was a female in her forties, about five foot six, slim build, in light blue jeans and a blue argyle sweater. A red coat was pulled around her. It was casual clothing, but she looked well-preened. Katie was unsure why she was clutching her coat   the interview rooms were by far the hottest place in the station, no aircon, just heat.

Helen Blake then removed her coat and sat back down, folding it neatly across her lap. She was attractive in a tired sort of way, hair pulled back too tightly, skin pale beneath expertly applied makeup. Her hands were clasped together, knuckles white.

Katie slid into the chair opposite her. 'Mrs Blake. Thank you for coming in.'

Before Katie could speak, and a little too eagerly for her liking, Helen looked up sharply. Her eyes were red-rimmed but dry.

'What's happened? You've found him, haven't you? Is he dead?'

Katie kept her voice even. 'Why would you think that, Mrs Blake?'

'It's Helen. Call me Helen.'

'Helen, why would you think that?'

'I heard about a body being found in the Cathedral. Michael went to a meeting in town last night. We do volunteer work at the Cathedral   he does the accounts. He was supposed to be home by midnight. We have an Uber Family Account, so myself, Michael, and our son can use it. I saw he booked an Uber for twelve fifteen, but it was cancelled just past midnight. I'd fallen asleep, but I woke around three thirty, needed the toilet, saw that notification, and tried to call him, but no answer.'

For a moment, Helen's face crumpled   not into grief, but into something stranger, harder to read. Shock, perhaps. Guilt.

'Helen, yes, we have had a body found in the Cathedral, but the ID on him shows it to be someone else, that I cannot disclose at this time as his family have not been notified.'

She pressed her hands against her mouth, shook her head, and whispered, 'No. Not Michael.'

Katie's pen stilled over her notebook. Helen had said Michael again. Why was she convinced this was Michael?

'Helen, can you tell us about the meeting Michael was going to?'

'But you said it's not Michael,' she said quizzically.

'Your husband is still missing, and we need to take details to try and help us find him.'

Katie was acutely aware of the surname, but didn't want to directly ask if they had a relative called Edward not subtle enough.

'He was going to Derek Mkhize's apartment on Queen Street, I think. There have been a number of discrepancies showing in the Cathedral ledgers over the last six months or so. About eight thousand pounds has been moved and unaccounted for. Derek is a verger. He's no accountant, but he tries. Michael used to help with the accounts; his brother used to be an accountant also in the family business. I don't know all the people that were going to be there. It's not like him, not to come home.'

Which was different from her initial call to the police, when she said he sometimes went off for a day or two.

CHAPTER 4

Katie noticed the use of the phrase 'Michael used to help with the accounts', which made her wonder. 'Helen, when you said Michael used to help with the accounts, did he stop doing that recently?'

'No, no, he still did it now and then.'

Hmm. Not 'does it'. She was assuming this was Michael. Why?

'What was Michael wearing when he left yesterday?'

'Black suit, maybe a cream argyle sweater. We both love argyle, we love it up there. We spend at least two weekends there a year, so quiet.'

'Helen, if we can stick to the description,' another voice interjected.

Helen looked agitated. 'He had on his full-length black Ede and Ravenscroft coat. It cost him almost a thousand pounds. I told him off at the time; he said we were strapped, and I got mine and Ewan's winter coats from a charity shop because he didn't want me spending too much. It made him look like an undertaker, and now look, he's dead and will need one himself.'

'Helen, the male we found was not wearing that distinctive coat.'

Katie's phone buzzed in her pocket. She took it out. It read 'call me'. It was Rook.

'Excuse me, one minute, I have to take a call.' She opened the door and DC Briggs almost fell in. 'Can you take over here, please?' she said, wondering why he had pressed himself against the door of the interview room. This was the only interview room where the spy hole did not give you a view of the people sitting around the table.

Briggs composed himself and walked in. Helen looked up and then down, a flicker of recognition passing over her face.

Rook informed Katie that the coroner's secretary had called. The system was back up and running and Edward had no reports of any knee surgery. She relayed her conversation with Helen to Rook and discussed the next move. This was unusual; some might say unethical, but something was not sitting right with either of them.

As she walked back into the room, Helen was still sitting in the same chair, staring at the table. Briggs was sitting across the room. 'She hasn't said a thing to me,' he said, trying not to meet her eyes.

'Do you have a recent photograph of your husband, Helen, please? I think you were asked to bring a photo rather than a mobile phone image.'

'Yes, yes,' she said, fumbling in her handbag. She pulled out a small picture and handed it to Katie. 'That was taken on a funfair ride in Bridlington last summer. That's Ewan, our son, with him. It's the most recent paper photograph we have. No one prints photos nowadays, do they?'

She reminded Katie that they did, and that she still needed to nip into The Range on the way home.

The photo showed a male in his late forties, slick black hair with flecks of grey and a kindly face. A face Katie had seen before, not in a photograph, but in the flesh.

This was getting very confusing. The body had the ID of Edward Blake, the photograph on the licence matched the person on the flagstones, but the Bridlington photo also showed the same person. However, the scar and the dental records did not match him.

'Has Michael ever had an operation?'

'What's that got to do with anything?'

'Can you just answer the question, please?'

'Erm, not that I know of. I've been with him for almost twenty years, not been in hospital for any operation in that time.'

Katie opened the folder she had in her briefcase and removed a photograph of the deceased male. It was from the mortuary; he looked asleep but pale.

'Helen, I understand this isn't going to be easy. I'm going to ask you to look at something. I don't want to cause you any more distress, but could you look at this photo and tell me if it's Michael?'

'Is this going to be the body? The body from the Cathedral?' she whispered.

'Yes it is. If you don't want to look, you don't have to. We will have to ask someone to attend the mortuary to make a formal identification, but for now a photo is what we have.'

'Ok, show me.'

Katie pulled the folder to the middle of the desk and turned it to face Helen. Briggs was intently looking at her. She opened the folder and showed the ten by eight inch colour photograph of the face and shoulder of the dead man.

Helen's eyes flickered towards Briggs momentarily. There didn't seem to be any emotion. She cupped her hands over her eyes. There were no tears. 'That's not Michael.'

'Not Michael? You're certain?' Katie asked softly.

Helen's eyes flickered up. 'Of course I'm certain. I'm his wife.'

But something in the way she said it sharp, defensive made Katie's senses twitch. 'But this is the man in the photograph you just gave me.'

'No, that's Michael's twin brother, Ed Blake, in your photo. Oh God, where is Mike?'

'Mrs Blake, we'll need to go over Michael's recent movements. His work, his friends, anything unusual lately. Was there anyone who might have wanted to harm him?'

Helen swallowed. Her lips parted, then closed again. 'But he's only missing. You think someone… killed him too?'

Katie held her gaze. She wasn't going to challenge her. 'We're treating this death as suspicious, yes. Is it just a coincidence that your husband is missing? We may need to be concerned for his safety. If they were both at a meeting about a potential fraud, we will also need to try and contact anyone else who was at the meeting. They may be in danger.' Katie knew Helen wasn't telling the truth, but didn't know why.

Helen's eyes flickered downward. For just an instant, Katie saw relief before the grief mask slid back into place. Relief, as though something she feared had been solved for her.

Katie's pen scratched across the paper, her notes neat and precise.

Something here was badly wrong. Why was Helen confirming thc dead man to be her brother-in-law when it was her husband?

'Helen, do you have the contact details for any of Edward's family? We will need to notify them that the body has been identified as his.'

Helen flinched. Her face drained. That wasn't what she was expecting. What a mess this was becoming, she thought.

'I don't think I have them here. If I find them, I'll give them a call.'

'No, I think that's something we need to do now. Please, can you check your phone?'

Helen very reluctantly scrolled through her contact list. She slowed as she reached the P's, her finger hovering over 'Pam B.' She pressed down as though trying to delete it.

Katie grabbed the phone. 'What are you doing?'

'Oh, oh, sorry. I was just trying to copy it and paste it over to you.'

'Who is this Pam?'

'That's his wife. She lives in Blaby. They are separated and have been for some time.'

'Helen, we would like to offer you a family liaison officer to stay with you.'

'No, I'm fine. Please just find Michael, will you?'

Katie showed Helen out of the station, telling her she would be in touch later in the day if they found any trace of Michael. Which she knew they wouldn't, as they already had him, cold, in a fridge at the LRI.

'Alan, what do you think of her? We know the deceased is not Edward. Why is she saying it is? What did she say when you were alone with her? She knows that is Michael, and there was no emotion.' Briggs stopped. He looked a little caught off guard, but maybe that was just Katie's discrimination, as she had decided she didn't like him from the moment they met.

'She didn't say anything. I tried to get her to tell me about her husband, any conversations she had recently, was he concerned about anything. She didn't say a dickie bird, just stared at the bloody table. Didn't seem too bothered thinking her husband has carked it.'

'Well she wouldn't, as she couldn't have known at that point that he was dead, could she? Unless she did it.'

Katie wondered, 'Do you think he was having an affair? Is that why she wasn't upset, or maybe she was, and this was fortuitous?'

'Your thought process is twisted, love,' he said, avoiding eye contact and wandering ahead of her.

Katie wanted Briggs out of the way. Something about him was unsettling, and it wasn't just her prejudice. She spoke with Rook, who tasked him with speaking to Derek Mkhize about the meeting, the allegations, and what he knew about Michael and Helen, and then to Susan to confirm who had the keys.

Rook then called the other officers who were not already tasked into a briefing, where Katie explained the autopsy, the scarring, and the dental work, and Helen identifying the deceased as her brother-in-law Edward, when all the medical pointed to it being someone else, and from Helen's photo, being Michael Blake. Everyone was silent; they were as bemused as she was.

Lounds decided she would pay a visit to Pamela. It was easy enough to locate her. She had called in a domestic with Edward about two months ago, when she moved out to a rental flat in Blaby and he had found her there. He wasn't arrested, no crime report; she just wanted him removed, which is why this address didn't show up on PNC for him. She didn't want to call in advance in case she avoided her, but kept the number as a fail-safe in case the address was wrong.

Katie drove into the village, past the field where the fair used to stand. Now it just floods. More and more houses were being built around this area, ruining village life, creating more use on the services and infrastructure. There were protests when the council granted permission for the fourth housing development in six months in the area. But, as we all know, money talks, not the constituents' views, she thought.

It was starting to snow again. Just a light spattering was on the ground, being turned to mush very quickly with the cars and heavy footfall. She turned into Cross Street and could see the shops ahead. Above one of the charity shops was Pamela's flat.

She managed to pull outside the coffee shop in a parking spot and noted she had thirty minutes. She was in her own car, not a marked car, and couldn't afford a ticket or to be towed. She found her way through an alleyway to the rear of the shops and climbed the stairs to the flat.

She knocked on the door and a few more red paint chips fluttered onto the ground with the snow. Within a few seconds the door was answered by a female, late thirties, mixed race, about five foot eight, bigger build than her, wearing pink pyjamas with white hearts.

'I don't buy things from the door, love, sorry,' the female tried to close the door. Katie put her foot in and pulled out her warrant card.

'Sorry, I'm not selling anything. DC Katie Lounds, Leicestershire Police. I'm looking for Pamela Blake.'

'That's me, innit.'

'Perfect. Could I come in and have a word with you?'

'What about?'

'Your husband Edward.'

'Ed? We're estranged. What the fuck has he done?'

'Nothing as far as we can tell. Can I have a word in private, please?'

Pamela relented, let Katie in, and led her through to a small living room. The threadbare carpets and mishmash of furniture looked like it had come from the charity shop below. Once inside, Pamela eased considerably.

'Sorry, call me Pam. I was just making a brew. Let me get you one. How'd you like it, lovey?'

Now she didn't think Katie was a salesperson. She had a calm voice with a slight twang Katie couldn't place.

'White, strong, with one sugar please, Pam.'

'Take a seat. Move Clyde if he's in your way.'

Katie looked at the sofa. Clyde was a St Bernard, definitely in the way, but with a little encouragement he jumped off and onto the rug. Katie was pleased. She always kept a lint roller in her car. She'd pick another one of those up from The Range too.

She looked around the flat, assuming it was a stopgap. Either a short break from her husband or a stepping-stone to getting her own place if they finally split. The room was damp, with mould starting to form around the window, and it had a musty smell. The back wall and corner were cluttered: two yoga mats, a large heraldic shield, a dog bed, a folding e-bike, an array of kettles in boxes, a rolled-up well-used duvet, empty demijohns, and that was just the front layer.

The tea arrived. Pam sat down on the pink chair, Katie on the green settee, and Clyde on the tartan rug.

'When did you last see Ed?' Katie asked.

'When your lot got rid of him, he found me here a few weeks ago. Must have followed me from work or summat. He said he just wanted a chat, some advice,' Pam replied. She paused, and Katie let the silence linger. When Pam still said nothing, Katie prompted, 'Advice about what?'

'His brother, Mick, twin brother. When they were kids, the only difference was a birthmark on their shoulder. Ed was called Spot for years because of it. Their mum made them wear vest tops a lot so people could tell them apart.'

Katie scribbled notes as Pam spoke, while Clyde drooled all over her shoe.

'What did he want advice on?'

'He said he had evidence that Helen had been cheating on Mike and wanted to know if I thought he should tell him, confront Helen, or do nothing.'

'Did he say who she was having an affair with?'

'Nah.'

'Do you know what he chose to do?'

'He said he was going to speak to Helen. Didn't want to upset his brother and ruin his marriage if it wasn't as he thought, even if they weren't best buddies.'

'And did he? Speak with Helen, I mean?'

'I don't know. I haven't asked him to ask.'

'Why did you call the police?'

'He asked me if I would speak to Michael. I said no, it's none of my business. He started shouting, I pushed him out, and he was banging on the door and forced his way back in. He had been drinking, and he scared me. I left him because he hit me and threatened me. It had been going on for some time. He became distant, and I wondered if he was seeing someone else. I asked him, and he punched me and left.'

'Do you have children?'

'No. I've always wanted kids, but Ed can't have them. Something to do with when he was a kid, he said, an operation. I was disappointed but learned to live with it. I've always been a big part of Ewan's life as his aunty, which is nice.'

'Do you know where he lives at the moment?'

'No, he lives with his mum. Don't know where she is; they moved not so long ago.'

Katie put her hand into her handbag, pulled out her warrant card holder, and pulled a business card from inside.

'Thank you for your time and the tea. If you do hear from Edward, could you let me know, please, and ask him to call me too?'

'Yeah, no problem. It's been nice having some adult company for once, no disrespect to Clyde,' she said, laughing.

'Oh, one last thing,' said Katie as she walked to the door and noticed all the dog hair on her trousers. 'Have you noticed anything unusual about Edward? Upset, angry, scared?'

Katie leaned down and patted Clyde's big head as he continued to rub his fur on her trousers, then stepped out the door, back into the cold, blustery snow, and headed back to the office.

'He was a bit concerned about Michael saying he was defrauding the Cathedral, but that's all,' Pam added.

While Katie was at Pam's, DC Briggs made his way over to Queen Street. He had already spoken to Derek, who was eager to help and would have tea and homemade coffee and walnut cake waiting for him.

There was no worry about parking at Queen Street Quarter. Derek buzzed Briggs into their private car park and then into the flats. This was very salubrious for a sixty-year-old semi-retired verger. He had done a bit of checking on his way; a one-bedroom studio apartment would set you back £900+ per month. The facility had its own gym, residents' lounge, and more.

The flat door was opened. The smell of warm coffee cake filled the air and immediately made Briggs' stomach rumble.

'I'll get you a good sized slice, Sir,' said Derek.

The flat was spotless, clinical white, minimally but adequately furnished. It was a long single-storey flat, and you could see from the living room through the kitchen into the bedroom.

'Lovely accommodation, Derek.'

'Thank you. I get a good private pension after being injured when I worked on the docks years ago,' he explained.

Derek sat on one of the white leather chairs and Briggs took the other. The coffee cake sat between them on the table.

'Derek, did you recognise the dead man that you found?'

'No, sir, he was face down. We didn't turn him; didn't think we should. It was clear he was dead, with all the blood. Once I'd had a quick look and seen the mess, I took Susan over to the seating area for a cup of tea to calm our nerves. Susan's a nervous sort; she was the one who called the police.'

'I understand that you had a meeting here last night about missing money from the Cathedral's accounts. Could you tell me about that, please? What was being said? Were there any suspects?'

'I can do that. Freddie and his wife Elenor. A young lad I only know as Nick; Enoch, we call him Kay. James Ratten, a warden, and Michael and Edward Blake. They are brothers, accountants   well Edward is. Michael worked for him for a while, but he just wasn't that good. Michael had been doing the accounts while Edward was having respite from a terrible bout of flu, he said. I hadn't seen Edward for a good few months, but we'd emailed him the details and he just turned up.'

Briggs paused to take it in. 'Did Michael and Edward come together?'

'No, Sir. They don't get on. They used to, but when I last saw them a couple of months ago they were arguing, barely spoke a word to each other. Michael had been doing our books. Edward accused him of cooking them, skimming funds and trying to make it look like it was his company. Michael wasn't happy. He said, 'All you do is accuse me. You have no evidence of this, and you have no evidence of the other thing either. ''

Michael had a taxi booked for midnight. Ed took his phone from him and cancelled it. He said he wasn't leaving until they got to the bottom of the missing money.

They had all calmed down. As they went through the books, it became clear that a number of entries showed money being removed or paid to a firm for building work. The handwriting was different from usual, and no such work had been carried out on the Cathedral by those companies for quite some time.

'What happened to the ledgers after the meeting?' Briggs asked.

'I don't know who took them. Maybe Ed; he was one of the last to leave. Next time I saw them, they were on the nave floor with blood trickling onto them.'

Briggs also collected a list of all the people who had keys to the Cathedral before taking his leave, and took another piece of coffee and walnut cake wrapped in a napkin.

'Oh, before you go, Michael's coat is still here. Strange, as he put one on before he left. But this one, expensive coat, boss, even I know that, has his wallet in the pocket. His wife rang me at about five am asking if he had left, as he hasn't come home.'

'Had he left by then?'

'Yes, he came back in with Ed just after midnight. He was irate. Nick gave him a tablet, he said it was a herbal calming relief tablet, and he settled down. They all left by 2 am after we had a takeaway delivered.'

Briggs took the coat, checked the pockets. There was only the wallet, as Derek had said.

When he returned to the station, he logged the property in the register and recorded it under the incident related to the recovery. He had already been through the wallet but found nothing of particular interest: a driving licence, a photo of him with Helen and their son, a library card, a Lloyds Bank credit card, a Sainsbury's reward card, and £120 in cash   four £20 notes, three £10 notes, and two £5 notes.

They convened in the briefing room and gave their updates. Still no contact from Edward. Had Pam or Helen not contacted him, or had they, and for some reason he was laying low? Why had Pam and Helen not contacted each other? There was no suggestion they had fallen out, just their husbands.

DI Keene burst out of his office, his stomach still bursting out of his shirt, into the briefing room.

'Not solved it yet, Lounds?'

'Not yet, Sir. Enquiries are creating more questions than answers.'

'Go home then, you lot. Fresh eyes in the morning.'

The team started to drift from the room.

Katie stood in the station car park, staring at her Honda Civic. Something was wrong.

She always reversed in straight, careful, as she did lining up desks back in her teaching days. But tonight the car was skewed, jutting into the white line as if someone else had slotted it in a hurry. That wasn't her.

She unlocked it, slid into the driver's seat, and froze. Her reversing mirror was moved.

She adjusted it automatically, hand trembling. A faint, greasy fingerprint smeared the inside of the windscreen. Not hers. But the car was locked.

'Long day?' Reeves's voice carried across the car park. She gave a tired grin, coffee cup in hand.

Katie forced a nod. 'Yeah. Just need some sleep.'

She didn't notice her hesitation. She wanted to mention these things to Jane, but thought she would sound ridiculous.

She sat for a few minutes while the car heater cleared the screen. It had started to frost over again. She pulled out of the station, up around the one-way system, and out onto London Road. The traffic light changed to green, and she went straight ahead, only realising she had again driven by The Range. The drive home was uneventful, with the usual amount of traffic for that time of night.

When she got home, she double-locked the door, fed Monty, cleaned out his litter tray, made herself some pizza, and sat on the sofa with a glass of rosé, eyes fixed on the black screen of her phone. Minutes later, it buzzed with a new message.

A photo. Her, in the car park. Taken from the shadows, just an hour before. Reeves in the background.

CHAPTER 5

Bright and early the next morning, everyone was gathering in the briefing room. Updates were shared by the team.

There had been a visit to Edward's accountancy business in Oadby, where they spoke to an office manager named Charlotte. She confirmed that Michael Blake had worked there until about six weeks ago. There had been a shortfall in the bank, and the VAT returns had not been completed correctly, which would likely have been flagged by HMRC as potential fraud if one of the junior staff had not spotted it. Ed had blamed Michael and dismissed him.

Michael wasn't a natural numbers man; he had been given the job by Ed as he had disappointed the family, never having a stable job, racking up debt, going from job to job, and he tried to do the brotherly thing. Michael had popped into the office about six weeks ago, and he and Ed had had a blazing row. She hadn't seen Michael since.

She had also told them that last Tuesday, Ed had mentioned he was taking a week off and he hadn't been to work since then. Charlotte had tried to call him, but his phone was off.

SOCO had confirmed that on St Martins East, there was a small patch of blood. The item had appeared under the melted snow, about thirty metres from the Cathedral's main entrance. There were no results yet to confirm whether it matched the body. CCTV footage was being checked, but coverage in the area was limited.

Helen Blake had identified the coat found at Derek's as belonging to Michael. She maintained that she had not seen Edward for months and was unaware that he had attended the meeting. Helen had also provided bank statements showing several large withdrawals from their joint account over the past couple of months, which she claimed had nothing to do with her. She said it was more likely Michael because of his debts and whatever other trouble he had gotten himself into.

Freddie and Elenor had been spoken to, as had Enoch 'Kay' Mkhize, and everything checked out. Freddie and Elenor had walked home as they also lived in the centre, and CCTV showed them in their accommodation by 00:50 and not leaving again. Kay had slept on his dad's sofa. He also confirmed that 'Nick', whom he had only seen a few times at the Cathedral, had given Michael a 'Kalms' tablet after his argument with Edward.

The Cathedral key sets were all accounted for from personnel who should have them, but one set was missing from within the Cathedral Office.

Lots of progress was being made, but not as to why Michael had been killed, Helen still maintaining it was Edward (she had not yet been disillusioned of that, and the press had not yet been given the deceased's name). Edward was 'missing' after being known to have a number of arguments with his brother over the last few weeks. It appeared he, Edward, the assumed victim, could be the number one suspect. Had he told Michael about suspecting Helen cheating on him?

Katie was sitting in her office when Keene came in to give her a ribbing about not making any progress and then left again, heading to a huddle with Briggs in the corridor.

Jane Reeves knocked on the door. 'We've had a phone call from Edward Blake. He says he's heard that his brother is dead and wants answers. He wouldn't say where he got the information, but he's on his way to the station now and he's not happy.'

Helen must have called him, Katie thought. She was the only person, apart from the officers, who had seen the crime scene or the photographs.

'Thanks, Jane. Let me know when he arrives. You can come in for the interview if you want.'

'Thank you. Don't you want Briggs? He's more experienced.'

'No, Jane. I want you in there with me. Another female intuition might help; I've felt mine has been a little off recently.'

'When he arrives, take a statement from him about his relationship with his brother, what happened on the night of the meeting, and where he has been since. I think we will go to the mortuary to ID the body if he is willing. After that, I'll make the calls to arrange it.'

Katie sat at her desk, papers laid out in neat, deliberate rows. Michael Blake's life was far less polished than his brother's. While Edward ran a successful accountancy consultancy with an impressive list of clients, Michael's record told a different story: brief spells in accounting, a series of failed ventures, and debts that never seemed to go away.

Michael had once worked for Edward's company, but was sacked six weeks ago.

Katie tapped her pen against the desk. Whatever had gone wrong between the brothers, it hadn't been small.

Katie called the mortuary and was put through to Dr Malik's assistant. It was confirmed they could attend for a viewing at 12 noon, despite it being a Saturday, for which she was grateful.

She got a call to say Edward had arrived, had given a brief statement, was very vague, and he was angry, so she went down to see him.

It was as if she was looking at the body on the flagstones: more alive, but still.

'You lot haven't even bothered to tell me my brother has been murdered and you're chasing me around like I'm a suspect, snooping into my business and my marriage, what the '

'Mr Blake, if you can calm down. We have tried to call you, as has your wife and your office manager. No one could get in touch with you. We haven't yet had anyone officially identify the body as Michael. Would you be willing to accompany us to the mortuary to do that?'

'I suppose so, as long as it doesn't take too long.' That was a strange reaction; he may have fallen out with his brother, but identifying a family member at a morgue was a big thing, and he just seemed completely detached and uninterested.

'Who told you that your brother was dead? Nothing has been released to the press.' No answer.

Reeves got them a pool car and drove. Katie was in the front passenger seat, Edward in the rear. 'Mr Blake, who told you that Michael had been murdered?' Again, he did not reply. 'Mr Blake?'

'I'm not under arrest; I don't have to tell you anything.'

'We are trying to figure out who killed him. I would have hoped close family members would want to find that out too.'

He slumped in his seat and under his breath, barely audible, muttered 'Huh, close.' He remained silent for the rest of the drive.

The three of them walked through the hospital corridors, the sharp smell of disinfectant lingering around every corner. People sat slumped in chairs, leaned wearily against walls, or lay on trolleys lining the hallways. A couple of young children were sliding down the corridor on their knees until a very embarrassed father hurried over to pull them up. 'Sorry, ma'am,' he muttered.

Neither Jane nor Katie was in uniform, yet Katie always felt she somehow looked like a police officer.

They turned into the corridor where the mortuary is and were greeted by Anika Parmar, a mortuary technician. Katie explained that they were here for a viewing.

They were taken into a small rectangular room with a pane of glass, covered by a curtain. Edward walked halfway along the glass and stood there, hands in pockets, no emotion on his face. The curtains were opened and Anika asked if they were ready. She pulled down the cloth covering the face of the body, revealing it.

The head had been cleaned up so there were no signs of the blood or blunt force trauma, which had left a crater in the side of the head. His eyes had been closed, and the sheet rested neck level so the incisions were not plain to see. The skin was pale. It would be kind to say he just looked asleep, but he didn't.

Katie and Jane just watched Edward. Nothing, not a flicker. 'Mr Blake, can you identify that person, please?'

'That person? That person is my brother Michael Andrew Blake. Yes. Can we go now?'

Katie thanked Anika and told Edward that they needed to return to the station and get his ID statement done. He reluctantly agreed, and they walked back to the car, in silence.

Before they got into the car, Edward said he needed to make a phone call. He walked a few metres away from them and appeared to be having a heated conversation with someone, then got back into the car and they drove back to Euston Street.

Upon arrival, they asked Edward to wait in the front office while they secured an interview room. When Jane returned ten minutes later, he was standing with James Parker, a well-known and rather awkward local solicitor who never looked particularly pleased to be anywhere. If the Mr Men character Mr Grumpy had a real-life counterpart, it would be James Parker.

Jane showed them both through into the interview room where Katie was waiting to take the statement, with a list of questions.

'Ah, DC Katie Lounds,' said Parker.
'Detective Sergeant,' said Katie.
'My apologies. I thought Briggs was your boss last time I saw you with him.'

Another snotty man who didn't believe women were capable of having men work under them, she thought.

Edward completed the proforma ID statement.

'I just have a few questions for you to assist us with our enquiries,' she began.

'Read out the list of questions, and I'll discuss with my client whether he wishes to answer them,' Parker interjected sharply.

'Mr Parker, your client is not under arrest. He is assisting us as a witness to the murder of his brother, but his or your continued obstructiveness will increase our suspicion that he may be involved in some way.'

'Read the questions, or we are leaving. As you said, he is not under arrest, he does not have to stay here.'

Katie opened her notebook.

'We would like to know about the meeting on Wednesday night, the allegations made about you or Michael tampering with the Cathedral accounts.'

'Why did you leave without your coat? Michael was wearing it when he was found.'
'Could you show me your driving licence?'

'Where have you been for the last few days? Not your wife, your mum, your business have been able to contact you.'

Edward was getting increasingly annoyed. He was struggling to contain it. Fidgeting about in his chair, he tried to stand up a couple of times, and Parker put a hand on his shoulder.

'Who do you think would want to kill Michael?' 'Tell me about your relationship with Edward and Helen.'

'Could it be possible that, as he was wearing your coat and you are twins, that you were the intended victim, Mr Blake?'

That last question made Edward spring to his feet, his face flushed with anger.

'Me? Who would want to kill me? What are you suggesting? Are you saying I should watch my back? What are you going to do about that?'

'We can arrange for a family liaison officer to stay with you for a few days,' she replied calmly. 'They'll help you through this while we investigate your brother's murder, and it will also offer you some additional protection, if you'd like.'

'I don't need your protection. Some namby pamby goody two-shoes looking after me? No thanks.' He refused to sit down, arms folded, jaw set like stone.

'You've had your statement,' he snapped. 'Michael's death is a tragedy, but dragging me in here is harassment.'

'We've not dragged you in here. You wanted to speak with us. We asked you to come in and you did.'

'My brother is dead, and you parade me around like a criminal?'

'No-one is parading you around like a criminal or anything else. You are being asked a few questions about what your brother was doing a few hours before he was murdered. It is purely routine to try to find out what happened to him. Don't you want us to find out, Edward?'

'Purely routine? How many times have I seen that on TV? Purely routine is an excuse to say 'we think you're the killer and want you to slip up. ''

DC Reeves leaned back in her chair, expression unreadable. 'We're just trying to establish some facts, Mr Blake.'

'The fact,' Edward shot back, 'is that you misidentified him in the first place. Typical incompetence.'

Katie kept her tone even and controlled.

'The facts, Mr Blake, are these: the body was wearing your coat and had your wallet and driving licence, complete with your photograph. You and your brother are twins. His wife identified the body as you. We established quite quickly through medical records that it wasn't you, but your sister-in-law is still insisting otherwise. At no point did we release any confirmation regarding the identity of the deceased.'

She paused, watching his reaction.

'So, when did you last see your brother, Mr Blake? Either at the flat that day or before then?'

Edward's eyes flicked to her, cool and dismissive. 'Michael ran his own life. I'm not his keeper.'

She noted the tightness around his jaw, the way his hands clenched when she pressed for detail. He was hiding something, though whether it was grief or guilt, she couldn't yet tell.

His solicitor murmured something about cooperation, but Edward cut him off. 'No more questions. Unless you're charging me, we're finished.'

Katie watched from the corridor as the pair swept out. She didn't miss the brief, heated exchange Edward had with the solicitor on the steps, words she couldn't hear, but the anger was plain. A man with nothing to hide didn't need to shout like that.

Back in the office, Katie laid out her observations: the body had likely been moved to the Cathedral, inconsistencies in Helen's testimony, Edward's evasions.

Keene gave a dismissive snort. 'The wife's grieving, the brother's angry. You're seeing ghosts where there aren't any. He probably cut through the cathedral grounds and got caught up in a mugging gone wrong. Let's not turn this into Shakespeare.'

Briggs added, smooth as ever, 'He's right, Katie. Sometimes the simplest answer is the right one.'

Katie bit her lip and snapped her notebook shut. They weren't listening. Not yet.

It was late when she reached her car. The rain had washed the streets clean, streetlamps glimmering in the puddles. She checked the driver's seat instinctively. Still where she'd left it.

She exhaled. Maybe she had imagined it before.

Night had fallen by the time Katie reached her street. The rain had stopped, leaving the pavement slick under the streetlights. She went to unlock her front door and froze.

It was ajar. Just an inch. But she always checked it. Always.

Her hand tightened on her torch as she stepped inside, every nerve on edge. The hall was quiet. The kitchen undisturbed. She checked each room, her breath held tight in her throat.

Nothing. Monty, where was Monty? She didn't care about her belongings, but Monty. Frantically, she searched room to room, calling his name. He didn't appear, not even at the shake of his biscuit tin. At last, she found him crouched behind the day bed in her second bedroom cum study.

Scooping him up, she carried him downstairs, holding him close before setting down his food. As he ate, she wondered what he had seen, who he had seen. If only he could talk. Though, knowing Monty, his only words would probably be 'feed me.'

Had the person who opened the door been inside? Monty wouldn't have hidden if someone had merely unlocked it. What had they touched? Had they taken anything, or left something behind?

She locked up, rechecked doors and windows, and went to bed. It took a while to drift off, with everything running through her mind, and still more than a little on edge.

CHAPTER 6

The following morning, rain streaked the windows of the station, echoing Katie's mood. She poured over the notes from neighbours and colleagues of Michael Blake, each statement pieced together like an incomplete jigsaw.

Michael had grown secretive in the weeks leading up to his death. Meetings appeared and vanished without explanation, and there were sudden withdrawals from their bank account, large sums taken out over several days. Someone had known something he didn't want revealed. Someone who had power over him.

Katie scribbled in her notebook, each word deliberate, and her green eyes scanning for a pattern. Her thoughts were interrupted by Keene's gravelly voice.

'Still chasing shadows, Lounds?' he asked, hands on hips. 'Mugging. End of story. You're wasting hours on what-ifs.'

Briggs, playing the diplomat, intervened. 'Boss, perhaps we let DS Lounds follow this lead. If nothing comes of it, fine. But a little diligence won't hurt.'

Katie forced herself to nod, though anger simmered beneath her calm exterior. What was he playing at? She caught Reeves watching her from across the room, a quiet signal of solidarity. It was small, but it mattered.

What was it they were missing? Who wanted Michael, or even Edward killing, if it were a case of mistaken identity? Who had either of them wronged so badly that someone thought death was the answer? Or were they right? Was it a mugging? He may have stumbled into the Cathedral, a sanctuary, but someone followed in there and finished him off. But that doesn't explain how the ledgers got back in there if Michael didn't take them. Someone from the meeting was in the Cathedral. Or why they planted the candlestick why bother? If one of them, Michael or Edward, had been stealing from the funds, why kill him? Why not out him, report him to the police? Or was one of them getting close to the truth of who did it?

There were more questions than answers.

Katie knocked on the brown wooden door that was at an angle, opposite the Blakes' house. A dog was barking inside, a smallish one she guessed. The door opened, and a tan-coloured cockapoo leapt out onto the doorstep.

'Percy, don't be jumping up, lady darling,' said the occupant as she stepped out.
'That's okay,' replied Katie. 'I love dogs. Cockapoo?'

'Yes, he is, Percy. He's only eighteen months old. He's still very puppyish.'

'I am Detective Sergeant Lounds. We have been doing some house-to-house speaking to neighbours to see if they saw or heard anything suspicious in the last few days in relation to your neighbours over there,' she explained, pointing at the Blakes' house.

'Yes, I know. I saw the police cars there the last couple of days. No-one is saying what happened. Please come in, have a coffee. I've just baked some cookies. I was going to take some to Evelyn over there, but she went out about twenty minutes ago, in a red car I haven't seen before maybe a taxi.'

Katie stepped over the threshold into the hallway; she could smell the freshly baked cookies. The hallway was nicely decorated, muted pastel colours, a dresser on the left, and some family photos on the wall on the right. She could see the photos included the lady who let her in, a man, probably her husband, and photos of two girls, ranging from them being babies up to about eighteen or twenty years old.

'I'm so sorry, so rude. I didn't even introduce myself. Jennifer Barnes-Halford. Call me Jenny. Come through into the kitchen.'

Jenny trotted across to the kettle, which she reboiled quickly. She took some fresh cookies from the oven and put them on a plate, indicating for Katie to sit on a stool at the kitchen island. She sat down; Percy was jumping up, probably at the smell of the cookies.

The kitchen was quite large. The colour palette wasn't as quiet as the hallway. It was purple purple everywhere: toaster, fridge, freezer, cup holders, all purple.

Jenny placed a purple coaster on the marble countertop, and onto that she placed a large purple coffee mug. There was a purple sugar bowl next to it. Katie helped herself to a large spoonful and gratefully took one of the cookies. It melted in her mouth macadamia and white chocolate, perfect.

'So, the Blakes,' she sat down on a chair on the opposite side of the table. 'Percy!'

Percy got down and was given his own cookie, which he took off, tail wagging, into his basket.

'I don't want you to get the wrong impression. I'm not one to gossip.'

'No, of course not, Jenny. It's helpful to have vigilant people in the community.'

'Well, Helen has a couple of gentlemen callers. Sometimes I get a bit mixed up because her husband looks very much like his brother. Occasionally Michael drives away, and then ten minutes later the other one arrives. There's also an older man, a bit scruffier but trying to look professional and younger. Sometimes she doesn't want to let him in, and other times she pulls him through the door.'

'Can you describe this second man, Jenny?'

'He's older than her. Well, he looks it. He looks in his late fifties but keeps himself in shape. He's bigger than my Owen, about six foot one, dark brown hair, a bit stocky.'

'Does he arrive or leave in a vehicle?'

'I've seen him once in a grey car, left it at the top of the street. I'm not very good with cars, but usually he walks down from Willoughby Road, so he is either local or parks on the main road. If he's up to no good with Helen, maybe he doesn't want his car to be seen on people's cameras.'

'What makes you think he's up to no good with Helen?'

'Oh love, sometimes she lets him in, and then within minutes the front bedroom curtains are drawn. Doesn't matter whether it's day or night. I don't suspect she's taking him up there for a cup of coffee,' she said with a glint in her eye.

'Do you know Helen well?'

'Not that well,' she paused and rolled her eyes as though trying to remember something. 'I've done cleaning for her once or twice. My husband's business is a carpet cleaning company, so I've cleaned her carpets. Downstairs is immaculate. I've not been upstairs.'

'What about Michael?'

'He argued quite a bit with his brother. They argued on the front a week or so ago. Edward said something about 'it all coming out if you have 'and 'ruining the business. 'I couldn't hear much more as Malcolm next door turned on his strimmer.'

'Well, Jenny,' said Katie, getting down off the chair and giving Percy a pat on the head, 'you've been really helpful, and I appreciate your time and the coffee and cookie.'

'You are welcome. If you need to know anything else, just call me.' She scribbled her number on a paper bag, slid another cookie inside, and handed it to Katie. She was not supposed to accept gifts from members of the public, but coffee and biscuits while talking to a witness did not really count as a gift just hospitality.

Jenny showed her to the door. 'Thanks again,' Katie said. Katie left the house and walked down the drive to where her car was parked. She got into her car and put on her seatbelt. Out of the corner of her eye, she saw Jenny back at the window watching. 'Well, she is the sort of neighbour you need sometimes. Doesn't miss much,' she thought.

She had a quick look around. A few houses had camera doorbells, and another couple had CCTV. She noted the numbers in case they needed to check later.

The drive back to the station was uneventful; the traffic, for once, was light.

Katie sat at her desk, the glow from her computer screen illuminating her face in the otherwise dim office. She scrolled through Michael Blake's financial records once more, searching for anything she might have missed. A series of payments caught her eye transfers to an unfamiliar account. The amounts were small enough to seem routine, yet frequent enough to suggest that someone had leverage over him.

The team meeting was tense. Keene, leaning back in his chair, his large cumbersome frame dominating the room, shot her a glare.

'Lounds, I don't know what fantasy world you're living in. Rumours aren't our job. Stick to the facts.'

Briggs interjected smoothly, 'Boss, perhaps we give DS Lounds some leeway. If it leads nowhere, we can regroup. Sometimes rumours are the key because they are true.'

Katie clenched her jaw but stayed silent. She wondered why Briggs was backing her again.

Keene's scepticism was more than professional doubt; it was the wariness of a man unused to women in authority. Even though he was senior to her, she was not someone he could boss around, he was discovering. She didn't crumble under his demands and put-downs like some might.

Reeves, standing at the side, offered a subtle nod, a quiet reinforcement. Katie's shoulders relaxed slightly. She was not entirely alone.

Katie confided in Reeves that evening, away from the others.

'I keep thinking I'm missing something, that I'm failing him… failing everyone,' she admitted quietly.

Reeves placed a reassuring hand on her shoulder. 'You're meticulous. You notice things others do not. Do not let Keene's attitude or the chaos get to you. You're doing this right.'

Katie drew a steadying breath. Reeves' quiet confidence helped to centre her. She knew she could rely on someone, even if the rest of the station questioned her judgment.

'I did notice there didn't seem to be a mobile phone at the scene. No-one is without their phone nowadays.'

'Nothing was booked into property?'

'Not a phone. No.'

By nightfall, Katie followed a lead to a secluded warehouse tied to Michael's financial dealings.

She made her way to some units off Illiffe Road in Oadby.

Rain slicked the pavement, making each step cautious. There were a few lights on in some buildings, no cars around. She weaved her way through to a unit she had seen noted. It looked abandoned.

Every instinct screamed that she was being watched. She should have really known better than to come out into the middle of nowhere, on her own, given what had been happening to her.

A shadow shifted near a doorway across the lot. Katie froze, heart hammering. Whoever was out there knew she was coming. The stalker? The killer? Someone closer?

Her flashlight cut a narrow path across the lot, the beam catching nothing but dripping water and discarded crates. Yet the feeling of being observed was suffocating.

Katie's whole body twinged. She was meticulous. She doubted herself. However, she had seen patterns others missed. She would find the truth.

From the shadows, someone smiled faintly.

The building was not accessible, no CCTV around it. She would return in the daylight and get Brenton to do some digging.

CHAPTER 7

The next morning, Katie got some of the team together, minus Briggs, who had reported sick. She wasn't sure if she imagined herself relaxing a little, knowing he wasn't there.

They had had a forensic report to confirm that the blood on St Martins East was Michael Blake's blood, so that was where the attack started. There was no CCTV of use around there, and she had asked the PC to widen the parameter of the trawl.

DC Reeves had asked Helen to attend for another chat, but she had refused.

'I think we need to bring Helen in, as a suspect, not a witness this time.'

'How do you link her to the murder?' DI Rook asked.

'I'm not thinking of arresting her for murder, but for perverting the course of justice for now deliberately wrongly identifying the victim and sending us off in the wrong direction. If she were involved, she may want us to think it was Edward, as that would distance her from motive.'

DI Rook accompanied Katie to the arrest. He picked her up in the car park, and they made their way down Aylestone Road, through Glen Parva and Blaby, and along Winchester Road into Countesthorpe, where Helen and Michael lived. Speed humps that hadn't been there before caught her attention.

They passed the school where Katie had taught many years ago. It had been a good school and a strong start to her career. As they drove by, she noticed that the High School that used to stand next to it was gone. The memories were a mixture of the good and the terrible, some of which still lingered with her to this day.

'What do you make of all this, boss? Sorry, Duncan?' she asked.

'I really don't know yet. There's a reason why she identifies the wrong brother. When you've been married to a twin for eighteen years, you know them subtle differences. Michael was clearly having money problems. Edward wasn't a fan of his brother. Is it a family feud? Was it to do with the Cathedral funds?'

'It's as though leaving him in the Cathedral was significant, maybe. He wasn't initially attacked there, so why not just leave him where he fell?'

Although Katie had worked in the village for several years, she did not know where Stonelea was. Their sat nav took them past the school, where Winchester Road became Willoughby Road, right on the edge of the village. Stonelea was a side street, a cul-de-sac lined mostly with detached properties, almost certainly carrying a high price tag. She did a quick Google search of recent sales the houses were between £400,000 and £600,000.

'How does a failed accountant and a part-time nursery nurse afford to live here?' she wondered aloud.

They slowed down to pull up to the correct house. As they got out of the car, Katie briefly saw what appeared to be two shadowy figures in the window. One turned and looked out, obviously saw Katie and DI Rook, and they both disappeared from view. There was a grey saloon-type car parked a few doors down without a rear registration plate. She noted this. She didn't know why, but something wasn't right. It was old, a bit decrepit, and looked out of place in this street.

Katie knocked on the door of the very smart, detached, double-fronted, double-garaged property. It took a couple of minutes before the door was opened.

'Hello Helen, can we come in, please?'

'I told you this morning I don't want to talk to you again. I'll call my solicitor if you keep pestering me.'

'I can understand you are upset, given the grave circumstances,' said Rook.

'Can we come in, please, or do you want us to do this on the doorstep? Looks like a nice area. Wouldn't want the whole village gossiping.'

With an audible sigh, she stepped aside and let them in, at the same time taking a good look outside. As the door shut, Helen showed them into the living room.

This house was a very nice property, three, maybe four bedrooms. She could see a through lounge/diner, which led into a large conservatory. The décor was fresh and clean. The furniture was matching and spotless. The creams and browns made a very elegant living room. There were a number of photographs on the wall and the mantelpiece, each immaculately lined up with the next as though someone with OCD had been in charge. There were a lot of photos of a young boy at different stages Ewan and family pictures, but also pictures where it appeared to be Helen, Ewan, and Edward.

'Helen, who stood at the window with you as we pulled up?'

'Er… no-one. Nothing to do with you.'

A sudden roar of a car engine caught their attention. Both Katie and Rook moved through the main reception room to the large front window and saw a grey saloon speeding out of the cul-de-sac.

'Who was that?' Rook asked.

Katie said nothing, her eyes following the car as it disappeared from view.

'Okay, Helen, it's 09:48 hours, and I'm arresting you on suspicion of perverting the course of justice. You do not have to say anything, but it may harm your defence if you do not mention, when questioned, something you later rely on in court.'

'What… what the fuck? My husband's dea…'

'Let me finish. If you do not mention, when questioned, something you later rely on in court, and anything you do say may be used in evidence,' Katie told her the grounds for her arrest.

On the table, she saw an iPad and a pink iPhone and collected them both.

'What are you doing? You can't arrest me. You can't take my phone. Have you got a search warrant?'

'We don't need one. You've been arrested at this address. We have the right to search for evidence.'

'Evidence of what?'

'Evidence of the offence you've been arrested for and any related offences.'

Once they had checked that the house was secure, they took Helen to the police car. They didn't handcuff her, to give her some dignity, and they were in a plain car.

Once they arrived at Euston Street, they led her through to the chute and placed her in a holding cell. After she was booked in, Custody contacted the DSCC to arrange a duty solicitor for Helen. Now all they could do was wait, hoping it was not James Parker.

The mobile phone and iPad were handed to a triage-trained officer, who immediately requested recent contacts, messages, and call logs.

'See if you can access the doorbell footage. I want to know who was at the address when we arrived, please.'

'Yes, Sarge,' came the reply.

There were a number of messages, which seemed to be coded, not full sentences. Helen's responses were terse and frightened. There was a call at 08:35, which lasted eight minutes, then the final text at 08:54 that read, 'Here, let me in.'

Her musing was interrupted by PC Owen walking up to her.

'Sarge, Blake's solicitor is here.'

'Thanks, Rick. Jane, are you sitting in on this interview? Rook has a multi-agency meeting to go to.'

'Yes, happy to,' replied Reeves.

Reeves collected the solicitor and went into the interview room.

'Sarge, this is Eric Balogan from Worthy and Co.'

Greetings were exchanged, and Balogan was provided with the custody record and a written disclosure outlining the reasons for Helen's arrest.

'Are you intending to make a decision today on my client, or will she be bailed?' he asked.

'We intend to bail her with conditions,' replied Katie.

'Thank you,' he said.

Reeves fetched Helen from her cell and left her with Balogan for their consultation. They were both given cups of custody coffee, which, in Katie's opinion, was unlike any other.

About twenty minutes later, Balogan emerged, confirming they were ready to go.

There were no windows in the interview room, but they had managed to get the biggest one. It was warm, despite being below zero outside. It was always warm and, as always, smelt of those who appeared to have an aversion to soap and hot water.

DS Lounds opened: 'Mrs Blake, we've confirmed the man found in the Cathedral was not your brother-in-law but your husband, which you've already been told.'

Helen's hands tightened in her lap. 'Michael?'

'You know that. When I arrested you, you said, quote, 'What, what the fuck? My husband's dead, 'before stopping yourself.' Silence.

'Do you remember saying that?'

'Why did you say that?' Silence. Katie studied her carefully.

'Raises questions, doesn't it? When we first spoke, and subsequently, when being shown a photograph, you confirmed that it was Edward why?'

Helen's lips parted and then pressed shut again. Her gaze fell to the table. 'I… I must have been confused. They looked so alike.'

'That doesn't explain why you said Michael on arrest. Up to this point you have sworn it's Edward even after looking at the photo.'

Katie didn't move. She let the silence stretch, a tactic she'd learned long ago. Silence always cracked something.

Finally, Helen whispered, 'Edward was… involved. He was always around. Always interfering. He made my life hell.'

'How so?' Katie prompted.

Helen's chin lifted, her tone sharper now. 'Michael and I had our problems, normal marital problems. However, Edward enjoyed it. He would come round uninvited. He would undermine me in front of Michael, say things, insinuate things. He liked watching me squirm.'

'What things would he say and insinuate?'

'That I had picked the wrong twin. If I had wanted a go-getter, a money earner, someone good in bed, I should have had him.'

Katie wrote in neat, deliberate strokes. Demeaning. Puts his brother down in front of him.

'Did Edward ever threaten you?' she asked.

Helen hesitated. 'Not in so many words. However, I always felt he could. And Michael never stopped him. It was as if Edward had some hold over him.

Katie closed her notebook slowly. 'You didn't like him.'

Helen's eyes glittered. 'I hated him.'

'There seems to be a number of photos displayed in your house of yourself, Ewan and Edward. No Michael. That tells a different story, not someone you hate.'

'Ewan's uncle. Sometimes Edward would come round and offer to take Ewan out for the day or for a weekend. Ewan wouldn't go without me.'

'But why display the photographs?' She had no answer. At least not one she wanted to share.

Katie thought she would go for the jugular and just ask the question she wanted to, outright. She centred herself in her chair, looking directly at Helen.

'Did you want to kill Edward, or have him killed, and kill the wrong brother?' Katie suggested, watching Helen for any reaction.

'No, of course not. I wouldn't get that wrong. I wouldn't pick the...' She stopped herself, realising what she had almost said contradicted what she had just claimed. 'I mean, I wouldn't want to kill either of them. I loved Michael and I put up with Edward.'

'Having seen pictures of Michael and Edward next to each other, and seeing both in the flesh granted, one alive and one not I can see the differences. So why, after so many years of marriage, can you not tell the brothers apart?'

'I was in shock. In the photo, he the body, Michael was wearing Edward's coat. I didn't want to look too closely at the picture. I saw the coat, I assumed...'

'Do you think it's reasonable to assume someone is dead based on what coat they are wearing?'

'No, no, of course not. But now the shock has passed, I can see. Back then I was running on adrenaline. Does it really matter? He's dead, he's dead.' Helen covered her eyes with her hands and sobbed dry sobs, with no tears.

'Yes, Mrs Blake, it does matter. In our opinion, if we can tell them apart from a photo, so can you after twenty years. By telling us it was your husband, it could lead us away from the truth. Is that what you wanted?'

'No.'

'Is there something you don't want us to find out, some reason why you gave us the wrong ID?'

'No, nothing, I swear.'

A few more questions were asked and avenues explored before Katie asked the last question.

'Do you admit or deny the offence of perverting the course of justice?'

The door to the interview room opened before she was able to answer. DC Briggs, who was supposed to be off sick, stumbled in.

'Oh, sorry Lounds, I didn't know you were in here.' He looked directly at Helen.

'Need me to sit in?' he asked, all easy smiles.

Katie returned the smile. 'Not this time, Alan. We're nearly finished here.' He looked put out, then left.

Helen looked terrified and reached out, touching Katie's arm. 'Please don't leave me with him. He scares me. He wasn't very nice last time.'

Katie let the silence stretch, using the same technique she had employed in the classroom with fidgeting pupils. Reeves shifted in his chair but remained silent.

Finally, Helen whispered, 'You wouldn't understand. None of you would.'

'Try me,' Katie said, calm but firm.

Helen's shoulders trembled. 'Michael... Edward... They were both liars. All I wanted was peace, a life without their games and lies.'

Katie leaned in slightly. 'Peace or safety?'

Helen froze. For a moment, Katie thought she might finally spill. Her eyes darted again toward the observation window. Then she looked down, voice flat. 'It was me. I killed him.'

The solicitor jumped in. 'Mrs Blake, I must advise that you don't say anything more until we have had another consultation,' interrupted Balogan.

'Yes, that's absolutely your right, Helen. Shall we stop the interview for you to speak with your solicitor?'

'No, no, please, I killed him.'

'Mrs Blake,' repeated Balogan.

Katie tapped her pen once against the file. Something was badly wrong. A true confession never sounded this rehearsed or came this easily, especially when she hadn't been arrested for murder.

Katie changed tack. 'Where were you Wednesday night into Thursday, up to three to four a.m.?'

Helen blinked. 'At home. Alone.'

'Anyone visit?'

'No.' Too quick, she thought.

'If you were at home, how did you kill him?'

'I went out. Sorry, I didn't know the time I killed him. Me.'

'How did you know where he would be? You said you called him when he wasn't home.'

'Find my iPhone. We both have each other's.'

Katie studied her, noting the clipped answers, the lack of grief, and the fear hidden under defiance. She was a quick thinker.

'How did you kill Michael, Helen? Please take me through it,' Katie asked, knowing that only the killer would know the detail.

Helen swallowed. 'I killed him. I just killed him. I followed him into the Cathedral. I didn't know why he was going in there, maybe to meet a woman or to steal some money. I followed him in and hit him and he fell.'

'What did you hit him with?'

'There are some stones near the altar, I think. One of those. Hit him on the head and he fell.'

'You hit him inside the building?'

'Yes, inside, so no-one would see. I followed him in,' she insisted.

'What did you see? I mean, if you were following him to see what he was going to do, why did you hit him before you actually saw what he was there for?'

'I'd picked up a stone, as it was dark in there. I didn't know if someone would attack me. However, he started to turn around, he saw me, and I panicked and hit him. Didn't mean to kill him, just knock him out. Maybe when he woke up, with a headache, he wouldn't remember who it was.'

'What did you do with that stone?'

'Put it back near the altar.'

'In what position did he fall?' Helen paused, as if thinking.

'I can remember, yes. Like your photo, he stumbled back, tripped, fell on his back and hit his head.'

Lounds and Reeves both knew this was not true. The body had been found face down when the cleaner arrived, and he had been stabbed.

Lounds continued, 'What did you do then? Did you move anything?'

'No. I took the keys from his hand, ran out, and locked the door behind me.'

'Is there just one door?' Lounds asked, pausing for thought.

'The main entrance has a big, heavy wooden door and a metal door.'

'Which did you lock?'

'Both.'

'Why lock the doors? How would he get out?'

'I don't know. I don't know why I did it, any of it. I suppose he could have got another set from the office.'

'How did you know where he would be?'

'I saw he'd booked an Uber for twelve fifteen from Athena. He hadn't come home, so I went there, used 'Find my iPhone, 'and followed him to the Cathedral.'

'Did you not think to stop him and ask him what was going on?'

'No, I wanted to see what he was doing.'

'Why would you be suspicious? Doesn't sound like you gave him a chance to show you what he was up to,' queried Katie.

'Money, women, you know, men things.'

'If you had stopped him and taken him home, he would still be alive now, as the killer wouldn't have got to him.' She was stumbling, and both officers and the solicitor knew it.

'I killed him.'

Both Lounds and Reeves knew that was all lies. Why had she admitted to a murder she didn't commit?

'Okay, I think we will end the interview there. You are denying perverting the course of justice.'

Helen looked bemused. 'Deny that, but I killed him. Don't you want to ask more questions?'

'No thank you, not at this time. Anything you wish to add, Mr Balogan?'

'My client is under a lot of pressure. She has not had legal advice on murder. She is visibly shaking, and she does not know what she is saying.'

'I understand, thank you. If there is nothing more, the interview is ceased at thirteen forty-eight hours.'

Helen was booked back in and returned to her cell.

'DS Lounds,' said Balogan, 'I'm concerned about my client. She could be having a breakdown. That was a very unusual switch. I think she needs to be assessed.'

'I don't believe that she killed her husband, Mr Balogan. Rest assured, if I did, I would have arrested her for it.'

Reeves remained in the custody suite, and Katie made her way back up to the office. As she was about to open the door to the stairs, Briggs stepped in front of her.

'You've arrested her? She is grieving. She doesn't know what she's saying. What did she say?'

'Why are you here, Alan? You took the day off sick.'

'None of your business. I knew we were strapped. Felt a bit better later on, so I came in. And this is all the thanks I get. Answer my question. What did she say?'

Katie let the door close behind her and started to climb the stairs, Briggs' face pushed up against the glass in the door watching her, fuming.

CHAPTER 8

A while later, Helen Blake was released on bail with the condition that she should not contact Edward Blake directly or indirectly.

'DI Rook is looking for you, Katie,' said Jane.

'Thank you, I'll pop in now.' Katie walked up to the inspector's office and knocked.

'Come in.'

He got up as she walked in and popped his head out of the door. 'Tom, over here, son. Meet DS Katie Lounds.'

Through the door came a sharp-looking man, early thirties, around six feet, gym build, with wavy dark brown hair and a slightly northern accent.

'Yes, boss. Afternoon, Sarge.'

'Katie, this is TDC Tom Ilkley. He's just back from paternity leave. I've brought him into our team while we are dealing with the Cathedral job, an extra pair of hands for you.'

'Great,' said Katie, holding out her hand. Tom shook it firmly, friendly. 'Where would you like me to start?'

'Tom is very good with tech, Katie. So if you've got CCTV, money trails, phones, or tracking, he's your man.'

'Nice to meet you, Tom. Confusing job body in the cathedral, ID'd the wrong twin by his wife, his wife has now confessed to murdering him in a way that he wasn't murdered.' She walked him as she talked over to the desk of DC Jane Reeves. 'Jane, can you bring Tom up to date, please?'

'Of course. We could do with another pair of hands. We've just got all the CCTV from the Queen Street area, and do you want a coffee?'

'I'll make them. How do you take yours?'

'Strong, lots of milk and two sugars, please.'

'Sarge?'

'Call me Katie. No, I won't, thank you. I've got to nip out shortly.'

Tom went off to make the coffees, and Reeves looked confused.

'I've looked through the crime scene photos and the property recovered by us and SOCO. No phone. Was a phone recovered from the scene? Helen said she called him around three thirty a.m., and we know he had it around midnight when the booking was cancelled. He must have had it with him when he was attacked. Looked on our property system, nothing.'

'Strange. I've got the phone number for it. Have a search through the attending officers' notes and see what was booked into property. Maybe it's been misfiled.' Misfiled or deliberately taken she considered.

'Get onto the service provider and see if we can pull the records of the calls and texts over the last few weeks.' She scribbled down the number and 'EE' and handed it over to Jane.

'We have Helen's phone now. Get Tom to install the Find My iPhone app and see if you can map the route from Queen Street. If you can, take Tom and walk the route, note any cameras we may have missed, and check sightlines. Show him the cathedral so he has a firsthand view of the location.'

'Will do,' she said as Tom returned with two full, steaming mugs of coffee.

'Katie,' said Rook, 'Enoch Mkhize, I think you spoke to him about the meeting. His father has reported him missing. He was supposed to come to his flat last night and didn't, not answering his phone. Was due at the Cathedral this morning for work, hasn't turned up.'

'I'll give him a call, pop over and see him; it'll give me a chance to look around the last place that anyone saw Michael alive.'

Through gritted teeth, 'Alan, have you got keys? I need to go to Queen Street. Witness Enoch reported missing, there's no keys on the board.'

'I've got some. I'll drive you,' he said with a smile.

Strange, she thought, as two hours earlier he was about to lay her out when she let the door shut in his face. It made her feel a little uneasy. However, keep your friends close but your enemies closer, she told herself.

She walked out into the snow, which was falling again. It was dark, but the snow lit everything up. She pulled up the collar of her green wax jacket and walked over to the 2014-plate Corsa that Briggs already had running in the car park.

Initially, the journey was quite stilted; neither said a word.

'So who do you think we should be looking into more deeply, Alan?' she proffered.

'I think you're barking up the wrong tree with the wife. She's grieving, she's all over the place. She wouldn't have had the strength to do it and move the body. I'd say the brother. If Michael was stealing or swindling clients, it would look bad on his business, as it's still 'Blake Bros Accountants. 'He's a more likely candidate, and he was off the radar for a few days before the murder and after.'

He had a point.

'Michael's bank accounts show that he had been withdrawing money regularly, not spending it on anything tangible. Possible blackmail who could be blackmailing him?'

'Maybe not. Maybe he's paying for another woman somewhere.'

They pulled up to the entrance, used the intercom, and were let into the car park again by Derek, who then buzzed them into the flat. Katie could see that the front of the block had cameras, and there were also cameras inside and in the lifts.

Katie and Alan walked into the white, clinical, minimalist apartment and were invited to sit down. This wasn't Katie's idea of a comfortable home. She felt she was making the place look messy being there; she perched on the edge of the white chair, trying not to crease the immaculate white satin cushion.

Tea and cake were provided, which they both took gratefully, eagerly in Alan's case.

Derek explained that Enoch had been uncontactable, which was very unlike him as his life revolved around his phone. It was also unusual for him not to go to the Cathedral; he hadn't missed a day of work in four years, even though it was voluntary. Derek had spoken to Enoch yesterday morning and noticed nothing unusual. Enoch had a job at midday but was expected at his dad's by six p.m. He was a stonemason working near Stoney Stanton that day. He contacted his boss, clocked off at about four thirty p.m. as usual, and then disappeared.

Katie completed all the missing-from-home questions got a picture of Enoch, the contact numbers she needed, and told Derek to let them know as soon as he heard anything, which he agreed.

They were up to leave, and Alan stepped out of the flat and started to walk towards the lift. Katie stopped and said, 'Oh, one last thing, Derek. Not about Enoch. We've checked and spoken to everyone who was at the meeting on Wednesday, except someone called 'Nick. 'No one seems to have a full name for him.'

'I don't either. Enoch started working with him, and when some work needed doing at the Cathedral, he started to do the odd day here and there. His name will be in the ledgers somewhere; he got paid.'

'We'll have someone ask the question. Thanks, Derek. We will be in touch.'

Katie caught up with Alan, and they took the lift down to the first floor and back out into the car park. It was still snowing, a little heavier now, and beginning to settle. Alan held the door open for her, and they got into the car and began the journey back.

'I wonder who this Nick is? Links to Enoch, who is missing, was there when Michael left, and no one has a full name for him yet.'

'Sounds like a jobbing handyman to me. No one has raised any concerns about him.'

'Alan, you arrived at the Cathedral before I did. We seem to have a missing mobile phone. Did you see it near the body? Did you see one of the uniform pick it up?'

'No. Now you come to mention it, it's strange that everyone has their phone with them twenty-four-seven. Maybe one of them picked it up, put it in their pocket, completely forgot about it, and then off on rest days.'

'No problem. I've got Ilkley onto tracking it as we speak; we'll locate it.'

'Probably inside someone's stab vest in their locker.'

Alan was driving a little too fast now for her liking, given the slow snow and the blizzard that was coming down.

It was getting late, and the late shift had enquiries in hand. The Missing-from-Home team were dealing with Enoch, so Katie made her way home. When she arrived outside her house, she realised her handbag was still at her desk. Damn, second time this week.

Still, she had her phone, work laptop, and house keys on her car fob, so she could manage without the rest for the night.

The door was locked, the place looked like she left it, and her car hadn't been messed with. It was a relief.

Monty came running up to her, jumping up her leg.

'I know, do you want your din-dins, Mont?'

'Meow,' he replied, and sat down next to his bowl in the kitchen.

Katie switched on the kettle and put Monty's food out for him.

She grabbed her phone, too tired to cook, and ordered a fish and chip delivery. She went and was changed and sat down with her laptop while she waited for the food. Food was coming from Oadby, so she had a good few minutes. The fifteen to twenty minutes delivery time it offered instantly changed to thirty-five to forty-five when she had confirmed the order!

She clicked onto the CCTV from Queen Street Quarter Apartments from the night of the meeting into the early hours. Just having a quick skim through, it was surprisingly clear.

The usual CCTV in town would show a grey blur in human form; this showed actual people.

She made a few quick notes:

- 00:04 Michael stands in the foyer; Edward comes out to him, they exchange words, looks heated. Edward puts his hand on Michael's shoulder; he shrugs it off. Edward then goes back to the lift area. Michael follows three or four minutes later.
- 00:35 James Ratten leaves. He had already been spoken to; was at East Midlands Airport by 01:50, checked in by 02:20. He agreed to come to the station to do a statement when he returned.
- 00:48 Delivered.
- 01:38 Freddie and Elenor leave, arm in arm. She waves to the man on security; he nods and smiles at her. Freddie oblivious.
- 01:41 Michael leaves carrying a leather bag. Where is that bag? Wearing Edward's coat.
- 01:52 Edward leaves. He has a rucksack, is not wearing a coat, just his suit jacket, and is also talking on his phone.
- 02:02 Unknown male (possibly Nick) leaves.

Katie paused and tried to zoom in. There was something about his face, something familiar. She could not quite place it. She saw him talking on his phone as he walked out of the building. Note to self: ask Jane and Tom if they recognise him.

She continued to watch until there was a knock at the door. No one else left the apartment, and by the time she finished viewing at 02:30, no one had re-entered.

The fish and chips with mushy peas were exactly what she needed after a non-stop day of false murder confessions, disappearing witnesses, bickering brothers, and fraudulent accounts. She finished her food, scraping the last of the peas from the tub with the remaining chips. At £18 delivered, she was determined to make the most of it. She was annoyed with herself if she had thought to pick it up on the way, it would have saved a few pounds. Damn, she had forgotten to go into The Range again.

Just as she was about to take her rubbish out to the bin, she saw an envelope hanging out of the inside of the letterbox. It was handwritten: 'Katie.'

Her heart raced as she carefully opened the envelope and unfolded the piece of A4 inside. On it was a short message: 'Be careful where you go alone.'

Panic surged through her. Had it been pushed through the letterbox while she was back, or while she was away? Knowing her landlady at the farm didn't go to bed early, she dialled her number. It took only six rings before it was answered.

'Angela, it's Katie. I'm sorry it's getting late; can I ask you a question?'

'Of course, my lovely. What's the matter?'

'Did you see anyone come to mine today?'

They have a shared drive down from the country lane; the main farmhouse is on the left and the barn is on the right. From the kitchen window of each property, you could see the other.

'I didn't see anyone, no love. Is everything OK?'

'I've just had something pushed through my door, a letter, hand-delivered.'

'No, love, sorry.'

'Ok, thank you, Angela. Goodnight.'

'Oh, Katie, love, now I think of it… About eleven a.m., there was a car. I was hanging out the washing when it started to pull onto the drive and then stopped. It reversed and parked, almost blocking it. I am glad it wasn't tomorrow when I've got to…'

'Oh, not much more. It waited there. I went back in and made a sandwich. I hadn't fancied one when I got up, a bit sickly this morning, but by eleven I fancied a bacon butty, streaky bacon and smoked. You've got to have smoked streaky, haven't you, pet?'

'I agree, nice and crispy. Did you see anyone in the car?'

'I can tell you're a detective. When I'd made the sandwich I looked out and it reversed back onto the drive and then went off down the street didn't see who was in it.'

'Can you describe the car at all?'

'I'm not very good with cars. Grey, dark, slate grey I think they call it, and long. Aye, longer than mine.' Angela had a 2007 Nissan Micra.

'Did you see any part of the number plate?'

'No, love, I didn't see one.'

'Thanks, Angela. Sorry to disturb you. Have a good night.'

Katie checked and rechecked the doors and windows before she went into the bedroom. Monty was already curled up on the bed, right in the middle, challenging her to disturb him. He was calm and relaxed she was not.

She was meticulous in many ways. Before she climbed into bed, she got clothes out of the wardrobe and drawers for the morning. She set her alarm bright and early.

Steadfast, solid and reliable, and most of all sensible, she always had been.

CHAPTER 9

The incident room buzzed with low chatter, whiteboards crowded with names, arrows, and grainy photos. Katie stood at the front, marker in hand, addressing the team.

'Edward Blake's financials show repeated payments to accounts over the last six months. They weren't tied to any of his past businesses. Amounts varied five hundred here, a thousand there. Consistent enough to suggest extortion due to round numbers, not casual spending.'

Reeves looked up from her notes. 'So he was being blackmailed?'

Katie nodded. 'Potentially. Someone wanted to keep him quiet.'

She tapped the board, where copies of bank transfers were pinned. 'We need to find out what leverage they had. Was it personal? Professional? And, more importantly, who benefits from him being gone?'

The room quieted. The unspoken implication hung there. Helen Blake's name glared from the board.

Briggs shifted in his chair, voice casual. 'Look, we're circling Helen because she makes an easy target. Sure, she hated him. However, this kind of blackmail? It smells corporate. Business rival, someone he shafted. Could even be a former partner.'

Katie studied him. His tone was smooth, persuasive, but she didn't like the way he dismissed Helen so quickly. 'We'll explore every avenue,' she said firmly.

Briggs flashed a disarming grin. 'Of course. Just don't want us barking up the wrong tree too soon.'

'Is there a right time to bark up the wrong tree?' TDC Tom Ilkley approached her.

'Yes, Tom.'

'Sarge, I went through some of the Blakes' joint account yesterday. There are a lot of cash withdrawals, but there are also four payments to a hotel, The Greyhound in Market Harborough. I checked the CCTV for when the card was used and have some footage,' he said, handing her a folder.

'Thanks, Tom. Did you and Jane get anywhere with the route from Queen Street or the phone data?' Katie asked.

'We've got a couple of bits of footage to collect today, and we are told the phone data will be later today.'

'Good job, thank you.' Tom left the room. He was good, worked off his own back, didn't need prompting, and thought outside the box as they say. She hoped they would be able to keep him.

Before opening the file, she looked out into the office. Keene wasn't in. Rook was in his office, and Jane and Tom were at their desks. Alan was nowhere to be seen.

She walked out with her laptop, stopping at the screenshot of the male leaving the Queen Street apartments.

'Team, could you have a look at this face? Do either of you recognise him? There's something familiar.'

They both took their time, zooming in on the image.

'No, sorry,' said Tom.

'There is something familiar. I don't know if he looks like someone I've dealt with before. Can you email me the picture, Sarge? I'll keep it in mind.'

'I will.'

Katie's phone pinged. No Caller ID. She picked it up and swiped to answer, but the call ended as soon as she did. Another ping followed. She clicked on the message it was a photograph of her, sitting on the sofa, eating her chips with Monty by her side. She felt a wave of panic roll over her and had to sit down.

'You alright, Sarge?' said Reeves.

'Yes, sorry. Not had anything to eat for twenty-four hours, better get something.'

'Oh, did you have a look at the images from the CCTV that Tom gave you from the hotel?'

'Not yet, I'll have a look.'

Katie flipped through the file. The hotel's name tugged at her memory. The photograph inside confirmed it: a dark-haired woman stepping out of a car, her face turned just enough for recognition. Helen Blake. She continued to watch the footage, seeing Helen walk into the front of the pub. The camera switched to an internal view and followed her to a table, where a dark-haired man sat with his back to the camera. She kept watching, but the man did not turn fully, only sideways.

Michael? Why go in separate cars? Then she saw it he was wearing a very thin t-shirt, and beneath it, faint but visible on the left shoulder, the birthmark. This was Edward.

Katie's chest tightened.

Helen had been meeting Edward in secret. But why? To argue? To plead? To conspire? To blackmail?

And why had she never mentioned it? She just said she hated him. But she looked quite happy in his company here.

Katie knew there was some tension between Alan Briggs and Helen Blake; she didn't know what. It seemed Helen didn't like him, but he seemed protective of her. Was he just leading her down the wrong path because he wanted her job? What was it?

She didn't really want to take Briggs to speak to Helen, but Tom and Jane were otherwise engaged and Briggs had the car, which he needed to go and speak to Enoch, who had apparently turned up at the Cathedral with a ledger.

'Alan, would you be able to drive me to Helen's, please? I just need to ask her something about payments from their joint account being made at a pub.' She showed him the picture from the hotel, carefully covering the birthmark.

'Looks like a husband and wife out for a meal. Why do you keep pestering her for nothing?'

'It's not nothing. It's a murder investigation. There was a large amount of money withdrawn whilst at that location, and I want to ask about that.'

Reluctantly, he agreed. She got into the car with him.

The car hadn't been used yet that morning; it was cold, the heater wasn't working, and as she sat there, she realised she could see nothing ice covering the windscreen. She remained seated and let Briggs deal with it, swearing as he scraped it with his warrant card.

During the drive, Briggs tried to make small talk.

'Can't see a ring. Married, kids?'

She was a little taken aback. He hadn't asked her if she took sugar in her tea but had launched straight into her private life.

'No, neither. Always been too busy with work for a relationship to work long days, working rest days, called out in the night, missing birthdays, like we all do. But for me, knowing that, I didn't want to start anything I couldn't commit to fully.'

'That's me all or nothing.'

'You?' she asked, not expecting a reply.

'Married twenty-two years, happily divorced, daughter Amelia, son Dom, both grown up and flown the nest.'

'I'm a dog man, you're a cat woman we were always going to clash,' he laughed, a crude laugh.

When had she told him she had a cat? Second thoughts she was always telling people what Monty got up to. It's a cat parent thing.

'What type of dog?'

'XL Bully, fully legal, registered as supposed to be. Called Beckham. Little bastard he is.'

'How long have you lived in Leicestershire?'

'All my life. Grew up in a council house in Aylestone, moved over to Thurmaston about twenty-five years ago.'

'Oh, didn't we need to get on the bypass?' she said.

'No, straight through the village, it's quicker,' he said. No need for a sat nav he knew this side of town.

They pulled up a house or two down from Helen's.

'I won't be long, just a couple of questions. You wait here,' she said as she undid the seatbelt and made her way to the drive of Helen's house.

A moment later, Helen was walking towards her.

'Come to arrest me again? Going to charge me with murder now?'

'No, Helen, I don't think you killed him.'

'I told you what I did.'

'I know, which is why I know you didn't do it.' She looked quizzical, but Katie didn't clarify.

'I've just got a couple of things to ask you if you have a few minutes.' Helen led Katie around to the back of the substantial property.

Helen's hands shook as she lit a cigarette on the back step of her house, the smoke curling against the cold. Katie stood opposite her, arms folded, watching.

'You met Edward,' Katie said flatly. 'At the hotel. More than once. Why?'

Helen exhaled, smoke trembling in the cold air. 'I hated him.'

'That's not what I asked.'

Her eyes darted away. 'He… he said he'd tell Michael. About us.'

Katie stilled. 'About what, Helen?'

Helen's lips pressed into a tight line, her voice low and heavy with shame. 'I made mistakes. I saw him once, twice… when Michael and I were at our worst. Edward never let me forget it. He threatened to ruin me if I left Michael, ruin Michael if I told. He had me trapped.'

Katie scribbled furiously, stepped closer, tone sharpening. 'So he blackmailed you?'

'No. He wanted me to carry on seeing him, that's why I was going to the hotel; I didn't want him at the house in case Michael came back. He started out by saying he thought I was having an affair with someone, and if I didn't sleep with him, he would tell Michael. I've just got myself in such a mess, such a mess, and now Michael is dead.'

'Who did he accuse you of having an affair with?'

'He'd looked at my phone messages. There was no name attached to the number, but he'd read them; he didn't know any names.'

'There was a large sum of money that Edward withdrew at the hotel that night. Is anyone blackmailing him?'

'No. He said he owed someone, but it wasn't a hundred percent kosher, so he needed cash rather than a bank transfer. He didn't say what. I asked him when he came and sat down with hundreds of pounds.'

Footsteps crunched on the gravel. Briggs approached with easy confidence, sliding between them like a mediator.

'Enough, Katie. Can't you see she's terrified? Dragging this out won't help.'

Katie's jaw clenched. 'We're not dragging it out. We're getting the truth.'

Helen looked at Briggs, eyes wide with gratitude for the interruption, then turned sharply. 'I don't want him here.' She walked to the back door and locked it behind her.

Back at the station, the board glared at her: Edward, Michael, Helen. Red arrows criss-crossed between them. Motives. Lies. Secrets.

The team's mood was shifting. Briggs had their ear. Reeves still backed her, but Briggs muttered that Katie was too hard on Helen, too focused, too personal.

It's not me who has a personal interest in Helen, Katie thought.

Leaning against her desk, she rubbed her temples. For a moment, she considered deleting the photos, pretending it wasn't happening, pretending she wasn't losing sleep.

Instead, she turned to Reeves.

'Can I trust you?'

Reeves frowned. 'Of course.'

'Meet me at Morrison's Café in twenty.'

Katie walked over to Morrison's and into the café, bought two teas, and waited. She sat in the corner near the trays, giving her a full 180-degree view of the café and the shop.

Jane turned up and sat down. 'What is it?'

Katie unlocked her phone and slid it across. The photos: her outside the station with Reeves, her at the Cathedral, a picture of the note pushed through her door. She told her about the house door being open and her car seat moved. Reeves stared, colour draining from her face.

'Bloody hell, Katie… why didn't you tell anyone?'

Katie's voice was barely a whisper. 'Because if they know I'm being watched, I'm compromised. They'll think I'm distracted, vulnerable. That I can't lead.'

Reeves looked her straight in the eye. 'You are being watched. Moreover, we need to deal with it. Whoever this is… they're already too close.'

Katie exhaled shakily. For the first time, the weight lifted slightly. Someone else knew.

Deep down, though, she couldn't shake the thought that it wasn't just intimidation. Whoever was watching her could be part of this personal, or trying to scare her off? That wasn't going to happen. She was going to get to the bottom of this murder, no matter what anyone else said or did. First murder in Leicestershire she had to make her mark.

'I initially thought it was Briggs. He was at the Cathedral, had access to the parking at work, and could easily have followed me home. When we went to Helen's the first time, a grey car sped off. I knew someone had been with her before we arrived. Then my landlady saw a grey car on our drive yesterday morning, around the time the note was put through. Briggs was off work then; he'd called in sick.'

'But you don't think that anymore?'

'I don't know. It's a mess.'

'I mean, he's strange. I don't feel comfortable around him arrogant but what's he got to gain? He's not going to scare you out of a job. He'd be better off trying to hamper the investigation. But the car park has public access, so far you've had nothing a random member of the public couldn't have done?'

'Apart from my phone number. It's my personal number. But I've got another concern: why I left teaching, why I left Leicestershire, could be related.'

'Go on.' Jane frowned, sipping her dark brown tea and dunking a digestive she'd pulled from her bag.

'I worked at a school locally. One evening, after a meeting, I left late about 7 pm. I was walking out to my car and saw two students arguing on the playing field. I walked towards them. The taller boy kicked the other; he fell to the floor, on his back. I saw the aggressor raise something shiny and pummel it down on the lad. He crumpled. I screamed as I ran toward them. He turned, looked at me, then ran over the fields, over the fence, gone.'

'Jeez. What happened?'

'He'd been stabbed, bleeding heavily, no one else around. I called an ambulance, tried to stem the bleeding. Ambulance came, police came they worked on him for some time before blue-lighting him away. I was told the next day he'd died, stabbed to the heart.'

Reeves was open-mouthed.

'I was the only witness. I knew both boys both in my class. I, of course, named him: Stephen Reading. He was arrested sixteen. I had to give evidence in court. He denied it was him, got his dad to claim he had already collected him from school, that he was at home; his uncle confirmed it. They made out I had it in for him as a troublemaker at school, and my last report attested to that behaviour.'

Katie paused, sipped her tea, and took one of the digestives poking out of Jane's bag.

'The police found blood on the sole of Stephen's trainer when he was arrested, and CCTV showed him buying cigarettes at a local shop around seven-fifteen, so he wasn't at home. Despite all that evidence, his father still blamed me. Stephen was convicted and sentenced to twelve years. As he left court, his dad, Courtney Ellis, told me he'd hunt me down, that I'd ruined his son's life, that I would suffer for the rest of mine.'

Not long after, my windows got put through at the house. My car was smashed in the school car park. CCTV was inconclusive, but I knew who it was in the footage. I moved back to Yorkshire. A few years later, I got an email through my work account:

'Yorkshire isn't that far away, twelve years is a long time. '

Attached was a photo of me opening my front door.

'Katie, you have to tell someone. Not Keene Rook. He has your back.'

'I can't say I suspect or suspected Briggs. How much extra grief would that bring me? I don't want to move on again. I don't know if it's Briggs or if Ellis has located me or even Stephen; he'll have been released a while ago. Whoever it is knows where I live, where I work, and follows me.'

Changing the subject to lighten the mood, Katie asked, 'So Jane, tell me a bit about you? I've not had a chance to sit down with you yet.'

'Single. Was in a long-term relationship; she wanted kids, I didn't. We drifted apart. I didn't think I could commit with this job, and I love the job.'

Katie knew the feeling.

'I go to the gym, like crafting, ride scrambler motorbikes, and play rugby on weekends when I'm not working. Very untidy and have a great habit of hacking people off without trying,' she laughed.

'Sounds like you're busy. What made you join the job?'

'Dad was in for twenty years before he was medically retired. Loved it. He used to tell us stories from his jobs; it sounded so exciting, so I joined and haven't looked back since.'

They continued chatting for a short while before heading back to the station.

CHAPTER 10

Katie sat at her desk trying to get her head around it. Notes on the board – Michael dead. His wife confesses but hasn't done it – initially says it's Edward – why? Helen meeting with Edward, money exchanging hands. Edward threatens Helen. Who else was Helen seeing? Had Helen meant to kill Edward but because of the coat and the dark got the wrong man? However, she couldn't have gotten him into the Cathedral. Michael potentially swindled the church. A mysterious, eerily familiar young man at the Queens Quarter, who has disappeared. Michael potentially fiddling the accounts, potentially looking bad on Edward's family business, Edward disappears for a few days after the murder and for some reason is very irate when we ask him about it.

What was she missing?

She needed the phone data from Michael's number; she needed his phone and the leather bag he was carrying.

CCTV from near the Cathedral was being processed.

She probably needed another chat with Helen but didn't think it was the right time to approach that again, she would give her a bit of space.

No-one had yet been able to clarify who 'Nick' was either.

The incident room buzzed with quiet energy. DS Katie Lounds stood at the head of the table as the forensics officer laid down a plastic evidence bag, the heavy brass candlestick inside catching the harsh light.

'Prints came back,' the officer said, sliding a sheet toward Katie. 'Multiple hits. Derek Mkhize, Edward Blake… and DI Briggs.'

Katie's brow furrowed. 'Briggs?'

'Clean match,' the officer confirmed.

'On the ledger, Susan Callaghan, Pamela Blake and Derek Mkhize.'

'Thanks, Tom, very helpful. Any luck with the CCTV and the route on the iPhone tracking?'

'We are just looking through some footage now.'

Katie decided she would speak to all the owners of those fingerprints, except Briggs, he could wait and she didn't want to show her hand too soon. Derek was at the meeting, going through the ledgers, so that was explained.

Briggs was in the office when she walked in to speak with Jane; she ignored him and went to speak with Jane. 'Could you get Edward and Pam over to Mansfield House for me this afternoon, do them about half an hour apart. Edward first. If you and Brenton take Susan here, please. I don't want to bring Helen back in yet, but Andrew suggests she could have been seeing someone else.'

It was going to be a long day, Katie wanted these interviews done this afternoon.

DS Reeves made arrangements for Edward and Pamela Blake to attend Mansfield House Police Station later that afternoon for interviews. Katie planned to take the Blakes herself and leave Callaghan with Reeves, who was due to come to Euston. Derek handled the accounts, so in the meantime, they would deal with the other matters.

Katie made her way over to the City Centre Station, she parked up in the last space in the back car park, the front was full – she secured the two interview rooms on the ground floor. Her intention was Edward in one, Pamela in the other, flitting between the two hoping they didn't see each other.

Knowing it might be a long afternoon and she hadn't yet eaten, she popped across to Tesco and got herself a meal deal. She just loved the cheese and onion and mayo sandwiches, so she picked one of those, a packet of plain crisps and a cold coffee in a cardboard tube. She paid and walked back over to the station and ate some of her lunch while she was waiting.

About ten minutes later, her phone began to vibrate, unknown number, with a little trepidation she answered, 'Hello.'

'Is that DS Lounds?'

'Yes.'

'Marilyn on the front desk. An Edward Blake is here for you.'

Relief.

'Thank you, I'll come and get him.'

Katie walked through the corridor into the front office; cold metal seats don't help in the winter. There were a few people sat around, a couple obscured by newspapers, and an angry young man at the probation counter with a can of Special Brew.

Edward seemed a lot more relaxed and didn't bite her head off at being asked to come. She also noted he hadn't brought his solicitor with him.

'No Parker?' she said, reaching out her hand.

He took her hand and shook. 'No, I understand I'm not being arrested, I want to help.'

'I've had to double park, there are no spaces in the car park, is that okay?' She looked out of the window and saw his blue BMW parked in front of a works van.

'If you leave your keys with Marilyn, the lady at the end desk of the counter, she can hold them. If they need to move it, an officer can do that while we are in the interview, if that's okay with you. Alternatively, there is a multi-storey car park less than a minute away.'

'No, that's fine, I'll leave it here, I don't trust multi-storeys, and you never know who is hanging around.' Edward walked over to the desk and handed over his keys. Marilyn looked up at Katie and smiled, and she nodded back her thanks. Sorted.

Katie led Edward back through the corridor into the interview room. It was a very small room; Monty wouldn't have been able to be swung in there! There was a table, three chairs and the recording machine and some clutter in the corner.

'Have a seat, Edward.' He sat, removed his gloves and jacket and folded it onto the seat next to him.

'We have had some forensics back and would like your input.'

'You are not under arrest, but I am going to speak to you as a significant witness – are you sure you don't want to have a legal advisor with you?'

'No, thank you.'

Katie set up the machine.

'Please can you confirm your name, date of birth and current address,' she asked.

'Edward Stephen Blake, thirtieth March nineteen seventy-five, living with my parents at Elm Tree Road, Cosby, Leicestershire.'

'Edward, thank you for coming in again. We've had some forensic results back from the cathedral.'

'I told you before, I haven't set foot in there for ages, but depending on how good old Susan is, my fingerprints could be anywhere.'

'Can you explain why your fingerprints were found on the candlestick recovered near your brother's body?'

'That's… no, that can't be right. I have not been near the place. Not since…' (hesitates) 'Christmas.'

'The prints were fresh. No dusting, no smudging. Not something that's been sitting there since Christmas.'

'Then someone's made a mistake. Maybe… maybe Michael? We're twins, after all. Couldn't you have mixed them up?' He was floundering.

'We checked. Identical twins don't share fingerprints. Yours are distinct.'

'Look, maybe I went in, all right? Just once. To check something.'

'Earlier, you said you hadn't been in the cathedral 'for a while. 'Care to define 'a while '?'

'It was a couple of weeks ago, maybe Monday or Tuesday. After hours.'

'Why didn't you mention that before?'

He sat back in his chair and puffed out his cheeks, looking embarrassed. He loosened the blue polka dot tie around his neck a little. He pulled his chair into the table, put his elbows on the desk and rested his head on his hands.

'Because it looks bad, doesn't it? My brother is dead, my prints on the bloody candlestick that killed him. I didn't kill him! I tried to think fast and tripped myself up.'

'Learn from that, Edward, you can't trip yourself up if you're telling the truth.' She paused; there was no response, so she carried on.

'What were you doing there?'

'I… I thought Michael was dipping into the cathedral's accounts. I went to look for proof. I didn't find anything, but I must have touched the candlestick without thinking. There are a few of them and they get moved around. There's one on the shelf near the door to the office from the nave; maybe I straightened it as I walked by. I don't know. I panicked when you asked before, so I said I hadn't been there.'

'You lied to us once. If you lie again, I'll know. If you want me to believe you had nothing to do with your brother's death, I suggest you start giving me the truth,' she said sternly.

Taking a deep breath. 'That's the truth. I didn't hurt him.'

'Did you take the ledgers to the meeting?'

'No, no, I didn't want to make it that public, I was hoping I could find out what had happened and if it were Michael, try and get the funds back in before it was reported and then try to make out I'd figured out where the missing funds went. I went hoping they could resolve it and it wasn't anything to do with them.'

'Why did you want to do that for him? You didn't get on.'

'No, you're right. A while back I thought Helen was seeing someone else, so I told him. He became hostile, said he didn't believe me and we argued in the cathedral. I hadn't seen him much until that meeting. But he was still my brother, and as he was still linked in name as a partner in the business, it would look bad on us if it got out.'

'Can you explain to me about your coat after the meeting? It appears Michael took yours. Did you not try and stop him, after your entire wallet was in the pocket?'

'I didn't see him leave, we had words after the takeaway, I went to the bathroom, when I came out he had gone. I didn't even look for my coat at that point. When I did come to leave, not long after, I couldn't find it. Saw his expensive Ede and Ravenscroft coat that he was always bragging about and realised he must have put on mine. I don't get it, his cost an arm and a leg; I don't know why he would pick the wrong one!'

'Michael's bag is missing, did you see that at the flat?'

'No, but I wasn't looking.'

'Did you go looking for him when you realised he had your coat?'

'I called him a couple of times but the phone went to voicemail. Most of the others had left too, don't forget, wasn't just him who could have taken it,' shrugging his shoulders.

'Oh,' something was dawning on him. 'I've asked before, you don't… you don't think I was the target, but because he had my coat on him…?'

'We have nothing to suggest that at the moment. Both of you have connections with the Cathedral, not a coincidence that he was found there, but if someone was after you, I can't say.'

'The ledgers which were used at the meeting were located in the Cathedral as you know. Michael didn't take them back there. Did you? Did you go to the Cathedral after the meeting?'

'No, no,' he said very sharply, piquing Katie's interest, but she wasn't going to pursue that now   let him think she believed him until she got some more of the CCTV back.

Katie's phone buzzes again. 'I'm just going to nip out and take that, Edward, if that's OK with you.'

'Yes, go for it.'

The phone call is to inform her that Pamela has arrived. She collects her and puts her into another interview further down the corridor and asks her to wait, and returns to Edward.

'Are you in a terrible hurry? I just have someone I need to speak to but would like to ask a few further questions.'

'Can I go and get a coffee?'

'Yes, if you could be back in 30 minutes, we'll get it wrapped up today and you'll be on your way.'

She stopped the recording and showed him out, hoping he would return.

She then collected her things and went into the room where she had shown Pam.

'Am I being arrested?' she asked. Today she looked more put together, as if she no longer fit the flat she was living in. Her hair was freshly styled, curled neatly, her makeup carefully applied, and she wore tailored trousers with a short white blouse and a red duffle coat. Even her voice sounded different, more controlled, Katie thought.

'No, not at all. You are a witness, but we have had some information come back and I need to ask you about it. You are not under arrest, you are a witness at this stage, but I intend to record the interview   if we need to make it into a statement later, we can.'

'Ok.'

Katie started to type the information into the recording machine. 'How's Clyde?'

'He's a bugger, malting, always malting. He's a big daft oompah lumpah. It was fine when we lived in the big house in Knighton, but he fills half the flat. However, I am not getting rid. Hairs, a fortune in food, but he is my baby.'

'Ok, ready to go, Pam, if you are?' She nodded confidently.

'Please can you state your name, date of birth and address for the machine?'

'Pamela Louise Blake, eighth July nineteen eighty-five, flat above Charity Shop, Leicester Road, Blaby.'

Introductions done. Pam didn't want a solicitor either.

'Pamela, forensics have placed your fingerprints on the ledger recovered from the cathedral floor. Can you explain how they got there?'

Pam straightened herself in her chair, trying to look more confident. 'Yes. Edward asked me to fetch it. I was in town, I work at the King Richard III Centre. The nursery I was working at was struggling and let two of us go. I've only

had this job since just before Bonfire Night. He rang, said he
needed to check something in the accounts.'

'So you went into the Cathedral yourself?'

'That's right. I thought nothing of it. I've been in there
plenty of times. There was no one about, so I just took the
ledger. I do some work there now and again, voluntary work,
so I can get in the office   I have a key.'

'Did anyone give you permission?'

Pam shifted slightly in her chair. 'Not formally, no. But
Edward's an accountant, and they are accounting books, so
I trusted he had a reason. He said he couldn't get away from
his other work that day, and since I worked opposite, it made
sense.'

'Where did the ledger go after you collected it?'

'I took it home and left it on the kitchen table for him.
He said he'd be coming round. He spent the evening playing
with Clyde and going through it, making notes. I left him to
it and went to bed. The next morning it was gone   I assumed
he had taken it back himself.'

'You didn't return it to the Cathedral?'

'No. I never touched it again after that night.'

'Pamela, did you look inside? Did you see what was in
the accounts?'

'No. Numbers make my eyes swim. I just fetched it. I
did not pry; those numbers wouldn't have meant anything to
me.'

'Why do you think Edward wanted it?'

'He told me he was worried about Michael. Those things didn't add up, that money was being shifted about. He wanted to be sure.'

'Did he tell you what he found?'

'He just said he needed more time. That he thought Michael wasn't being straight. I wasn't there when he finished and left I was already in bed, didn't even hear him go.'

'Did Edward seem nervous? Afraid?'

'Yes. Jumpy. He said he hardly slept that week, thought people were watching him. Oh my God someone didn't kill Michael by mistake, when it was Edward who thought he was being followed? Does that mean he is still in danger?'

'We can't say that. Apart from Edward, who knew you'd taken the ledger?'

'No one. At least, I didn't tell anyone.'

'And to be clear, you never took it back to the Cathedral?'

'No. That must have been Edward. He must have returned it himself. He took it from me.'

'When did you get it?'

She paused for a few moments, looked at her watch as some people do when thinking of a date. 'Couple weeks ago now. I think it was a Monday.'

'Pamela, can I ask you something directly?'

'Of course.'

'Why would you do this favour for Edward? You and he are estranged. My records show that only a few weeks ago, you called the police to have him removed from your home.'

'Yes. That's true. He had turned up drunk, shouting. It frightened me.'

'So why help him now? Why collect this ledger when he asked?'

Pamela paused, took a breath. There was a look of regret in her face. 'Because… because it wasn't like that this time. He wasn't shouting. He sounded desperate. Tired. Like he needed someone to trust him, just once.'

'Even after what happened?'

'Edward and I may be finished as husband and wife, but I still remember the man I married. I thought if I helped him with this, maybe he'd calm down. Maybe he'd stop hiding from shadows.'

'I know it's personal, but it might play a part   why did you separate?'

She looked prickly, her eyes slanted a little; Katie had hit a nerve.

'I thought he was seeing someone. Money kept going from our account Thursday nights. I challenged him, he started drinking, shouting at me. I just kept pushing him, told him he was as bad as his brother, cheating and squandering money, and he slapped me. He told me not to be so stupid a hysterical woman. I asked him why he was going to a hotel in Market Harborough. He said it was a pub and he entertained clients there, and I was thick. I told him I was going to leave him and take the boys until I felt I could trust him.'

'Did those thoughts go away? Did you think he had changed?'

'I wasn't sure. I just hadn't seen him like he was that night.'

'You thought this would help him getting the ledgers?'

'I hoped so. I didn't want him knocking on my door again at midnight, demanding I listen. I thought if I just fetched the books, he'd leave me alone.'

'Did he tell you exactly what he was looking for in the ledgers?'

'Just that he believed Michael was moving church money where it shouldn't be. That if he could prove it, he'd finally have peace of mind.'

'And did you believe him?'

'I didn't know what to believe. But I know how he gets when he thinks someone's deceiving him. I thought… better to help than have him spiral further.'

Katie believed her about the ledger part anyway.

CHAPTER 11

With that, Katie ended the interview. She thanked her for coming and walked her into the corridor. She made sure Edward was in the front office and let Pam out the side door so they wouldn't see each other. She didn't seem to notice the BMW. She was either texting or looking for something on her phone as she walked out of the car park, maybe ordering an Uber, she thought.

She then returned to the interview room, set it up again for Edward, and went to fetch him.

'Thank you for your patience.' She could see, once again, it was wearing thin. He had bought with him a sandwich ham and cheese on doorstep wholemeal and a Costa Coffee. 'Don't mind if I eat this, do you? I've not eaten today.'

'No, go ahead.'

She restarted the interview.

'Edward, we spoke before about the ledger. I now have a verbal statement from Pamela. She says you asked her to fetch it from the cathedral, so you didn't go to get them.'

'She wasn't supposed to tell you that.' 'So you admit it?'

'Yes. I asked her. I didn't want to be seen poking around again, thought it would make people suspicious of me.'

'You realise that puts her in a very difficult position? A ledger with her fingerprints on was found metres from your brother's body, on the floor with blood on it. You're estranged. Just a few weeks ago, she called the police to have you removed from her house. Why involve her at all?'

Edward was becoming defensive   because he had been caught out in a lie, or something else?

'Because she still listens to me, even when she says she hates me. I couldn't go myself. Michael would have known I'd asked for them. On the other hand, Derek… or one of the bloody vergers. They all watch me.'

'Why did you need the ledger so urgently?'

'Because I knew something wasn't right. Money is going missing. Transfers that didn't make sense. I wanted proof.'

'Pamela says you told her it was Michael misusing church funds.'

Edward hesitated, sat back in his chair, chewing the huge sandwich and gulping it down with the strong coffee, making Katie wish she had one. 'I thought it was him. He had access; he was always desperate for money. But '

'But what?'

'The entries… some of them… they didn't look like Michael's doing. The timings, the accounts. It was too slick. Michael's too… careless. This was careful.'

'So who do you think it points to?'

'Once I'd seen it, I didn't believe it could be him.'

'Yet you let Pamela believe it was Michael.'

'Yes, it was a hunch. I hadn't confirmed it wasn't.'

'So you manipulated her?'

'I didn't manipulate her, I asked her. I just needed the damn book! I didn't know he would be murdered and that book be left there.'

'Why didn't you tell me that earlier? Why let me think you collected them? What difference would it have made?'

'I realised I shouldn't have got her involved, so I said I went and took them. I want to get back with her; I don't want a broken marriage. I've made mistakes and although I don't deserve a second chance with her, I've got to try.'

'So, I ask you again, when did your fingerprints get onto the candlestick?' She didn't believe for one minute this was the murder weapon, but someone had bloodied it and planted it to try and make it look like that's where the murder happened.

'Must have been when I returned the ledger. There's one on the ledger cabinet. It was a couple of weeks ago. They move things around the place. One needs cleaning or repairing, so they put another out of the office in its place.'

'Okay, I know it looks bad, me misrepresenting things.'

'Lying about things, Edward, let's say it how it is,' she corrected him.

'Lying. I'm sorry. Are we done now?'

'Nearly. Where did you disappear off to after you left the meeting in the early hours of Thursday? No-one could contact you.'

'I know, I know that makes me look suspicious. I went off to an Airbnb I'd booked, wanted some space. I've moved back in with my parents. I wanted to have some time alone, no distractions, turned the phone off to go over what I saw in the ledgers and what was said at the meeting. If I'd have known Michael was dead, I wouldn't have gone   it made me look dodgy.'

'Who told you Michael had been killed, Edward?'

'Helen did.'

'When did she tell you?'

He looked for a moment as if he was trying to recall. 'Friday, I think.'

'Tell me about you and Helen.'

'Sorry?'

'Tell me about yours and Helen's relationship   how you get on.'

'Sister-in-law.'

'Edward, we've spoken to Helen a couple of times. I wouldn't want you to 'misrepresent 'yourself again. She said you were having an affair. We have footage of you both at The Greyhound.'

Colour drained from his face and he bowed his head, looking into the coffee cup intently.

'It wasn't an affair, not really. I felt sorry for her. Michael was all over the place, spending all their money. She never went anywhere, didn't have many friends, and he didn't like her having friends. He said they were just vultures because she lived in a nice house, in a nice area, and had money. I met up with her one day for a meal. Ewan was at school, Michael had done one of his disappearing tricks. One thing led to another. She was upset, I comforted her, and, well… yes, we booked a room. Mr and Mrs Blake   no lies there.'

'You said 'had money '. We know they have a nice home, but his finances weren't great?'

'No. Helen's grandfather died about two years ago. He was a well-off man, had a business. In the will, it said to sell it and give the funds to Helen. She got over £300k, but she only put a fraction of it in the joint account and told him that was her inheritance. She knew he'd waste it all if she put it all in. She said she wanted an 'escape fund '. If Michael continued to embezzle, waste funds, go on benders, she wanted enough money to get out and not be beholden to him.'

'How often did you meet?'

'It was only five or six times. Michael started asking questions about where she had been   he claimed he had a tracker on her car and would find out, so we couldn't risk it anymore.'

'Did you think she was seeing anyone else, Edward?' She let that linger for a while. No response.

'We have been told that you suspected she was having an affair and were going to have a word with her to tell her to stop, or that you were going to tell Michael. Were you going to taunt him knowing you were seeing her, or think there was a third man involved with her?'

'No, it was just me. You've spoken to Pam, haven't you? What did she say? I told her that to throw her off the scent. I wanted to get back with my wife. If she heard rumours of an affair relating to Helen, she wouldn't suspect me then, as she thought I already knew about it.'

'What a mess you've made, Edward, and you are making our investigation into finding the killer of your brother difficult withholding information and lying to us from the start.'

'I know, I know.'

'What about some large amounts going out of your account and their joint account?'

'Helen knew what a mess Michael had made of the business. He took a lot from it, I just couldn't prove it, but she knew. She was giving me small amounts to feed back into the business to balance the books, and I was withdrawing cash from my personal account to put into the business account. That is why, when the issues were raised about the cathedral accounts, I thought it had to be Michael, but I'm not too sure now.'

'Ok, thank you for your time, I do appreciate it.'

'I know you're just doing your job. I'm sorry about the other day, I was rude.' 'Thank you, interview ceased.'

Katie showed Edward into the front office where he picked up his keys and made his way out to the car park and watched him get into his car. He didn't look back once.

Meanwhile at Euston Street.

DS Reeves had been notified by switchboard that Susan Callaghan had turned up. She went to set up an interview room and DC Brenton went to fetch Susan.

He also fetched everyone a cup of hot chocolate, a small cup, at least it was Cadburys.

Susan was still looking very pale and nervous, not dissimilar to when she tried to comfort her after finding the body.

'Just try and relax Susan, you're not under arrest, we just need your help.' 'Yes love, sorry Ma'am, no sorry err Officer.'

'It's Jane, call me Jane.'

'Thank you, just need warming up a bit, it's biting cold out there.' 'How did you get here?'

'Walked mainly, my husband drops me off at the cathedral and I don't drive.' 'That's a long walk.'

'I got a bus to Morrison's and then walked, sorry.'

'Ah ok, don't worry, we will give you a lift back when we have done.'

DS Reeves explained the procedure to her, confirmed she was not under arrest, was not a suspect interview but she could have a solicitor if she wanted. She declined.

'Ok Susan, let's get on with it shall we?'

DC Reeves opened with:

'Susan, I know you've given this account before, now we have you on tape please can you tell me what happened when you went into the cathedral on Thursday morning?'

'I went up to the doors and noticed the gate was unlocked. I thought that was odd, but the big wooden door was locked, so I entered the cathedral. I picked up my cleaning bag and walked into the building. Then I saw that body near the altar. I panicked, screamed, dropped my cleaning things, and went closer just to make sure it was a body. However, what else could it be? I ran out to raise the alarm, only to be met by Derek coming in. I told him what I'd found, he took a few steps into the nave and saw it, then he came back to me and took me over to the seats, got us a cuppa and then when I caught my breath and my heart stopped beating ten to the dozen I called you. I had a wander around a bit, I still couldn't believe there was a body, I peeked around the corner, I didn't touch him Officer, and I didn't.'

'Forensics show your prints weren't on the candlestick. How do you explain that with you being the cleaner?'

'I never touch the candlesticks when cleaning, only dust around them, I'm very careful with church objects, especially near the altar. If I do have to handle artifacts, as I call them, I put on my silk gloves so I don't damage or rub anything; some of them are hundreds of years old you know.'

Reeves listened carefully, then asked:

'Susan, your fingerprint has however been found on one of the ledgers that was on the floor of the nave, it is a fingerprint in some blood, how can you explain that?'

Susan sat there, tearful, thinking. 'I think I remember seeing the ledger on the floor of the nave. Without thinking, I picked it up to put it back on the table. It shouldn't have been there, but I wasn't thinking straight. I don't even remember doing it. I must have touched blood on the cover before lifting it. You're not going to arrest me for tampering with evidence, are you?'

'No, don't worry, we just need your help to understand what about the scene may have changed.'

'Derek said he picked the ledger up off the floor, can you be certain that it was you?'

'Oh god, oh I shouldn't say that should I? It could have been that he picked it up and gave it to me, or I picked it up and gave it to him. I can't rightly remember,' she paused. 'I think I did that as I walked past before I sat down for the tea, I was in a tizzy, didn't think, just picked it up, didn't see any blood. Maybe it was already dried, or I wiped my finger on my dress, it was dark brown, it wouldn't have shown. There's a place for everything and everything in its place. It belonged in the office, so I was going to take it there, but then panic took over and I sat down, but whether I put it down or gave it Derek, I can't remember, I'm so sorry.'

'Why didn't you tell us this before?'

'I didn't think about it at first, then played things over in my mind, was terrified and ashamed, worried I'd be accused of tampering. I thought admitting I'd touched something near the body would make me look guilty. It's all I've thought about for days, walking in there and finding the body, it's just me, I clean, I tidy up, put things away, that's what I do. My Ray says if he puts his tea cup down whether he's finished or not it will be in the washing up bowl before he realises it's gone.' Susan was still shaking.

'I think I need you in my flat Susan,' said Reeves, trying to reassure and relax her.

'Do you know anything about the Blakes' disputes over money or cathedral accounts?'

Susan shook her head. 'I keep out of family business. I know Michael and Edward argued often, sometimes even in the cathedral, but never about details.'

Brenton asked, 'When you found the body, did you know straight away whether it was Michael or Edward Blake?'

Susan shook her head again. 'No, no, I didn't. I didn't even know if it was one of them. I saw the body, the blood, and I almost fainted. Derek had to sit me down and get me a cup of tea. I didn't even know it was one of them until I heard your officer, the handsome young man with the ginger beard and tattoos, say the driving licence was Edward's. They look so alike, don't they? It was only when I saw the coat again as I walked out that I thought it might be Edward like he said. He wore that grey wool one all the time. But I couldn't be sure. I didn't like to look again.'

Brenton carried on. 'So at that moment, you weren't certain who it was?'

'No. Even after hearing the name Edward and the coat, I hadn't seen his face and didn't want to look.'

'You mentioned before that Edward had been in the cathedral a day or two before. What was he doing?'

'He asked me some questions… about who'd been around, whether the ledgers had been moved. He seemed worried, but I didn't press. Not my place. He went into the office and I carried on cleaning.'

'Did you get on with Edward?'

'He was polite enough. But he always seemed a bit tense. Guarded. Michael was warmer. He'd stop, ask after my mum, and pass the time of day. Edward never did that.'

'So you preferred Michael?'

'I suppose so, yes. He seemed more human, he was a bit daft, forgetful, forgot to put the cash register away, put the bibles on the wrong pulpits, that sort of thing. I didn't know either of them well.'

DC Reeves then interjected. 'What about Derek?'

Susan smiled. 'Oh, Derek is lovely. Always helpful if I'm carrying something heavy, or if I've run out of polish he'll find me some. He remembers birthdays too. Kind, really. Makes a proper good brew as well. Not everyone can do that, you know. I mean, did you know some people put the milk in first? Abomination,' she said, giggling to herself.

'Do you think he could have been the one stealing from the cathedral?'

She laughed. 'Derek? No. Not in a million years. If anything went missing, he'd be the one trying to sort it out. He tried to help out with the basic day to day accounts, but numbers aren't his forte if you know what I mean?'

'And yet the ledgers suggest someone was moving money about. Who do you think it was?'

She shrugged. 'I don't know, Detective. People higher up than me, that's for sure. It's not my world.'

'You mentioned that others sometimes come and go. Does anyone stand out?'

She nodded. 'There's a man, well boy, he's about twenty two to twenty five I'd say… Nick, I think? He comes into the office sometimes, in dirty dusty dungarees. I don't know his surname. He makes me uneasy. Can't say why, he's never done anything wrong to me, but when he's about, the room feels colder, if you know what I mean.'

'What makes you uncomfortable?'

She fidgeted with her hands and looked a little embarrassed. 'Just the way he looks at people. Like he's weighing you up. Gives me shivers. I've only seen him two or three times. I'm there six days a week, only part time, a few hours a day, tides me over. Sometimes you don't know do you, it's just a feeling.'

'DC Brenton, anything you would like to ask Susan while she is still here?'

'Yes, you've said before both of the Blake brothers would come to the cathedral and they both had roles to perform, what about their wives? Helen and Pamela?'

'Pamela, common as muck, doesn't know how she got with Edward. 'Muck and brass attract, 'is that what they say? But having said that, she was pleasant enough. She filled in a day here and there with the cleaning if I wasn't around, and she would come in when we had special days or additional functions to help out. Her dog is lovely, Clive I think his name is, something like that. Funny name for a dog that…'

'Thank you, and Helen?'

'Helen is a kind lady, she helps out when we have an Eucharist, she would do little guided walks with the public around the building. She sometimes looked like she had the weight of the world on her shoulders, poor love, she must be beside herself with Michael gone.'

The interview was wrapped up and DC Brenton gave Susan a lift. She went home, being interviewed by the police was enough excitement for the day and she wanted to get home and tell Ray all about it.

CHAPTER 12

After the interviews Katie went into the back car park to get her car and started to make her way back to Euston Street. Her paranoia still getting the better of her, before she clicked the fob she checked all four doors and the boot. She sat in both front seats and checked the mirror. Everything was as it should be. In reality it was a locked private car park; if the person stalking her had interfered with her car here, it would have to be a cop. And only one cop fit the bill in her mind. It was rush hour, snow had started to fall, and the roads were mushy. Vaughan Way was rammed as usual; she was going nowhere fast. Traffic continued inching towards St Nicholas Circle, not far from the Cathedral. The grey buildings looked even greyer in the dull darkness lit by street lights.

She was still crawling up to the bend, where the underpass was an option, and she looked to her right. The traffic in that lane, going under the underpass, had started to flow a little more as it split from the traffic going the other route. By now it was too late for Katie to swap lanes to get to the underpass. Three lanes of traffic with a moderate flow would have been difficult enough to manoeuvre, but not in this traffic, so she was stuck with what she had.

She noticed a grey estate car. As it drove by her the driver seemed to look her way. The inner light was on; maybe she imagined it, maybe it was just a bored driver stuck in traffic having a look around, pretty much the same as she was doing. It was a younger male, in his twenties, but then the car was no longer parallel. Even though three lanes over, she could no longer see his face; it was only a glimpse. There was a second male in the car in the passenger seat; he looked away as she looked at their car. She could see the rear of the vehicle as it went into the underpass. No registration plate. Damn. Is this the car that was at Helen's, that had turned around in her drive, potentially leaving the note at her home? Her heart rate sped up almost immediately. Is he following her again, who is he?

She knew that both roads would converge again at the junction of Newarke Street, but she also knew he had taken the quicker route and would reach those lights before her.

The red lights ahead of her changed. The cars started to move onto the busy roundabout.

'Come on, move, drive!'

She was yelling at the cars in front, but they were only inching forward. Only a few cars got through. Katie's light was barely amber when she went through it, but she made it through, only to be hampered by buses in the layby. Typical, never one coming when you want one, and then two in your way when you don't. She wished she was in a marked car with blues and twos, but she wasn't and there was nothing she could do about it. She manoeuvred around the buses, went around the left bend, and towards the traffic lights on Southgates. There were a good few cars ahead of her, and the lights were about to change to red.

She then noticed that the grey car without a rear plate had already gone through a red light and was on Newarke Street. By the time the lights changed twice and she got onto Newarke Street, the car was nowhere to be seen. She hit the steering wheel, grinding her teeth. It had to be the same car, didn't it? A sudden thought came to mind. She didn't actually know what car Briggs drove. She made a mental note to check in the car park. Surely he wouldn't park a car with no registration plates in the police car park.

She warily continued slowly up Welford Road, past the gym and then past Leicester prison, watching all lanes of traffic as she did. There were no more sightings of the car. She would also ask Tom to take a look at the cameras on Vaughan Way and Newarke, approximately seventeen thirty-five she thought, when he would have come around.

She eventually made it back to the Station ten minutes later. The snow had yet again turned to rain, and as she made a little effort to jog into the station she got caught, as her fob wasn't working at the rear gate.

She went into the changing rooms on the ground floor, and, angling her head under the hand dryer, attempted to dry her hair before it plastered itself to her head.

Making her way upstairs she passed Tom Ilkley.

'Had some results back from the CCTV and the Track My iPhone.'

'Go on.'

'It seemed to sit still until about three a.m. in the middle of nowhere on the tracking app. It turns out that it is in St George's Churchyard near the Curve. Looking at some footage, it shows Michael walking from Queen Street, slipping on some black ice and stumbling into the churchyard. Looks like he may have knocked himself out for a while.'

'Ok, anyone around or go through there?'

'A couple of people do, but nothing unusual.'

'I've been down there with Briggs and behind a tree a few metres into the churchyard, but out of sight from the path, a brown leather satchel.'

'Did you find it or Briggs?'

'He did, I was walking the path.'

'When you went to the location did either of you take your own bags?'

'Eh, sorry Sarge?'

'Did you or Alan have anything in your hands?'

'No, why?'

'It doesn't matter, carry on, good work.'

'It was soggy, but it's definitely his, matches what he left the Queen's Quarter with, and had his Cathedral badge and some other bits of paperwork in, with his name on.'

'Did you open it there and then?'

'No, Briggs passed it to me, I bagged it, we then drove on to check some other locations. When we got back, we opened it on the desk.'

Why was she suspicious of Alan, what made her think he was involved? She couldn't quite put her finger on it. But the niggling doubts were there.

'We've seized footage from Halford Street at around three ten. He is walking very slowly and keeps clutching his head. No one bothers him. He then cuts through the market, as seen on the bank CCTV. Quite a few people about. Then he goes onto Hotel Street, by The Friary. He goes into St Martins and then he is lost. He goes into some of the cobble side streets and we haven't been able to find any further footage. Guildhall Lane camera down.'

'Great work. Does anyone interact with him, follow him, any unusual vehicle activity at all?'

'Not that we can see. As he turns into St Martins, he stops and looks around for a couple of seconds, looks behind him, and then walks on. He had his phone in his hand, so we know he had it at that point. I watched the footage for about fifteen minutes after that, and it was not obvious what, if anything, or who he was looking at. No identifiable or suspicious vehicle movements either. No other angles.'

'Thank you, we need to check everything as you know, appreciate your diligence. Anything on Michael's phone tracking since then?'

'No, it hasn't shown up anywhere. I've set up an alert on the laptop that if it does turn on and a site is located, I'll get a notification.'

'Great idea, thanks Tom. You off now?'

'Yes, Rook said we can regroup tomorrow and see what we've got.'

'Have a good evening. Tom, I haven't asked and it was rude of me. You've been on paternity leave, boy or girl?'

'Little boy, Reuben, my first. He's awesome but doesn't sleep too much at the moment.'

'He'll grow out of it,' she said, as though she had no idea about anything to do with babies. Monty grew out of not sleeping too well when she initially moved; that was close enough. 'Congratulations, have a good evening.'

'Thanks Sarge, you too,' and with that he was gone out the door.

Katie made her way, soggy, into the office. She was ready for home.

'Afternoon Alan, Jane around?'

'She's out with Brenton, went to the Cathedral for something or other. Call from the Dean, so they've gone out to see him.'

'Have you any update for us? I've spoken to Tom about the CCTV and that you've found Michael's bag. Good work,' she said through gritted teeth. He was as surprised as she was to hear those words come out of her mouth.

'There was a USB stick in the pocket of the bag, but it's encrypted, so I've taken it down to the tech people to try and bypass. Oh, and Ratten came in, he's back from his stag do.'

'Did he have anything to say of any interest, anything different to what we already have?'

'I've emailed a copy of his statement to you. Nothing really. I'm off. See you tomorrow.'

Katie walked into her office, quite bemused at the normal, civil interaction between her and Briggs. No weirdness, no defensiveness. Hmm.

She pulled out her seat and switched on the laptop. It took time to whirr to life; it's as though the police only get equipment when it's about obsolete in every other place.

Eventually she was able to get into her emails and clicked on the one from Briggs, scanned the statement through; it was unremarkable.

'This is the statement of James Richard RATTEN. I am making this statement in relation to the events that took place on the evening of Wednesday eighteenth into Thursday nineteenth January two thousand and twenty-three.

I am a Warden at the Leicester Cathedral. My role involves pastoral care, building maintenance, and financial stewardship. I am to assist in keeping records and helping with congregational matters.

I attended the meeting, which was in relation to irregularities in the accounts. Money had been moved, paid to unused or unidentified contractors, and petty cash missing.

Also present Michael and Edward Blake, Derek and Enoch Mkhize, and a male I do not know, whom I think was called Nicholas.

The ledgers were scrutinised and it was noted that around £8,000 appeared to have been misappropriated. The entries did not appear to be those of persons who regularly write in the books. It looked awkward and jittery, potentially written left handed.

Nicholas was pointing the finger at both Edward and Michael; they were passing the buck. Edward said he was an accountant and knew how to do accurate accounts and made pointed remarks about the accounts at their own business and Michael's underhand behaviour. Michael retaliated, saying Edward always tried to cover up by using him as a scapegoat and accusing him of things without evidence. He added, 'It's not just accounts, it's women too.'

Derek Mkhize said that he or his son would look into 'D Barton Ltd' and 'Cohesion Maintenance', which were the companies that appeared to be receiving payment for work that was never authorised or undertaken.

Michael and Edward did leave at one point and were arguing outside, but they came back shortly after.

A takeaway had been ordered, but I left before its arrival as I had a taxi booked to take me to the airport.

This is all I remember from that evening. Signed

James Richard RATTEN

The only thing that was clarified was that the 'other thing' that Edward was accusing Michael of was something to do with a woman, possibly the affair that he was going to speak to Helen about.

Katie closed down the laptop and made her way down to the changing rooms, changed her shoes, put on her coat and made her way back outside into the cold and wet. She turned up the collar of her green wax coat to rush over to her car, which she had deliberately parked as close to the gates as she could get it. The last shift had started a number of hours ago, but the car park was thinning out. All seemed in order with her car; it was where she had parked it. She opened the door and looked at the seats and the rear-view mirror, all ok. With a little relief she got into the car, started the engine and drove out of the station car park, up the hill, around the one-way system, remembering as she pulled onto Putney Road, 'The Range'.

She pulled into the car park where Halfords and The Range were situated and made her way into the store. She located the aisle with picture frames so many different ones. She picked up a silver-coloured 10x8 ' frame with some scrolls etched into it; she also picked up a black one and stood looking at them for a moment, and decided on the silver, and then went to find the lint rollers. She picked up two packs of those and went to the counter to pay. She then got back into her car and started to make her way home.

She was crawling along the A6 into Oadby and was feeling very hungry; she hadn't eaten half of her meal deal from earlier due to the interviews. At the last minute she switched lanes to nip into Sainsbury's to get herself a ready meal. She was also kicking herself, as she promised when she moved new place, new Katie, new start that she would be healthy, but she just didn't have the time when there was a live murder investigation.

After manoeuvring her way around the store, she found the ready meals, tried to pick the ones that sounded a little healthier, and settled on the 'Gym Kitchen Thai Green Chicken Curry Ready Meal for 1'. That, she thought, was the closest she would get to a gym for some time.

She paid, made her way back to the car and carried on home, pulling into her driveway a few minutes later.

Angela was putting the rubbish out when Katie drove up to park her car. She got out with her work bag and ready meal.

'Katie love, I'm so sorry for not getting back to you. It's absolutely fine if you want to get a cat flap put in the back door. It will be lovely to see Monty strolling around and enjoying the sun in the summertime. It's been a few years since I lost Tonka; I've often thought about getting another one.'

'Thanks for that, I'll look into it when I get a minute.'

'You're always on the go, love; that job of yours will have you in an early grave if you don't mind.'

That might be more true than you realise, she thought to herself.

'I know, I need to pace myself. First things first is food. Thanks again for getting back to me, I appreciate it.'

'You're more than welcome.'

Katie unlocked the front door and walked into her home. Monty immediately appeared, rubbing himself around her legs. 'Give me a second, boy, let me put all this down.'

She hung up her coat, took off her boots and put on her slippers, her bag and phone on the table, and she took the food into the kitchen.

Monty was jumping up the side of the work counter as Katie emptied his sachet of food into his bowl and replenished his biscuits. She then looked at the instructions on the pack and put it in the microwave. It was only going to take about six minutes, with a stir in the middle.

There was a ping from her mobile phone; her heart sped up a little. She was being ridiculous; she got messages from many people.

As she clicked into the WhatsApp notification, two pictures started to load. The data clicked into Wi-Fi and the pictures appeared. She wasn't being ridiculous.

One of a silver photo frame with etched design. One of a pack of lint rollers.

The ping of the microwave made her jump, dropping her phone onto the sofa. 'Shit, shit,' she said to herself.

He was letting her know that he was always close, always watching, even when doing something mundane like buying a lint roller. Whoever he was.

Katie ate her food, though all of a sudden wasn't feeling hungry anymore more sickened. The more she ate, the more her stomach gurgled, her heart rate not settling. She sat for a couple of hours in the window, watching the entrance to the drive, scrolling through her laptop, trying to take her mind off it. She couldn't turn her brain off.

She was still shaking when she went to bed. The electric blanket wasn't on and it was cold upstairs, making her shiver even more. Monty came up and cuddled into her on the bed; she held him tight. Scared. She eventually fell asleep.

CHAPTER 13

Wednesday morning came around much too soon.

Katie was woken from her sleep by Monty, yowling for his food and treading over her chest. 'Mont, it's half past six,' she said, turning her head to look at the clock. Half past six meant nothing to Monty; when he wanted breakfast, he wanted breakfast. So Katie got up, went downstairs, put the kettle on, and put some food out for him. He chomped at it, purring away. She looked out of the kitchen window. Some heavy snow had fallen overnight, about three inches deep judging by the piles on the bird bath and garden table.

Katie popped two slices of wholemeal bread into the toaster and got some butter and blackberry jam out of the fridge. She sat down with her tea and powered up the laptop.

With a little trepidation she looked at her phone nothing. Relief.

When she opened her emails, she saw a number of new ones. One from Colin Swift; he was one of the officers in the digital hub who was to be examining Helen's phone.

The toast popped out of the toaster, almost burnt   just as she liked it. She spread it with butter and jam and then sat back down at her laptop to have a look at what Colin had to say.

It read:

Evening Katie, I've sent the full report to Tom Ilkley who requested it, but as you authorised it, I thought I would summarise the main findings so far.

1. Edward Blake's phone number, as we have it, is in the phone   it is only used for family matters as far as texts show.

2. There is an unidentified number where messages suggest they may be meeting or having an affair; these have been protected in a 'for my eyes only' folder. There are some similarities between the text and writing style and Edward's messages.

3. There is a second number which has regular contact with her   07966553433. These messages are brief, some explicit, potentially a second suitor?

4. This mobile phone remained connected to the Wi-Fi at the home address on Stonelea, from 5pm on Wednesday 18th through until 9:45am on Thursday 19th.

5. There is a log-on to 'Find My Phone - Michael Blake' at 02:18. No response from the app.

6. At 03:31, 03:44 and 04:01 there are outgoing calls to Michael Blake's known number.

7. Interestingly, at 00:30 and 03:46 there are calls to the 433 number. Only the latter call is answered and it lasts for just four seconds and the recipient hangs up.

8. At 04:08 the phone texts the 433 number: 'What have you done, wtf have you done?' No response back.

9. The last call from 433 to this phone was at 09:12 on Monday 20th and lasted three minutes.

10.   All of the calls mentioned were made from this home address.

All the messages have been downloaded into the report.
Hope that's been of some use.

Yours,
Colin

Well, Katie ran through her head, that means, unless
Helen has been very clever and left her mobile at home,
gone into town tracking him using another phone, killed
him and come home again to make calls, she wasn't the one
who attacked him.

But she clearly thought her mystery number could be
involved in something. She wouldn't have known what had
happened at that time, or that it was Michael. Had she sent
someone to hurt Michael or Edward? Had she known, maybe
her lover had gone to speak to Edward, but on realising she
couldn't get hold of Michael, a mistake had been made?

That last call from the unknown number was less than
an hour before Helen had been arrested. Was it someone who
knew she might be spoken to again, warning her off
speaking, or did someone try to blackmail her to admit to the
murder to cover for them?

Just when she thought she was answering questions,
more were coming out of the woodwork.

Having caught up with her emails, she finished her toast
and went and took a shower. She got dressed and decided to
leave early; the snow would be slowing the traffic, so she
thought she would get ahead of the game and make her way.
She put on her wellington boots, put her shoes into a bag,
picked up her bag with the laptop in, and proceeded to her
car and out of the drive.

As expected, the journey was slow, the snow still falling. As she was early, the roads hadn't seen much traffic, so the snow was compacting rather than melting.

She pulled into the nearest petrol station to refill, even though she still had half a tank. It was a habit   below half, refill.

She once left home in Yorkshire with the petrol gauge already in the red, knowing there was a petrol station off the motorway about six miles ahead and thinking she should have plenty to get there. Halfway to the services, she found the motorway closed for an RTC. She and everyone else were diverted along a country route that seemed to go on for hours, sitting still or crawling, watching the little needle edge towards empty. The car juddered and coughed, but she was just able to pull into a layby in the middle of the North York Moors. That wasn't going to happen again.

As she went up to the desk to pay, taking her bank card out of her warrant card holder, she glanced at the newspaper rack. Last night's *Leicester Mercury* 'Love Triangle to Body In The Cathedral'. 'Ugh,' she thought, 'where have they got that from?' She'd have a read. She picked one up. 'I'll take one of these too, please,' she said to the girl behind the desk before presenting her card to the contactless machine.

She was the first one there when she arrived in the office. Having changed her boots for shoes, she went to the kitchen and made herself a cup of tea.

DC Dean Brenton was starting his day at the industrial estate which had been identified as having links to 'Cohesion Maintenance', one of the businesses that the cathedral's funds had been making payments to. He made his way directly from home in Loughborough over to Oadby; it was a long drive in the snow and, as the traffic got heavier, the journey got slower.

Parking up in the estate, he looked at the board which identified each of the units. None of them were 'Cohesion'. He pulled his laptop out of his bag, skipped through to the invoices which had been left with the ledger. 28th September 2022 £2,850 paid to Cohesion, Unit 14, and a further £3,800 on 18th November 2022. The invoices had been named to a Gordon Critch.

He had already done a search on Companies House no such business. He had searched the name 'Gordon Critch' no involvement with any company and didn't seem to be a resigned director of any company either.

Dean parked up next to Unit 14, which displayed the name JPS Motors. Getting out of his car, he realised just how effective his car heater was since he had it repaired. He put on his gloves, did up his coat and walked up to the doors of the unit. The doors were closed, but lights were on inside, and footprints in the snow suggested a couple of people had entered quite recently. One looked like a slim-footed, pointy-toed shoe probably a female and some big clompy boot prints.

He pressed the buzzer on the intercom. 'JPS,' came the woman's voice. 'Good morning, DC Brenton, Leicester Police. I wonder if I can come in and speak with you?' A buzzer sounded and the door clicked. He pushed it and it opened. He stepped in and was greeted by a robust lady in a grey wool pinafore dress and a grey cardigan. She was wearing short, thin-heeled grey ankle boots potentially a killer in the snow and ice, he thought. She matched the grey walls and the grey carpet; he wondered if this was done on purpose. 'Morning officer, Jane Hubbard, manager, come in.' She led the way into a small office, indicated a seat for him and took a seat behind a desk.

'How can I help you?'

'We have come across some invoices in relation to a current investigation that seem to have the address of this unit, but not your name   did your business change names recently?'

'No, we've been JPS for over fifteen years who are you looking for?'

'A Mr Critch, Cohesion Maintenance.'

'No, sorry, means nothing to me, but hold on, I wasn't doing the accounts last year.' She swung around ninety degrees in her swivel chair, which was also grey, and dialled an extension. 'Gary, can you pop in the office for me please?' She placed the phone back down.

Less than a minute later a man appeared: early 30s, dark wavy hair, slim, wearing dirty jeans and a checked shirt. 'Son, this is DC Brenton, he's after some invoices.'

'Detective, this is my son, Gary, he was doing invoices last year, but he has moved into stock management and fitting, that's why he is always dirty.'

'Mum! Good morning, how can I help?'

Brenton explained the invoices he had which indicated they were for a company at their address.

'Yes, hold on, that name is familiar,' and he disappeared out of the office.

A few minutes later he returned with some paperwork, which he handed over to Brenton.

Three invoices, all for Cohesion Maintenance, all paid invoices. All paid by Leicester Cathedral.

'Any idea of what they are for? Who they are and who Critch is?'

'No, when they arrived, I checked them against our outgoing invoices and against payments into our account and there was nothing matching. I didn't know if they were for us but the wrong company had put them on, so I held onto them to check and then forgot about them and left them in my tray. Unlikely the Cathedral would have paid us for anything, so wasn't surprised when they didn't turn out to be ours.'

'Do you mind if I take these?'

'Be my guest,' said Jane. DC Brenton slipped the invoices into an evidence bag.

'I take it you didn't keep the envelopes?' he asked, more in hope than expectation.

'No, sorry.'

'No-one has come to this unit asking about invoices or paperwork?'

'No, no-one, I've been on reception since December, Gary was in there before then.' Gary shook his head also.

'Well, thank you for your time, I appreciate it.'

'No problem,' they both said. Gary showed him out.

Whilst there, he popped into another six or seven units which had lights on, asking about the company name and the name Critch. A couple of places said Gary had asked them the same. The answer was the same everywhere. Never heard of them, never heard of him. He noted the places he had been to in case DS Lounds wanted him to try the others, but he thought it was a red herring, just a fake invoice to cover up for stealing. But why send one out to a fake address? Just leave an invoice in the Cathedral paperwork, less hassle.

With no luck, no further forward, he made his way back over to Euston Street.

The team were gathered together in the incident room.

Kate dropped the newspaper on the table. 'Has anyone spoken to the press? The press office have not issued anything to do with a love triangle. They have named the deceased as Michael Blake and seem to have the inkling that there was an affair.'

There were head shakes around the room.

'Maybe Edward, he isn't happy at the lack of progress, he thought his brother was cheating on Helen,' said Ilkley.

'Pot kettle he was sleeping with his sister-in-law,' said another.

Page three had further details and three photographs. One of Michael Blake, whether that came from a family member or social media was not known. Another showed the body bag being loaded into the black-windowed private ambulance. They had tried to get the van as close to the doors as they could, but those journos get into tight angles. The third picture was of her, DS Lounds, leaving the Cathedral and glaring at the camera.

DI Rook had been through the up-to-date position and he allocated some tasks during the briefing.

'Alan, can you go through the CCTV around St Martins? I want to know if Edward Blake did go home or went looking for Michael, or took the ledgers back. Can you also do some checks on this Nick please the male who was at the meeting but no-one appears to know anything about. His image from the Queen Street CCTV is on the briefing and on your emails.' Alan got up and walked out of the room; the CCTV and monitors were down the corridor.

'Tom and Dean, there are a lot of messages on Michael's phone, can one of you take texts and the other WhatsApp and see if you can find anything relevant please?'

'Yes, Boss,' said both.

'Jane, can you do a few more checks and searches on Pamela Blake? Her background, marriage and reports to the police other than the one we know of. Checks at the old address. We've not got a lot on her.'

'No problem, Sir, leave it with me.'

'Katie, take Helen's phone please. We've had the initial report from Colin, you've read the email. Can you do some cross-checking of numbers? Try to trace any unknown ones please. We've also got the download of the USB from

Michael's satchel if you can run your eyes over that when you get a minute. I know that's a mammoth task, but we need to make a start, it's almost a week and we don't have a clear suspect.'

'Of course. Yes, we have a few blurred ones though,' she replied.

DI Rook went back into his office and closed the door, sitting down at his desk. He looked at the evidence board. Something had to come soon, something that would point them in the right direction for answers instead of going round in circles and leading to more questions.

He hadn't had breakfast and had picked up a bacon and sausage cob from a trailer down the road, so he walked down the corridor to pop it in the microwave. Within about thirty seconds, that most wonderful smell of cooking bacon filled the room and drifted out of the open door into the corridor.

He went back into his office and put a battery in his radio. He turned on the intranet and searched for PC James Elliott, PC four six three five. Checking his duties, he was on an early shift.

He point-to-pointed him on the radio; it was answered right away. 'Go ahead.'

'PC Elliott, this is DI Rook, can you speak?'

'Yes, yes Sir, what can I help you with?'

'I understand you and your crew mate PC Kang were first to arrive at the Cathedral last week, is that correct?'

James sounded worried. 'Yes Sir, we arrived alongside PC Chester and PC Lucas. We were there for about fifteen minutes before CID arrived.'

'Tell me what you did please.'

'Yes, we walked in and straight ahead, where we were greeted by an IC three male, I think his name was Derek. He said the cleaner had found a body. Chester and Lucas initially waited outside. Derek walked us a little further in and we could see the body, face down, blood on the back of his head and some underneath his chest on the floor. I put on some gloves and bent down to test for a pulse; it didn't look likely but I tried his wrist and neck. Nothing. Close to where his chest was laying on the flagstones was a wallet; must've fallen out of his inside coat pocket maybe. I picked it up, looked at the driving licence and bagged it. I gave it to DS Lounds when she came.'

'Did you move any part of him?'

'No, boss, other than lifting his wrist to try for a pulse, but I put it back. My bodycam was on so you can see before and after.'

'Did you touch anything that was around?'

'No, as soon as I confirmed he was dead, I called up to control to confirm a dead body and request more mobiles and supervisory. Kang went over to Derek and the cleaner. I went to the doors and confirmed it to the other crew, who put the police tape up on the door and started a log. Chester did a wider cordon around the garden and the alleys at the side. I think other response mobiles then turned up to stand on the cordon.'

'Did you search the body further, check coat pockets etc?'

'No, I didn't. CID started to turn up, I don't know their names. The older man and younger female came first; the female went over to the witnesses and the male went and looked at the body. I don't know if he searched, I wasn't looking. I'd been asked to help out with camming the scene by the female officer.'

'Did you ever see a mobile phone at the scene that could have belonged to the victim, or hear anyone mention it?'

'No, I didn't Sir, sorry.'

'Thank you for your time James, over.'

CHAPTER 14

A couple of hours later, Jane came into the office where Katie and Rook were. 'Not a lot on Pam Blake, boss. She and Edward have lived on Balmoral Close in Knighton since twenty-seventeen. She called the police in twenty-twenty when his car was stolen from outside his business premises. She worked for a few months in Blake Bros Accountancy. She was a witness to an assault in twenty-nineteen when she worked at a bakery on Queens Road. She doesn't appear to have a driving licence. Had an expired provisional from two thousand and nine. She doesn't have much of an online presence, Facebook is all I can find. Nothing of immediate interest from what I am able to see from the public view.'

'Interesting,' said Katie. 'When she was interviewed she said numbers 'made her eyes swim 'when I asked her if she looked at the ledgers so obtained for Edward. Strange that she worked in an accountants for a few years then.'

'She might have been a cleaner, or a receptionist, I suppose,' added Jane.

Next to come in was Dean Brenton. He went through the WhatsApp messages from Michael's phone. There didn't seem to be much. Normal husband and wife messages between him and Helen, a couple where she was asking when he was going to be home, asking him where he was as she had called the office and they said they hadn't seen him that day. No accusations. There was a number between him and Edward, which clearly showed their differences. There was a thread of Edward telling him that he thought Helen was seeing someone else, Michael sniping back that he didn't suspect her; there was no evidence of that, etc. The last WhatsApp was Edward saying, 'Don't be so sure, sometimes you just don't know, spouses can cover things well.'

'Is he gloating that he was sleeping with his brother's wife? Was he suggesting he thought Pam was having an affair or did he really have evidence she was seeing someone else? We definitely know there is another number that she was sending spicy messages to,' mused Katie.

'It's not unusual for people to have a second phone nowadays, for various reasons,' added Rook.

Brenton continued, 'I know I wasn't tasked with this this morning, but when Tom and I started on the CCTV yesterday, there was definitely a blue BMW skirting the Guildhall area around three a.m. Didn't see a registration, could have been Edward's. More CCTV needed. There was also a grey Ford, no rear plate.'

Katie's heart started to beat a little faster. She glanced at Jane. 'What about it?'

'It was also doing circles around the same area. KP was all we could make out on the front plate. Hopefully Briggs will pick them both up. We've put it in the log he's got, so hopefully he'll trace it a bit further.'

'Good work, Dean. Can you take over on the USB please? I need Katie for something else.'

'Of course,' said Katie. She picked the evidence bag with the USB in and handed it over to Dean, with a printout of what she had already been through.

Alan was next to come back in, mug of coffee and a Chelsea bun in hand.

'Blue BMW is around Peacock Lane, Loseby Lane, traced it back to Charles Street around three a.m., and it makes its way towards Peacock Lane, Guildhall Lane area after that. Seems to be just driving around. Pulls into a side street off Guildhall Lane about three-fifteen, next seen Jubilee Square onto High Street about three-forty-five, where it stops.'

'Yes,' said Katie. 'Could be Edward's then. He did say he had been staying in an Airbnb in town and there are a few new apartment blocks around Highcross which have been turned into Airbnb.'

'Did you get the plate from all that footage?'

'There were plenty of good angles of the front and rear of the car. It looked, though, like there was some kind of reflector on it. I've asked for the ANPR photos,' added Alan.

'What about the grey Ford without a rear plate? Find anything on that?' said Rook.

'No, a couple of grey cars, but nothing specific.'

Dean looked at Katie quizzically and started to speak. 'But...' just as she raised a hand and gave a brief shake of her head. He stopped with a puzzled look on his face.

'Thanks, Alan. Let us know when the ANPR images come through,' said Rook.

Katie had earlier had a brief chat with Rook about her suspicions of something strange about Briggs' behaviour when it came to Helen and the missing phone. What is the connection between the car that had been stalking her and Alan? Why doesn't he want it tracing?

Katie's desk phone began to ring. She walked quickly to stop it going to voicemail. It was the control room, telling her she had a visitor sitting in the front office who wanted to speak with her about the accounts and ledgers for the Cathedral.

'Enoch Mkhize downstairs, about the Cathedral accounts.'

'I'll chase the ANPR and look at the CCTV again,' said Rook. 'You go and speak with him, you know more about the ledgers.'

'Yes, boss,' she said, picking up her notebook, a pen, and her phone as she headed down to the front office.

Opening the internal door, she could see a number of people in the front office. 'Mr Mkhize?' she enquired.

'Yes, ma'am, that's me,' said a very well-dressed male in a suit, waistcoat, shirt, and tie. He stood up and offered a hand to be shaken. Katie shook his hand. 'Come through,' she said, leading her way through the corridors and secured doors to the interview rooms. She took the second corridor of interview rooms; there were fewer rooms and it was likely to be quieter.

'Please take a seat. Can I get you a drink?' she asked her guest.

'I would love a coffee, black, two sugars, thank you,' said Enoch.

Katie disappeared out of the room to fetch the drinks, and Enoch started to set out papers onto the table, along with his iPad, which he logged into.

Katie returned with two paper cups of coffee and placed them on the table. 'Thank you.'

'I understand that you think you have discovered the missing or misdirected funds, Enoch?'

'I do, ma'am.'

'Call me Katie.'

'Katie, I scanned the ledgers at the meeting. I quite like figures and paper trails, but it was impossible to go through them with everyone arguing and bickering about who could have stolen it. Therefore, I thought I would take them home and go through them at my own pace, and I'd be able to nip into the Cathedral to check against anything else if I needed to. Some people were pointing the finger at my dad and I couldn't have that. He would never do that; he is the most honest, God-fearing man I know.'

Katie then asked, 'What did you deduce?'

'Ok, in late twenty-nineteen we had some works done on some walls in the rear of the Cathedral grounds, two separate attendances by workmen we had sourced.' There was a dispute about the workmanship and the invoices weren't paid. Twenty-twenty comes along and Covid. Those invoices were forgotten about, by us anyway, by the time she could all come back and access things. In twenty-twenty-two we received a letter from the Court; the building company had opened a small claim. The then Dean, The Very Reverend Andrew Bymarsh-Graham, had said to just pay them; the Cathedral didn't need the fuss. We have had a new Dean since September, The Very Reverend Peter Tasselthwaite, so he wouldn't have been aware. The office was told just to pay.'

He shuffled through his papers to produce the court documents and slid them across the desk. She picked them up and studied them. 'Cohesion Maintenance? But it was said that the Cathedral knew nothing about that company and that they don't exist on Companies House?'

'That's right,' replied Enoch, gliding through pages on the iPad. 'When the work was done, it was 'Emerald Incorporated Building. 'They were who did the work, three separate invoices totalling £6,650.' He slid the iPad over to show her three invoices in the name of Emerald. 'It turns out one of the directors of Emerald died and the business closed, and the surviving director had become 'Cohesion Maintenance 'but as a sole trader.'

'His name?'

'Gordon Critch.'

'So the office just paid out the money, two invoices made into one payment and a second invoice for the last one.'

'Yes, I see that, that makes sense.'

'Yes, doesn't it? It's such a relief.'

'The other two were easy, £760 to D Barton. In August last year, we had some renovation done and we hired two skips. For some reason the bank transfer was made to the boss of the firm, David Barton, instead of 'Leicester Skip Hire 'which was normally done.'

'The final one, £651.80, that was in August twenty-twenty-two, was a bankers draft, so no bank account details, but sifting through the paperwork, that went to Ray Callaghan.'

'Susan, the cleaner's husband?'

'The very same,' said Enoch, nodding enthusiastically. 'He attended an auction somewhere in Norfolk. There was a first edition book from the sixteen-hundreds or something, about St Martin's Church, which became Leicester Cathedral. He had permission from the Dean, the old Dean, to acquire it if he could with a budget of £800. He spent £651.80 including fees, and that invoice I've found misfiled.'

Katie looked at the obvious errors in disbelief, shaking her head. Could Michael have been murdered because someone thought he, or Edward if they got the wrong person, was stealing from the Cathedral funds, when no such theft had taken place?

'So there is nothing missing, just poor accounting methods?'

'Exactly that. It looks like it was Edward doing the accounts at the time; he really isn't much of an accountant. Emails show he was asking the secretary, Lynda Bloom, to pay invoices and enter the info into the ledgers. That'll be why the handwritten wasn't the usual.' He again showed her images and all the evidence, either in paper form or on his device.

'Enoch, you've done an amazing job and saved us a lot of work,' she said, shaking his hand again.

'You're very welcome. Like I say, I like numbers and paper trails, and I couldn't have my dad being accused of anything, or anyone else for that matter.'

She again thanked him as she packed away all his paperwork into his rucksack. 'Could you scan those bits through to me, just the bits which support what you're saying?'

'Of course I will,' he said. Katie handed him her card with her email address on.

'I appreciate you coming in, Enoch. I really do.'

'No problem at all, Katie. Thank you for listening.'

'Oh, Enoch, ring your dad. He's reported you missing as he hasn't heard from you and you didn't go to his place yesterday. I'll update and close our report.'

'Oh, sorry. I just got waylaid, head in the books and the numbers. I'll do it right away.'

Katie then let him out of the secure doors, and he made his way over to his car, the crackling frozen snow noisy underfoot.

Katie returned to the office and explained to Rook and Jane who were present. So no-one had been tampering with the accounts, but that doesn't mean it could still be a motive, if they believed someone had been.

'Do you think he's legit, not just created paperwork and explanations to get his dad off the hook?'

'No, I think he's straight.'

They still had a number of enquiries to make, and were waiting for results to come back. They would try and not have to bother any of the Blake family today with questions.

Michael's body had been released and his parents and brother had arranged a quick funeral. His father was Jewish; the brothers did not follow in their father's religion. Even so, it was to be a Jewish funeral. Michael took no religion himself. The parents, Lynda and Gordon Blake, had not been spoken to; they would have to be approached at some time, but not today. The funeral would be taking place at Jewish Gilroes in Leicester at two p.m. Officers were to attend mainly to watch, observe behaviours, and see who turns up.

Katie, Alan, and Jane were to attend the funeral. Always good to see what is happening, who is avoiding whom, anyone turning up whom they weren't expecting, or behaving in a way that would be suspicious.

Katie saw this as her chance to find the answer to one of her questions without having to ask, go searching, or follow him out of the station at the end of their shift. 'Alan, do you think we could go in your car? Mine had a bit of a rattle this morning; I think I might need oil, so I don't want to travel too far before I've popped into Halfords,' she lied.

He tutted a bit. 'Meet you out front in ten minutes.'

Katie and Jane walked out into the car park as Alan drove from his parking space in a blue Volvo V40, not a Ford. Katie opened the front passenger door. 'Could you both sit in the back? I've got some stuff on the seat.' She looked at the front passenger seat; he wasn't kidding. She probably had less stuff in her garage! The three of them made their way over to Groby Road, where the service was to take place. They parked up and made their way to the entrance.

Rain spattered down in a fine mist as mourners clustered beneath the grey stone arch of Gilroes. Black umbrellas jostled together like dark petals. Katie stood near the back, coat collar turned up, watching faces as much as she watched proceedings.

Michael Blake's coffin was simple oak, carried in by four men. Edward was at the front, his expression guarded and pale, Michael's absence making the symmetry unbearable for the congregation. An older man, whom Katie assumed was Michael and Edward's father, and two others who looked about the brothers' age, possibly friends or cousins, completed the pallbearers. Pamela and Helen walked behind. Helen's lips were pressed into a thin line, her hands clenched white around a handkerchief. The ladies didn't seem to be engaging with each other. Had they fallen out about something? Helen did have bail conditions not to contact Edward, but given the circumstances, nothing would be said.

Katie noticed DI Alan Briggs hovering on the periphery, his usual confidence muted, his eyes hidden behind dark glasses. He'd taken a seat not far from Helen, though they didn't exchange a word. Too close for comfort, Katie thought. As is normal in the Jewish faith, the coffin was sealed and there were no flower donations. The body is washed but not embalmed and usually dressed in a white shroud. The family had done this earlier today.

DC Jane Reeves slipped beside her, whispering, 'Everyone's watching everyone, aren't they?'

Katie gave the faintest nod. 'Funerals always strip things bare. Just watch.'

CHAPTER 15

The mourners gathered, the Keriah was performed, a black ribbon being torn, the service continued with prayers and a eulogy by a Rabbi and family members. As the Rabbi spoke, Katie's eyes roamed the pews. Derek sat stiff-backed, whispering now and then to a young curate. He seemed genuinely stricken, eager to show his grief. Susan, the cleaner, dabbed at her eyes with tissues, her shoulders shaking.

At the far edge of the congregation stood a young man, tall and lean, perhaps in his mid-twenties. He wore a smart jacket, but his eyes were nervous. Glasses framed his face, and a snood was pulled up to his nose, perhaps a defence against the chill of the building. Katie caught a flicker of recognition she couldn't quite place. He neither approached the coffin nor joined the line of mourners, nor did he speak to anyone; he simply lingered, observing.

She leaned slightly toward Reeves. 'See the lad at the back? Do you know him?' Reeves followed her gaze. She shook her head. 'Doesn't look like family.'

Katie kept watching him. Something tugged at her memory, not quite a name, but a familiarity she couldn't pin down.

After the service, groups huddled in the drizzle, talking in whispered voices. Katie edged closer to Helen, offering her condolences. Helen's eyes were bloodshot, her words few, but Katie caught her glancing past her shoulder.

Katie stepped aside, just in time to see Briggs move to Helen's side. The exchange was brief, a murmur, a hand brushing her elbow, but it spoke volumes.

And then the young man at the back was gone. Vanished into the rain without a trace.

Katie felt the unease flutter in her chest. Funerals were meant to bring closure, but this one only opened more doors.

Back at the station, Katie spread the attendance sheets across her desk. Every mourner had signed their name neatly in black ink, except for the one she was looking for: the young man from the back row, the one who had slipped away before the coffin was even lowered.

She rubbed her temples, frustration prickling at her. His face tugged at her memory; not recent, perhaps just a brief meeting or a passing introduction, but familiar enough to make her stomach tighten.

Reeves dropped a paper cup beside her. 'You look like you're seeing ghosts.'

'Maybe I am,' Katie murmured. 'There was a man at the funeral. Mid-twenties, kept to the shadows. I know I've seen him before.'

Reeves perched on the desk. 'Want me to check Gilroes CCTV?'
Katie nodded.

Two hours later, Reeves was back, laptop under her arm. 'Got him. Side door camera, leaving before the service ended.'

The still image made Katie's skin prickle. Collar up, hair damp from the drizzle, a guarded glance over his shoulder. Definitely the same man.

'Run him through facial recognition please,' Katie said.

Reeves tapped at the keyboard, the database whirring. Matches scrolled across the screen. Then a name appeared: Alexander Dominic Casey.

Katie repeated it under her breath. 'Casey…'

'Ring any bells?' Reeves asked.

Katie shook her head slowly. 'Not clearly. But I've seen him before. I just don't know where.'

Reeves leaned back. 'Want me to dig deeper?'

'Not yet. He's not on our radar officially. Let's keep this quiet, for now.'

She closed the file, but the unease stayed. Alexander Casey. The name sat wrong with her, just out of reach, like a half-forgotten song. And if he was innocent, why leave a funeral like a thief in the night?

Katie waited until the office had thinned out for the night before opening the file again. Alexander Casey. The name was ordinary, but the unease it carried was anything but.

She keyed his details into the PNC, careful not to mark the search with anything that would raise eyebrows.

Address: a house share on Narborough Road; a dingy property of rented rooms, not a family home. Family: mother, Angela Casey, Leicester. No father listed.

Katie frowned. Nothing unusual stood out on paper, yet his face stayed with her. She was certain she had seen him before, though she could not recall when.

Scrolling further, a red flag caught her eye: driving offence, drink driving. Licence revoked. Grey Ford Focus, registration KP56 PGT. Stopped in Oadby five months ago.

So he was off the road, or should have been.

Katie leaned back in her chair, rubbing her temple. Grey car. The grey car, she wondered, was he the male who watched her leaving Mansfield House? Could be. He was a bit generic, nothing outstanding about him. Her pulse picked up.

She drafted a quick note into the PNC: 'Grey Ford Focus KP56 PGT. Driver disqualified. If seen on the road, stop vehicle. Report immediately to DS Lounds.'

Then she rang the response sergeant, keeping her tone professional.

'Can you put that reg in tomorrow morning's briefing? Treat it as priority if it's spotted. No need for detail yet. Suspect it will only have a reg plate on the front.'

The sergeant agreed without hesitation.

Katie hung up, staring at the still image of Casey again. The more she looked, the more unsettled she felt.

She locked the file, shut the laptop, but the thought followed her home:

Why had Alex Casey been at Helen's funeral? And why did she feel like she already knew him? No-one in the whole investigation had mentioned a Casey, or an Alex or Alexander.

The briefing note had only been out a few hours when Katie's phone buzzed against her desk.

CALLER ID: Sgt Moffat (Response). She picked up at once.

'Lounds.'

'Katie, we've just had a unit call in a sighting. Grey Ford Focus, KP56 PGT. Two male occupants, both hooded. Vehicle pulled off Narborough Road, heading towards Braunstone Gate.'

Katie's pen slipped across her notebook. 'Any chance of getting them stopped?'

'They tried. The car sped off before they could. Not a pursuit-trained mobile. Registered keeper Alexander Casey, right?'

Katie kept her voice steady. 'Correct. Did they get a look at the driver?'

'Negative. Tinted glass on the driver's side only. One of the lads says the passenger leaned forward, like he'd clocked the panda car. Almost like they knew.'

Katie's stomach flipped. Too alert. Too aware.

'Tell all units to keep watch. No pursuit unless it's safe. The last thing we need is a collision.'

Moffat agreed and rang off.

Katie sat back in her chair, staring at the map pinned above her desk. Narborough Road not that far from the city centre.

The car wasn't supposed to be on the road at all. Whoever was driving it wasn't just taking chances, they were bold. Brazen.

She pulled up the CCTV still again, the blurred outline of Casey, half-turned. She felt the prickle at the back of her neck.

It wasn't just Casey. There had been two in that car. And the question that kept gnawing at her:

Who was the second man?

Katie stood in Keene's office, the map of Narborough Road spread across the table. DI Keene's brow was furrowed, hands planted firmly on the surface. DI Rook sat quietly to one side, arms folded, observing.

'We've had a sighting, grey Ford Focus, KP56 PGT. Alexander Casey registered. There were two occupants, and the unit thinks it may be linked to the other incidents.'

'Lounds, we're chasing nothing. You've got nothing concrete connecting this car to the murder, nothing at all. I'm not authorising surveillance for some disqualified driver who goes to a funeral.'

Katie felt her jaw clench.

'It's more than that, sir. I saw a grey car, possibly the same one. It was tailing me after I left Mansfield House, and now this.' She wasn't going to mention the vehicle being on her drive a couple of days before; she didn't want to disclose it as stalking just yet.

Keene's sigh was long, exasperated.

'No. Not enough. You need evidence first, not gut instinct. I'm off tomorrow. Get a move on with this. I want a murder solved. Leave this, Lounds. Don't act.'

Katie's shoulders stiffened, but she didn't respond. Keene left, slamming the door behind him.

Rook leaned forward slightly, his voice low but firm. 'You think it's connected?'

Katie glanced at him, eyes hard. 'Yes. The car at the funeral, the sighting with the second man, the grey car I felt followed me… it's too much of a coincidence.'

Rook nodded, resting a hand on the edge of the desk.

'Then do it. You have my authorisation while he's away. Covert surveillance. I'll get uniformed officers to cover it so you're not exposed. Keep it discreet.'

Katie allowed herself a small nod, relief mingling with tension. 'Understood, sir. I'll set it up immediately.'

Rook gave a brief, encouraging smile.

'Good. Keep your head down, Lounds. And report anything straight to me. I'll handle the fallout if Keene hears about it.'

Katie left the office, her mind already running through logistics, cameras, stakeouts, rotation of officers. The net was starting to close, and she was determined not to let the trail slip.

That evening, Katie parked a discreet distance from Casey's flat on Narborough Road, drizzle tracing slick patterns across the windscreen. The grey Focus was nowhere to be seen, though her instincts told her it would not stay gone for long.

DC Jane Reeves sat beside her, laptop open, surveillance logs ready. 'You're sure this is the place?' she whispered.

'According to the PNC and council records, yes. Everything points here.' Katie looked up at the windows above, three storeys of cramped flats, some lit, others dark. Shadows moved behind thin curtains, unaware of the watchers below.

'Have you set up the cameras?' Katie asked.

'Already. Two fixed on the street, one on the side exit.' Reeves tapped keys quietly. 'All angles covered.'

Katie glanced at her notebook. She jotted down small details: passing vehicles, licence plates, pedestrian activity. Every pattern mattered, every irregularity.

Hours passed with little action, the hum of traffic punctuated by the occasional shout or car door slamming. Then, a glint in the street caught Katie's eye.

'Focus. Kilo Papa five six Papa Golf Tango. Coming up from the south.'

Reeves leaned closer, typing rapidly to flag the vehicle. The grey Ford slowed, hugging the side of the road. Two figures inside. Katie's stomach tightened. The passenger, the one she had seen at Helen Blake's funeral, hunched slightly, watching the street as though calculating every move.

Katie whispered, 'Eyes on only. Don't engage. Let's see where they go.'

The car turned onto a side street. Katie followed at a careful distance, weaving slowly, keeping them in sight without being noticed. Every instinct screamed that the pair knew they were being observed, deliberate, careful, dangerous.

'Going into the industrial estate,' Reeves murmured, voice tight.

She made a small note:

Industrial estate. Grey Ford Focus. Two occupants. Possible link to Blake case. Observation only.

Katie exhaled slowly, eyes never leaving the car. This was just the beginning. If she lost them now, crucial evidence could disappear forever.

Katie stayed hidden in the unmarked patrol car, engine off, rain pattering on the roof. Reeves crouched behind the laptop, monitoring the cameras and the car's movement.

The grey Ford Focus rolled slowly into a dimly lit corner of the industrial estate. Katie's pulse quickened. The passenger, the young man she vaguely recognised from the funeral, stepped out first. Who was he? She wasn't sure, only that his movements were deliberate.

The driver, Casey, followed and pulled a black duffel bag from the boot. He and the passenger disappeared through the shadowed doorway of a warehouse unit.

Katie whispered, almost to herself, 'They're not just meeting. They're handling something.'

They stayed in position, keeping distance. Through the CCTV feed, Katie tried to see the face of the passenger, but the footage wasn't clear; it was dark with very little lighting.

'That's not random. Whatever's in there, it matters. They're hiding it, not transporting normal goods.'

Reeves swallowed, whispering, 'What now?'

She jotted a quick note:

Industrial estate, evening. Grey Ford Focus KP56 PGT. Two occupants handling black duffel bag. Metallic content. Suspicious movement. Observation continues.

Katie's hands trembled slightly as she closed the notebook. The stakes had just gone up. Whoever these two were, and whatever they were moving, they were connected to Michael Blake's case, and possibly more.

The two then got back into the Ford and drove back to the location of Casey's flat, pulled into a side street and went into the address.

Katie and Reeves left the observation to a uniformed officer in an unmarked car and headed back to the office.

'It's got to be the same car, Jane. No rear number plate. It's followed me, it's been to my address.'

'Have you told Rook about your stalker yet?'

'No. I don't want to, not yet. I can manage this. Yes, it scares the life out of me, but I can't let them think I'm showing any weakness.'

'It's not weakness, Katie. It's your safety.'

They spoke for a while. It was late. Katie told Jane to go home. Briggs, Brenton and Owen had already gone. They walked together into the car park.

'You look scared,' said Jane, leaning in to give Katie a hug. Katie was taken aback but didn't pull away. It had been a long time since anyone had hugged her, and the gesture felt unexpectedly reassuring.

'I'll be OK, thank you.' As she said that, there was a ping on Katie's mobile, WhatsApp. She looked at Jane, who raised her eyebrows, and Katie went to put it back in her pocket.

'Katie, look at it, is it the stalker?' She opened the message, a photo from an unknown number, a photo of her and Jane, standing at the funeral. Jane hugged her again. Katie could feel she was shaking.

'Please be careful if you're not going to report this,' Jane said.

They parted ways and made their way back to their respective homes.

Katie arrived home within about twenty-five minutes, the rain still drizzly. The journey was uneventful.

What was Alan up to, speaking to the deceased spouse at the funeral, denying there was any footage of the grey car, which was stalking her?

Approaching her front door, she stopped and turned around. No-one was there; she was quite sure she hadn't been followed. She had used her rear-view and side mirrors more in the last week than she had in the previous ten years, she thought. As she turned back, she saw her curtains twitch and her heart pounded, but immediate relief came when she saw Monty's face at the window.

She put the key in the door and turned it. It opened as it should; it had been locked.

'Monty, you nearly gave me a heart attack, boy,' she said, stroking his head before following him into the kitchen. He sat by his bowl, staring expectantly at the tray of sachets. Katie held up two options, and when he headbutted one, she tore it open and tipped it into his bowl.

Determined to have at least one healthy meal this week, she threw together a salad with salmon and new potatoes and sat down, watching House of Games on catch-up to eat it.

When she had finished, she washed her plate, made a cup of tea and opened her laptop. She had told herself no work this evening but couldn't help herself. An email from Rook, which she clicked on to open.

BMW driving around at around three a.m. in town is Edward Blake's ED19 PTR. The image of the plate isn't clear, as Briggs suggested; it may have some type of film over it. A shot from an ANPR camera shows Edward in the driver's seat and no-one in the passenger seat. The image was attached to the email. Yes, definitely Edward. Well, Edward or Michael, she thought to herself.

Grey Ford without the rear plate is on the footage and in the area of Jubilee Square, Guildhall Lane, Loseby Lane three ten to three twenty. So it was around the area where Michael was murdered, at around the time he was killed. Briggs said that car wasn't on the footage; it followed her home; it was at the funeral. Who the hell is Casey? What link does he have to me, Alan, and the murder?

She closed the laptop. It was getting late, and she checked the doors and windows. She went to the bedroom, got undressed, had a shower and set her alarm before going to bed. It was a particularly cold night, so she selected some fleece pyjamas, put the electric blanket on and went to sleep.

CHAPTER 16

It was another grey, damp morning greeting Katie as she woke, had a shower, fed Monty, dressed, and went back into the kitchen to make herself some breakfast. The windows of her Honda were iced. As she had time, she went out, started the car, and got the heater going. Her breath was almost freezing as she exhaled. The temperature gauge on the car said minus two. She hadn't been able to afford the version with a heated windscreen, and the heater wasn't as good as it should be, so she thought she would get a head start on clearing the windows and heating the vehicle before she set off. She locked the car door with the spare key and left it running.

She went back into the home and finished off her scrambled egg on toast. Monty was rubbing around her legs and running to the back door.

'Know you want to go out, Monty. Later on we'll have a walk on the lead. I'll get some quotes for a little door for you, buddy,' she said, picking him up and giving him a cuddle.

When Katie arrived in the briefing room, no one else was there. She went to the shared kitchen to make a coffee. Did she want a stained mug or a chipped one? Choices, choices. She really needed to remember to bring in her thermal mug. Opting for the chipped cup, she made herself a strong coffee and sat at her desk.

Inspector Rook came in carrying his own coffee and what smelt very much like a bacon cob.

'Morning, Katie. How's things?'

'I'm fine, Duncan. I'm just frustrated we're not getting anywhere. We just need that one little break, and I'm sure we will have this sorted.'

'It's coming. Sometimes it takes a while, but it will fall into place.'

'I hope so.'

'Right, Alan was in early this morning. I've sent him over to headquarters with the memory stick and CCTV. I wanted him out of the way.'

'Why?'

'You said that you had some suspicion about him, what with him not telling the truth about the grey car in the CCTV and that car turning up where you are. I've just been informed by the response sergeant that Alex Casey was arrested last night after a Fail to Stop in that car.'

'Oh, I was hoping we would be able to keep tabs on that for a while, see where it could take us.'

'I know, but once it's taken off and been driven moronically, they've had to bring him in. I've taken it from Uniform; it's obviously their remit, but as there's a potential link to our murder, I want it keeping in-house.'

'Yes, I understand. I don't feel comfortable doing the interview in case he has been following me, but I'm happy to look through the statements and draft an interview plan with Jane and Rick to incorporate some questions about the CCTV and following me, if that's in order.'

'Spot on. You can then monitor the interview. If you need to chip in, you can send them a message.'

Rook handed her a handover pack, which had statements printed out and some photographs. There was also some dash-cam footage from the pursuit to view. Also included was a printout of Casey's custody record. She studied it carefully, racking her brain as to why the face was familiar.

'Duncan, take a look at him. Does he remind you of anyone?' Rook took the paper and looked at it.

'No, not off-hand, sorry.'

She set about reading the statements and drafting an interview plan. Within half an hour, Jane Reeves, Rick Owen, and Dean Brenton had all turned up, complained about the cold, and made themselves hot drinks.

She spoke to them about the arrest and asked Jane and Rick to take the interview. Rick instantly regretted the thermal base layer underneath his suit trousers and pale blue shirt. The interview room heated up like an oven, especially when there were a number of bodies in there. He decided he was going to go and remove them, leaving Katie thinking that might be a good idea, as he liked to wear trousers which gave nothing any room to manoeuvre anyway, and with that extra layer he could barely sit down comfortably. Katie went through the plan with them and let them know she would be monitoring remotely.

A solicitor was called for Casey, as he had requested, and they waited for her to arrive before taking him into the interview room and allowing a consultation before the interview.

Reeves entered all the relevant information into the recording machine and pressed start. A little red monitored notification appeared on the screen, confirming that Katie and possibly Rook were listening in.

'Okay, it's eleven forty-three hours on Thursday the twenty-sixth of January.'

Reeves began the interview with the standard preamble, outlining the suspect's rights and entitlements. She introduced herself, as did PC Owen, who was taking notes.

Reeves sat on one side of the desk in a blue padded chair, facing Mr Casey, who occupied a black plastic one like those found in schools or libraries. He was tall and lean, not the sort who looked like he spent hours in the gym, but strong nonetheless. His T shirt sleeves were rolled up, showing his biceps, and his jeans were torn and dirty. He looked as grim as the room itself.

'Please introduce yourself with your name and date of birth.'

'Alex Casey. Twenty-third June nineteen ninety-seven.'

'You have a solicitor with you?'

'Leah Russell, Russell, Elliott and Co.'

The caution was explained, and Reeves began.

'So, Alex, you were arrested last night on suspicion of failing to stop for the police, dangerous driving, driving whilst disqualified, and having no insurance. Tell me what happened last night, say from seven p.m.'

'No comment.'

'Where were you at seven p.m.?'

'No comment.'

'What vehicle were you in?'

'The vehicle you made off in was a grey Ford, registration Kilo Papa five six Papa Golf Tango. Tell me about that.'

'No comment.'

'At present, that vehicle has been seized.'

'What? You can't take my car!'

'Thank you. So, to confirm, according to the keeper details, it is still registered to you?'

'No comment.'

'Does anyone else drive your car? Do you allow anyone who isn't insured to use it? You know that's an offence.'

'No. No one else drives it.'

'You were seen driving that car last night at ten twenty-five by a patrol unit, circling the industrial estate in Oadby. What were you doing?'

'Nothing.'

'Then why did you drive off when the police car approached?'

'Don't have to stop and chat to you, do I? I'm not into talking with strangers. Stranger danger and all that.'

'Not at first, no. But when you drove off and they followed you with lights and sirens, yes, you did have to stop. So why didn't you?'

'Ain't got a licence, have I?'

Reeves then led him through a series of questions about his driving: exceeding eighty miles per hour in thirty and forty zones, going through red lights, driving the wrong side of a keep left bollard, nearly colliding head on with a vehicle on a country lane, and throwing objects out of the window at the pursuing police car. He replied 'No comment' to each one.

'Who was in the car with you last night, who got out and ran from the vehicle?'

'No comment.'

'Why would he run?'

'Ask him.'

'I will, when I know who he is. Who was he?'

'No comment.'

'Okay, Alex. Tell me what you were doing between two and four a.m. on Thursday the nineteenth of January.'

'What?'

'Where were you at those times?'

'How the hell do I know? It's ages ago.'

'It's a week.'

'Tell me why your car was seen driving around the Guildhall Lane and Loseby Lane area of Leicester. You've already told me no one else drives it, so if we are to believe you, it was you doing that.'

'No comment.'

'Do you know Michael Blake? Or should I say… did you know Michael Blake?'

Alex visibly shifted in his seat, flicking a glance at his solicitor.

'No comment.'

'Do you know Edward Blake?'

His expression changed, and Reeves was certain he looked frightened.

'No comment.'

'Now, you've refused to give the PIN to your phone, but
'

'Too right. You're not looking through my private stuff. None of your business.'

'If you let me finish… but we have been able to access your phone anyway.'

'What? You can't! Tell them that's illegal without my permission,' he said to his solicitor.

She replied calmly, 'It is not illegal. If they believe it could provide information in relation to an offence that could assist you or them, they are entitled to access it.'

He stared at her as though it were her fault the law existed.

'So, tell me about the calls and texts you made between two and four a.m. on Thursday the nineteenth of January.'

'No comment.'

'The number zero seven nine six six five five three four three three who does that belong to?'

He began to look nervous.

'No comment.'

'Alex, this is serious.'

'No, it's not. It's driving stuff. No comment.'

'Who does that number belong to?'

'No comment.'

'Right. I am further arresting you on suspicion of aiding and abetting murder.'

'What? No! You can't do that. I'm leaving. Let me out. I haven't killed anyone!'

Reeves paused the interview, fetched drinks, and gave the solicitor time to speak privately with him.

'Interview resumes at twelve forty-eight. Same persons present. I remind you that you are still under caution.'

'Alex, I'll ask you again: whose number is zero seven nine six six five five three four three three?'

A long silence. Alex stared straight at her.

'My dad's.'

'What is your dad's name?'

'No comment.'

'Was your dad in the same area as you at that time?'

'No comment. I'm not aiding and abetting anything. It's not serious if you haven't done it, is it?'

'You're wrong, Alex. The same sentence applies. Aiding and abetting murder carries the same penalty as murder itself. Life imprisonment.'

'I haven't done anything. I haven't.'

'Then tell me what those calls and texts to your father were about. We know where your car was, we know you were driving, and we know where the murder happened, right near where you were. How are you involved in this?'

'I'm not.'

'Talk to me then.'

'My dad wanted to speak to someone. I'd seen that person in town. I was trying to tell him where to find the person. I was driving around 'cause I lost him, some streets are pedestrianised.'

'How did you follow this person in the dark, through the crowds of people?'

'He had his big, long woolly grey coat on.'

'And who was it that you thought you were following, to tell your dad where he was?'

'Edward Blake.'

'Except that person wasn't Edward. It was his brother Michael, who for some reason took his brother's coat.' She let that linger for some time.

'Michael was murdered around that time, possibly because someone thought he was the wrong twin because of the coat.'

Reeves could see beads of sweat starting to appear on Casey's brow. He wiped them away with his sleeve and looked very panicky, rubbing his sweaty hands on his jeans.

'Look, I know nothing about any murder. I'm nothing to do with it.'

'Why did your dad want to speak with Edward?'

'Something about a woman. I wasn't listening.'

'How do you know Edward Blake?'

'No comment.'

'I'll ask you again. Who is your father?'

'My dad would never kill anyone. He's a… no, he would never kill someone. No comment from now on.'

'But you've confirmed that your dad was in town, looking for Edward. You were directing him towards who you thought was Edward because of the coat, but it was actually Michael. Shortly after that, Michael was murdered. Can you not see how that looks for both you and your dad?'

'I've done nothing. I didn't know anything was going down like that. My dad didn't do it.'

'It won't take us long to confirm who uses that number. Don't you want to help clear your dad's name?'

'You find out then. No comment.'

He continued to answer 'No comment' to the questions relating to the offence. Reeves then changed approach and asked a few questions on Katie's behalf.

'Tell me about the last time you went to Great Glen, a little village outside?'

'Where?'

'Your car, which only you drive, was seen on the driveway of a farm, parked up for a few minutes. What were you doing there?'

He sat back, arms above his head. The sweating appeared to have stopped.

'Oh yeah, my mate saw a red Honda Civic with a for sale sign in the window. He said it had pulled into one of the farms and asked me to take him there so he could put a note through the door to ask about it.'

Reeves knew that was untrue.

'Alright, tell me more about that Honda.'

'Don't know… no, wait, yeah I do. We were in town the other day, me and my mate, and he saw it again. Knows the plate or something, I assume. We tried to follow it but couldn't change lanes at the underpass.'

'Do you know who owns the car?'

'No.'

'Have you seen the face of the driver?'

'No, no idea.'

'Is that the same mate who was with you last night?'

'No comment.'

'I'll ask you again, what's your mate's name?'

'No comment.'

'Have you sent any messages to the person who drives that car or owns it?'

'No. I don't even know who they are, so how would I know their number?'

'Who is your dad? Give me his name, please, if you want to help clear yourself. If your dad isn't involved in the murder, then you can't be aiding and abetting, so we can only work out if you are innocent if we clear your dad. Do you see?'

'No comment. You do your job yourself. I'm fine. I'm confident my dad ain't done nothing.'

Reeves asked him if he admitted or denied each offence. 'No comment' was given to all except 'aiding and abetting murder,' which was 'Deny. It's nothing to do with me.'

'Okay, I have no other questions for now. If you have nothing else to say…'

'No.'

'Mrs Russell?'

'No, thank you.'

The interview ceased at thirteen twenty-four.

Casey was returned to the custody desk, where he was booked in and put back in his cell while further enquiries were made. He was less cocky now than when he had been brought into the interview room at the start.

The custody sergeant reminded him of his rights.

'Are you sure you don't want anyone informed of your arrest? Your mum, dad, partner?'

'No,' he said, looking at Reeves.

Mrs Russell was shown out.

Reeves and Owen joined Rook and Katie in the briefing room.

'I think we just call that number, withhold the identity, and give it a call to see if "dad" answers.'

'Okay,' said Rook. 'Let's do that.'

Katie took out her work mobile, put in 141 before the number so her number wouldn't show up, and dialled zero seven nine six six five five three four three three very carefully. They waited. The phone began to ring. It continued to ring out.

'There is no one available to take your call. Please leave a message after the tone,' it said in a generic phone voice.

'Damn, at least we know the number is still live. Phone is still on.'

'We could try and get it authorised for a ping. They may go for it, given that it's potentially linked to a murder,' suggested Owen.

'I'll speak to Superintendent Wilde,' replied Rook and headed back to his office.

CHAPTER 17

They all went back to their desks to review the interview and consider any further leads or enquiries that could be pursued before getting a decision on Casey.

'I don't want him released before we've had a chance to look into the vehicle movements, his knowledge of the Blakes, and who his dad is,' said Katie.

'We could get a charging decision on the driving matters and see if we can get him remanded. Then he's going nowhere. It's too late for court this afternoon. We keep him in on the murder,' Owen offered.

'Or do we want him out, to see who he goes to see, who he tries to speak with, now he knows we're onto this number in relation to the murder?' said Reeves.

'Difficult one,' said Katie. 'Okay, Rick, can you do a bit more digging on the number and recheck the footage? Go a bit further, after the murder. See if the car is around then. See where it goes, whether it picks anyone else up.'

'Shall I ask Helen Blake about the number?' he asked.

'No. Don't alert her to the fact we may have suspicions about it. She may speak to the owner of the number. Check her communication with it, the texts. See if there are any clues as to who it might be. You've got lunch here, haven't you?'

'I have. The wife always makes me a packed lunch when she makes the kids' ones for school.'

'So what is it today? Jam sandwiches cut into triangles with the crusts cut off and a strawberry Frube?' laughed Brenton.

'Bugger off,' laughed Owen.

'Jane, have you got lunch?'

'No, got to nip out and get some.'

'Let's go over to the café, get something to eat there, and run over what we've got,' Katie suggested.

'Right-o, see you out the front in five.'

'Guys,' Katie said, addressing Brenton and Owen, 'I don't want anyone who's not in this room right now being told about Casey being in the bin. No one. Keep all the material away. Don't use his name in front of anyone else, and don't talk about that vehicle in front of anyone except the five of us.'

They both looked at her quizzically.

'Not even Phillips or Briggs?'

'That's right. No one other than us. Yes, I know it's an odd request, but I have my reasons.'

'No problem.'

'Yes, Sarge,' they said, as Owen opened his lunch box and pulled out a pile of triangle sandwiches without crusts. Brenton nearly wet himself.

'Child,' retorted Owen.

'Says you, with the baby triangle sandwiches,' he said, elbowing his colleague in the arm.

Katie and Jane walked out of the station and into the car park.

'Bit nippy,' Katie said.

'And icy,' Jane agreed.

'Okay, whose car is the least iced?' Katie asked.

They were parked close to each other. Jane's Peugeot looked the better option, so they did a quick blast of the heater and set off for the short two- or three-minute drive to Morrisons.

They parked as close to the entrance as they could without being in a disabled spot. They walked up to the counter, looked at the sandwiches and cakes, and then at the hot food menu. It was an obvious choice: they both went for the all-day breakfast with toast and tea. They paid and made their way over to a table in the corner, collecting cutlery, sugar, stirrers, and sauce on the way, and getting their tea from the machine.

As they sat down, Katie's phone pinged. She rummaged through her pockets until she found it. A new message. Blank. No number, no name.

She placed the phone on the table, glanced at Jane, and swiped it open.

'What's it say?' Jane asked.

Katie read it aloud.

'You won't catch me. Watch your back.'

Jane leaned over to read the screen, her brow tightening.

'That has to be the passenger from Casey's car,' Katie said. 'He knows he got away. That same car has been following me. I'm not buying Casey's story for a second.'

'Katie,' Jane said firmly, 'you need to tell Rook. That is a direct threat. No more hints or mind games.'

A lady in a white overall with a blue rinse came over to the table.

'Two breakfasts?' she asked.

'Yes, thank you,' they said almost simultaneously.

The lady placed them on the table and walked back into the kitchen. They looked at the fried egg, two rashers of bacon, sausage, baked beans, black pudding round, half a tomato, and two rounds of toast. It was very welcome, and the smell was divine. They both started to tuck in.

'How can you send a text message without your number showing up?'

'You can do it from the web. They can send it from a random made-up number or just through an app; they come through anonymously,' explained Jane.

'He was using a number ending four zero eight when he WhatsApped me the pictures. Now there's no number,' Katie said, holding the phone out so her friend could see the screen.

'Does that number come back with anything?'

'Nothing. All I can get is that it is with some company I've never heard of, "Coralla".'

'Never heard of them,' she agreed.

She knew one thing for sure: it wasn't Casey sending the messages. He was safely locked up in a cell with a camera watching his every move. But it was something to do with his vehicle, so the passenger, or the father? Neither of whose identity is known.

'What do you think of Casey? Any idea who his dad could be? '

'There must be some clues on his phone. He must have 'Mum' or 'Dad' as a contact. It can't be that difficult to work out who he is. '

Katie was philosophical. 'We are struggling. We've worked out there was no fraud, but that doesn't mean Michael wasn't killed because someone thought there was. We need a break. Where are we not looking? '

'Something's got to give. It's been a week. We still have the same possible suspects but nothing on any of them. Let's just keep digging; something small will turn into something huge, 'she replied enthusiastically.

They finished their food and made their way back to the station.

Katie walked back into the Incident Room, but before she reached her office, Inspector Rook beckoned her over.

'We need to make a decision on Casey, and I want it kept quiet, 'Rook said. 'Charge him with the driving offences and remand him. We'll get a crew to take him to court in the morning. The Superintendent has agreed to extend his custody clock for twelve hours on the murder, so the crew can bring him back from court into the cell. I've briefed the morning Sergeant. We need to keep this under the radar. I don't want anyone to know he is here. '

'Okay, good call. Can I go to the Magistrates in the morning? I want to keep an eye out to see if anyone turns up who shouldn't be there someone involved who shouldn't know he's under arrest. The other person in the vehicle, someone who isn't getting their phone calls answered? 'asked Katie.

'Yes, do that. We can cover it here; there's not a lot of new evidence coming in. Go home, take the phone records Helen's and Casey's and see what you can do. I'll pass you the phone number of whichever officers take him to court in the morning. '

'Thanks, Duncan. I'll get Reeves to go and charge him now. I'll put the file together properly and let you have it before I leave. Just one more thing, 'Katie then explained, not in full detail, some of the messages she had been receiving.

Katie ran the plan by Jane, whom she felt she could trust completely. Jane nodded, and Katie made her way downstairs to the Custody Suite.

'Afternoon, Sarge, 'Jane said to Sergeant Williams, the Custody Sergeant. 'I've come to charge Casey. ' 'Yep. I've had Wilde give me the update. We've had Casey's name taken off the board now there has been a handover in shifts, so no one here now other than myself, the Superintendent and you guys know he is here. '

Casey was fetched from his cell by a detention officer. He emerged half asleep, rubbing his eyes. He wore custody tracksuit bottoms, his hands tucked down the front as young men often did. He looked completely disinterested.

'Releasing me then? 'he grunted.
'No. '
'What do you mean, no? '

Sergeant Williams popped the charge sheets on the desk. Superintendent Wilde appeared behind the desk.

'Afternoon, Sir. 'He nodded. 'Go ahead, Reeves. '

Reeves then ran through the charges: failing to stop, dangerous driving, disqualified driving and driving without insurance. She cautioned him; he made no reply. Sergeant Williams informed him that he was being remanded to court in the morning.

Before he had the chance to kick off, as he was about to, Wilde stepped up to him.

'In relation to the aid and abet murder, having heard representations from your solicitor and speaking to the officers, I am happy that enquiries are still ongoing and expeditious. It is necessary to keep you in custody whilst those enquiries are done. I am therefore authorising an extension of twelve hours. You will be taken to court and brought back here for further questioning. If the court remands you, we will take you to prison once we have finished with you here. Do you understand? '

Casey punched the custody desk, kicking the wall, and was immediately grabbed by two uniformed officers, who swiftly returned him to his cell, where he started to thump and kick the cell door.

'DC Reeves, we've also had the request from DI Rook to block any calls for Casey. I grant that. ' 'Thank you, Sir, 'she said, picking up the paperwork and leaving custody. That meant Casey would not be able to make any telephone calls or have anyone told that he was in custody until the block was lifted. This was to ensure no one could interfere with their investigation.

Jane left the custody suite, and the smell of sweat, socks and microwaved curry behind her, and went back up into the office.

Katie had already left the station, jumped in her car, and cranked the heat up as much as she could. Despite there being something wrong with the heating, it did warm her up after a short distance. She didn't know how she felt about the grey Ford being off the road. At least she knew that vehicle, so she knew if she was being followed. Now, whoever it was could have a completely different car, and she would have a clue. She drove cautiously towards home.

Halfway home, Katie realised she had left her work mobile in her desk drawer, off. Never mind, she thought. If there's anything urgent, they will try her mobile or ping her an email.

Helen had been sitting at home, scared and confused. She had been getting some anonymous calls, just hanging up when she answered. She couldn't believe what had happened; this was never what she wanted. She knew it was all her fault she had been sleeping with her brother-in-law and the other man, whom she thought Edward knew about. Not for one minute did she think she would start this year losing her husband. He was always too busy with this scam, this scheme, gambling, to notice what she was doing, so no one would ever have found out about her infidelity. What you don't know won't hurt you, right? He wouldn't have found out if people hadn't started to stick their noses in.

She hadn't properly cried since she had seen the crime scene photo confirming it was indeed Michael her husband dead. For some reason, he was wearing Edward's coat. Did they mean to get Michael or Edward? She shivered. If the person who did it was who she thought, it was probably her fault. All he was going to do was have a word with Edward, not spill the beans to Michael.

A familiar number rang her phone. She just sat, staring at the mobile flashing and vibrating, hoping it would stop; she really didn't want to deal with him right now. It kept ringing and ringing, so she swiped the call away. It rang again, and again, and she did the same.

A text came through.

Just answer, will you? The police will think it's you, you know.

Leave me alone, she typed back, hands trembling.

You won't get away with this.
I haven't done anything. Leave me alone.
I'm coming round.
No, you aren't. Ewan is here.
No. Today is his football club until seven.
He's here. He's not going to football. He's terrified.

Someone is going to kill me, and his dad too. He hasn't left my side for a second.

Katie's stomach knotted. Every ping made her jump. The screen felt alive, threatening, a constant reminder that someone was watching, waiting.

The phone rang again. She swiped the call away and powered it down.

Ewan was thirteen, a sensitive boy. He hadn't wanted to be apart from his mum since he lost his dad. The only time he had stayed with Pam was for a few hours while Helen was being interviewed at that stage, however, Helen was still saying it was Edward who was dead, and Ewan wasn't aware it was Michael. He loved being able to see Aunty Pam… well, more than he loved Clyde.

Helen was panicking when her landline started to ring. She didn't know what to do for the best. She powered her phone back on and called Pam, asking her to take Ewan. Pam agreed. Helen drove her to the next village, terrified she was being followed, driving quickly and watching every car to see who it might be.

It was a straight, fast drive: out of her cul-de-sac, onto Willoughby Road, left into Cross Street, across the junction, and into the car park behind the flats. She made sure she wasn't being followed, got Ewan's overnight bag out of the boot, and took him up to the flat, knocking on the door.

Pam opened it within seconds. 'Aw, sweetheart, come in, 'she said, giving him a hug. He clung to her.

'Aunty Pam, someone killed Daddy. I want my Dad back. I miss him so much. '

Pam had tears in her eyes. 'I'm so sorry, love. I know you do, 'she said, still hugging him. Just as she did, Clyde lumbered into the porch, pawing at Ewan's leg and smudging him with his head. 'Clyde boy, 'he said, rolling onto the floor and play-wrestling with the enormous dog.

'Come in, Helen. You look like you could do with a coffee or something stronger. '

'Just a quick one, thank you. Coffee, that is I'm driving. '

She walked in and sat down. The flat looked cleaner. Matching throws over the chairs and sofa gave it cohesion, and it looked like it had just been hoovered.

'I can't imagine what you're going through, babe. I'm so sorry, 'Pam said, handing her a Lion King mug of steaming black coffee.

'You've nothing to be sorry about. I'm terrified. I don't know if it's something Mike did that got him killed, if it's a business thing and they may come after us next. It can't just be random, can it? He was in the Cathedral. '

'Who knows? He could have gone in there on his way to get a taxi to get out of the weather. Someone saw the door open, thought they'd go in to see if there was anything to rob, and met Mike in there, ' Pam said, trying to make Helen feel safer.

'I suppose so… there are so many things. I think I'm going mad. I keep seeing a grey car drive by my house. It's a dead end; the car isn't from my street. I don't know anyone with that car. I'm scared someone is watching me. '

'If you see it again, call the police. It could be a clue. You've got that lady detective's number, haven't you? '

'Katie? Yes, I have. I know I thought she was having a go at me, bullying me but she wasn't. She caught me out, and she's only doing her job. I need her to find out what happened. '

'Do you want to stay here tonight? '
'No, thank you. I need to get a few things straight while Ewan isn't here. But thank you. '

They chatted for another twenty minutes before getting up to go. Helen said goodbye to Ewan.

'Be a good boy for Pam, and I'll see you tomorrow. Love you. '
'Love you, Mum, 'he said, giving her a hug. Both had tears running down their faces. Pam tried to hold hers back as well.

Helen was shown out, walked carefully down the wet, slippery wooden steps into the car park, and drove back home. She drove up to the end of the street and back before parking, just to see if she could spot that car or him or anyone else. She couldn't. She went into the house, set the alarms, and went into the living room.

Briggs had been asked to check the bundle Katie had downloaded from Michael's USB. Rook told him it was in a file on her desk. He approached the door, saw through the glass that she wasn't inside, and went in. The main office was noisy, with PCs updating CCTV, witness statements, and house-to-house reports. Briggs settled into the comfy chair in Katie's office corner and opened the file.

Not long after, Helen turned her phone back on to try and call Katie to tell her of her concerns. She immediately saw nine missed calls. Her whole body started to shake. She wasn't sure why he had never hurt her or threatened her but something felt off. She thought he was involved, and if he was, it was her fault.

Scared, she grabbed her handbag and dug through it to find Katie's card. It wasn't there. She dug deeper. There it was, at the bottom with all the receipts. She dialled the number. It wasn't on. No message. No voicemail. She waited a minute, tried again, and again. Same result.

Ring the police, she thought. *Ask for Katie.* She called the number and waited.

'Which emergency service do you require?'

'Police, please,' she said, trembling.

'Leicestershire Police. How can we help?'

'I need to be put through to Detective Katie Lounds, please. I've tried her mobile it's off. Can you put me through to her office or her radio?'

'Your name, please?'

'Helen Blake.'

'Thank you. Give me a minute, and I'll try her office extension.'

The call clicked through and began to ring. After about six rings, it went to answerphone.

She launched straight into her message, not waiting to hear a word in reply.

'Katie, I need to speak to you. I'm being followed. I'm scared. He's trying to manipulate me. I think I'm going to die. I've taken Ewan away in case someone turns up. There's a grey car that keeps driving by and parking outside. It doesn't have a plate on the back, but I've seen the front KP56, that's how it starts. I haven't seen it for two days. Please, Katie, call me. Please don't bring him with you. I don't know what he's done. He's involved. I think he killed Michael. I need to tell you everything. '

The line went dead.

The moment the voicemail started, Briggs recognised the voice and listened intently. He leaned over to where the voicemail button was and clicked delete. The light stopped flashing. He didn't want Helen to be looked into too deeply; he felt sorry for her. He sat back down and continued to read through the file.

CHAPTER 18

Helen decided to take a bath, so she could relax a little. The house was locked, and she would nip upstairs for half an hour. She ran herself a bath with pink bubble bath and lay in the bubbles, keeping her face out of the water as she hadn't taken off her make-up. The hot water felt cleansing, and she began to relax a little.

Later, she got herself a glass of wine and curled up on the sofa in her pyjamas and dressing gown. It was early evening, but she didn't intend to go out again that night. She wondered how things had gone so wrong. She had a lovely house, plenty of money, and even though Michael had been a constant pain, a constant living mystery, she missed him.

She began to cry and reached for a tissue; man-sized tissues, Michael said they were better value than the scented women's ones she actually liked.

She was suddenly jerked out of her grief by a banging on the door.

'Katie, is that you?' she whispered at the door. No reply.

She moved to the window and tried to peep out of the gap in the curtain and saw a blue BMW parked outside.

'No, it's me, let me in,' whispered the voice.

'Go away,' she called, voice raw. 'I shouldn't see you.'

'Come on, it's me,' he replied, calm and soothing. 'You're safe with me, you know you are.'

After a moment, she unlocked the door. He stepped inside, closing it gently behind him. His shirt was damp from the rain, hair slicked back. He moved closer, voice low and reassuring, and pulled her into his arms. She felt a flicker of security, but deep down, she knew it wasn't real.

'DS Lounds is convinced you are involved.'

Helen's breath hitched. 'I didn't kill him. You know I didn't. You, of all people, know I didn't.'

'What do you mean by that?' No reply.

He placed a hand on her shoulder, steady, intimate. 'Look, I know you didn't do it. But if they push hard enough, they'll make it stick. You'll go down for it. They probably already know you were having an affair. You'd want him out of the way, prime suspect to the police. They always look at the spouse as a number one suspect. You've seen that on TV.'

Helen's voice cracked. 'What do I do?'

His eyes softened, but behind them something colder flickered. 'You trust me. I'll handle it.'

Helen didn't know what to believe, what to think, or who to trust. 'Should I go away, take Ewan away?'

'They will think you're running away. It'll make you look guilty.'

'I'm not guilty of anything, well, not murder. I don't know what the hell to do. What can I do?' she shrieked, breaking down in a flood of tears.

He had an arm around her to comfort her in the hope she would believe him too. 'I didn't touch Michael, Helen, you must know that, don't you? I wouldn't kill him, I couldn't kill anyone, even if he was your husband and stopped us getting together. I wouldn't cause that much grief to you and Ewan.'

She was confused; she wasn't sure. But she didn't want to challenge him or accuse him as there was no one there to help her if he got angry. 'I know,' she whispered and gave him a smile.

He placed his arm around her shoulder and guided her to the sofa. 'You've probably not had a good night's sleep all week, have you?' he asked.

'Not one, an hour here and there, that's it. I feel terrible,' she replied.

'I'll make you a hot chocolate. Take a couple of sleeping tablets while Ewan isn't here and get a good night's sleep. I'll stay until you fall asleep,' he said, walking into the kitchen.

'I don't want tablets, I can't take them like that.'

'You aren't going to get a good night's sleep without them, Helen. Trust me.'

He went into the kitchen, spooned two heaped teaspoons of cocoa into a mug, stirred a little milk into a paste, then topped it up and put it in the microwave. He took the sleeping tablets from the medicine shelf, took two out and crushed them up. When the microwave pinged, he added the powder and put it back in for thirty seconds.

He picked up the mug and the blister packs of tablets and went into the lounge. 'Come on, let me take you up to bed.'

He guided her up the stairs to her bedroom at the front of the house. He placed the mug and tablets on the bedside table next to the digital alarm clock and pulled back the covers. He helped her out of the dressing gown and she got into bed.

She was slightly propped up on the pillows, and he sat on the edge of the bed and handed her the cocoa. 'Drink it up. You'll feel so much better when you've had a good night's sleep.'

'Do you think I should speak to DS Lounds? I've not told her about any of this.'

'No,' he said. 'You'll just give them more ammo to think it's you. Tell them you're having an affair and we both become suspects. Neither of us killed him, so it's just diverting their attention from the real murderer.'

She sighed. 'You're right.'

Thirty minutes passed, and Helen was becoming sleepy. 'I'll let you get some sleep,' he said. 'I'll lock the door behind me and pop the key through the letterbox.'

He did as he said and left the address. Jumped into the car and drove off.

CHAPTER 19

Morning came around too soon, her alarm on her phone waking her up at seven thirty. Monty was curled up on her pillow and gave a shallow groan as Katie moved her head, nudging him awake. He stretched out his front legs, making biscuits against Katie's shoulder. The room was still virtually pitch black; she had invested in some blackout blinds to help her sleep. She stumbled her way to the bathroom, still squinting, half asleep, and began to get herself ready: teeth, shower, hair, dressing, feeding Monty, and putting the kettle on. She could see outside that there was a light covering of snow on the ground, but it was no longer coming down.

She had the feeling it was going to be a long day. She made herself two sausage cobs, one to eat now and one wrapped in foil for lunch, along with a bowl of pasta salad from the fridge. She poured tea into her travel mug, drank a few sips, and then carried it out to the car.

She started the engine and let it run for a moment. She placed her bag in the boot; she wouldn't be taking it into court. She put her work shoes in the passenger footwell, fastened her seatbelt, and set off.

She drove to the Magistrates Court and found somewhere to park in Newarke Street Car Park, knowing someone was stalking her, and she now didn't know what car they might be in. A multi-storey wasn't ideal, but it was daylight and plenty of people were around. There was no one waiting at the lift, but people were walking down the stairs, so she went with the stairs. She made her way to the Court and made a call to PC Phillips, who was transporting Casey. He told her Casey was already in the cells and they were waiting. She asked for one of them to join her upstairs as she didn't want to be seen in court herself.

It had been arranged for Casey to be on first, due to his custody clock. He did not enter any pleas. The admin was done, he was remanded for the offences, but given back into the custody of the officers to be taken back to the police station. Given the time left on his clock, the police applied for a warrant of further detention to keep Casey in court for another thirty-six hours. He was not happy, and he made that very clear to the accompanying officers, who had to restrain him on the floor of the car park and fasten his legs to stop him kicking out at them. He was then placed in the rear of the van like a rolled-up carpet, and they drove back to the cells.

When Katie arrived back in the office, there was an air of activity; people were rushing around.

'Incident 108, Sarge, 'Owen said. 'Edward Blake has reported his car stolen. '

She pulled up the incident log.

Incident Log 270123/108
Transcript Date/Time: 08:34 hours
Caller: Edward Blake, resident of Cosby, Leicester
Operator: Police, how can I help?
Edward Blake: Yes, I need to report my car stolen.
Operator: Alright, sir. Can I take your name?
Edward Blake: Edward Blake. I live in Cosby. My car's gone from outside my parents' house.
Operator: Okay. What type of car, and what's the registration?
Edward Blake: It's a blue BMW, registration ED19 PTR. I parked it last night, around seven o'clock, right outside my parents' place. Came out this morning, and it's gone.
Operator: Do you have all sets of keys?
Edward Blake: Yes. I'm the only one with keys. They're

here with me.
Operator: Was the vehicle alarm activated?
Edward Blake (hesitates, voice lowering): No. I don't think
so. It should have been, but it wasn't. At least, it didn't go
off if anyone took it.
Operator: Any signs of forced entry? Glass on the ground?
Edward Blake: Not that I saw. Just gone.
Operator: Alright, Mr Blake. We'll log this and get an
officer to make contact with you.

Katie opened her desk drawer and removed her work mobile phone. She switched it on. As soon as she did, it started pinging: missed calls, four of them, all from yesterday evening, and all from Helen Blake's mobile number.

'Damn it, 'she muttered and tried to call the number back, but it just rang out.

She turned on her emails. There was an email from control: there had been a call put through to her desk phone at seventeen twenty yesterday, from Helen's phone number. A voicemail that lasted fifteen seconds. She looked at her answerphone. Nothing there, no flashing light.

New voicemails zero. She tried Helen's phone again. No answer.

Katie's heart thumped. Helen had left her a voicemail. But her voicemails empty. No new messages.

She sat back slowly, her throat dry. 'Who listened to it? 'she whispered. There were only two possibilities:

A technical glitch unlikely.

Or someone with access had deleted it before she could hear it. The latter was most likely, she feared.

She scanned through the lists of incidents and calls into the police from five o'clock the previous day to now. There was nothing else from Helen.

Katie went to speak with Rook, but Keene was in the office. She wasn't about to waste time telling him everything that had happened, so she went to Jane and explained the missed calls, the missing voicemail, and not being able to get hold of Helen.

'I think we need to go round there. Can you grab a CID car, Jane? '

Jane went off into the Inspector's office to get a set of keys. Briggs walked in. She saw Owen and Benton were already at their desks, both with a pile of papers and their laptops open. She would leave them to it.

'Sarge! 'shouted Rick, who had been listening to the area radio. 'Call from Pamela Blake. She's been looking after Ewan for Helen. She left him there yesterday afternoon because she was scared someone was after Helen. She was supposed to pick him up for school this morning, but didn't. Pam took him to school and has tried repeatedly to call Helen, but can't get a reply. She's worried. She says she can't go check in person because she doesn't drive. '

'Has a mobile been assigned, Rick?' she asked.

'Yes, call sign Charlie Romeo five six.'

'Have they updated arrival?'

'Just updated. Yes, front door is unlocked.'

Shit, thought Katie to herself. Why did she forget her phone? What was Helen calling her for?

Jane came back with some keys. 'Sarge, crew on scene have called for an ambulance. Female at the address is unresponsive. '

At that moment, PC Phillips walked in.
'Ross,' said Katie, 'have you got a marked car?'
'Yes, Sarge.'
'Great, get us to Stonelea, Countesthorpe, will you? Fast. Jane, Alan with me.'

They virtually ran to the car park and jumped in the young PC's car. They took off at speed towards Helen's address.
They killed the lights and sirens as they entered the village, passed the college, and made their way to the cul-de-sac that they by now knew well. Pulling up at Helen's address, there was a paramedic's car and two marked police cars. Katie looked across the street and saw the curtains twitch at Jenny's house, the cockapoo peeking out also.

PC Phillips remained in the car, but Katie, Jane and Alan made their way into the address. They could hear voices coming from upstairs, so they made their way up the large sweeping staircase.

They entered the large bedroom. There was a queen-sized bed, if not bigger, with a cream duvet with a delicate lilac flower design on it. Helen looked very small in that bed.

Helen's face was pale, lips faintly tinged blue, but the rest of the scene was wrong. Everything staged, laid out with care. No mess, no signs of panic. The mug at the bedside had no drips, no stains on the duvet, no smears of chocolate on Helen's lips. Though it looked like she may have spilt a little on the pillow, a bit of a chocolate smudge.

Briggs let out a sigh. 'Looks like she couldn't take the pressure. Tablets, hot drink, bed. Peaceful enough way to go.'

Katie didn't answer straight away. She crouched by the bedside table, studying the scene. Her gaze lingered on the blister pack two blister packs, two missing from one, four from the other. But the packaging was too clean, no ragged edges from someone fumbling under stress, both placed neatly on the bedside table. And the mug perfectly in the middle of the placemat. Are you that meticulous if you are about to take an overdose? Maybe it was accidental.

'Sleeping tablets, Zolpidem. Quite strong, prescribed to her but last year according to the packet which is on the table,' said the paramedic, who had his digital tablet in hand, making notes.

'Has she been moved?' Katie asked.

'No more than to lift a wrist, put on a cuff. She's been gone a good few hours. No point in trying CPR or getting the defib on her.'

'She was frantic yesterday,' Katie murmured. 'She tried to reach me. If this was suicide, why try so hard to call for help first?'

Briggs gave her a weary look. 'Not everything adds up tidy, Sergeant. People change their minds.' Rather than just looking cocky or bored, was it her imagination, or did he look a little scared? Upset?

Katie stood slowly, her jaw tight. 'Or someone changed it for her.'

'Alan, could you go and organise SOCO and the coroner, please?' He walked out of the bedroom and down the stairs.

Katie scanned the room again. Something wasn't right. You don't lie flat on your back, duvet folded neatly, hands crossed on top. It looked staged.

The front door was unlocked. Helen wouldn't have gone to bed leaving it open, not when she'd been so desperate to reach her. There were no signs of forced entry. Someone she knew or trusted had been here.

Katie made a few calls.

'Jane, bag that mug and the tablets, will you? Tip the liquid into a container and seize that separately. Bodycam what you are doing, please. I want you to get that to the lab in Nottingham. Get someone to take it on blues. I've organised a fast-track forensic submission. Need the results back ASAP.'

Jane put on some blue latex gloves and took an evidence bag out of her pocket. 'Yes, Sarge.'

Dr Malik turned up quite quickly. 'You're keeping me busy, Sergeant,' he said.

'Yeah, and this one probably is down to me,' Katie thought to herself.

'Appears at first glance to be an overdose: open tablets, tablets missing. She was scared, but it doesn't feel right. How quickly can you do this one?'

'She linked to the other Blake?'

'Wife.'

'I'll pull it in this afternoon. Now you've got a double murder. She looks like she has some light bruising on her shoulder there,' Malik said, pointing at her left shoulder near the neckline. Katie could see three small, round, light bruises. He spent a few minutes looking her over, taking her temperature.

'Estimated time of death?' she hoped.

'I'd say roughly eleven p.m. to four a.m., but I'll be able to give you more when I open her up.'

SOCO turned up. Photographs were being taken, and the scene was being processed. Helen's body was then to be removed.

Katie looked on the bedside table. There was a photograph frame, an elegant black glossy frame, triangular in shape, and in it was a picture taken on a beach: Helen, Michael and Ewan. That poor boy lost his dad a week ago and now his mum is dead. A lump came to her throat. She blinked in an attempt to stop tears coming into her eyes.

'Sarge, there's a lady out front with a little dog. Says she needs to speak to you, strange goings-on she reckons,' said the PC.

'Jenny, she said her name was.' Ah, neighbourhood watch, thought Katie. Ideal. 'Thanks.'

Katie went back downstairs. Alan was sitting on the sofa looking at his phone. She left him to it. He was behaving strangely, even for Alan.

Outside, Katie was pounced on immediately. She bent down to stroke his head. 'Hello again, Percy, good lad.'

'Jenny, how can I help you?'

'What's happened? There were things going on last night. Is Helen okay?'

'I'm afraid not,' she knew within the next few minutes the body would be brought out, so all the curtain twitchers and those who were just brazenly standing on their lawns watching would soon see. 'What did you see, Jenny?'

'It wasn't that late, about eleven. I was just letting Percy out before bedtime when I noticed the blue BMW parked outside her house. A bit later, someone came on a bike, but I didn't see where they went. It was dark. They went to the car. I couldn't see what they did after that, but the bike was left at the side of the house. The car drove off after a couple of hours. I heard a car start around half past midnight. I looked out and saw it driving away. I didn't see when the bike left or where the rider went.'

'That's really helpful, Jenny. I'm always happy to find someone so observant,' she said.

Hmm. Coincidence or not? Helen's dead, Edward's car is at the scene. Edward reports his car missing. Edward's address is no more than a five- or six-minute drive from here.

'Thank you, Jenny. I may well need to speak to you again later today if that's alright?'

'Of course it is, love. Me and Percy will be in.'

Katie left the scene, leaving PC Phillips and the original attending officers. She took the marked car; Phillips would jump in with one of his colleagues later. Briggs was unusually quiet, reflective, concerned, Katie would say, more so than just dealing with any sudden death. She didn't say anything. They travelled back to the station in silence.

Briggs got out of the car in the car park and walked off, leaving the two ladies behind.

'You think he was the other person seeing her? He's pretty upset, even though he tried to fob it off in there,' were Jane's first words.

'I have my suspicions too,' replied Katie.

The ladies went into the station and sat at their respective desks. There was property to be booked in and notes to be written up.

TDC Tom Ilkley slid into his chair, flicked open his laptop and stifled a yawn. A red notification pulsed in the corner of his screen. He frowned and clicked it open.

The trace map for Michael Blake's phone appeared, red dots marking its signal.

• Twenty-three twenty-four hours: phone active, pinged to Stonelea (Helen Blake's address).
• Remained there for about thirty minutes after activation. Signal in and out.

• Zero twenty-one hours: signal moved, travelling south.
• Last known location: Hill Lane, Countesthorpe.

Ilkley's eyes widened. That wasn't random.

He got up quickly and crossed to DS Katie Lounds' desk, where Reeves was perched on the edge going over statements.

'You'll want to see this. Michael Blake's phone pinged last night Stonelea at eleven o'clock.'

Katie froze, her eyes narrowing. 'Stonelea… Helen's place, about the time Edward's car was there?'

'Yes. It stayed there for about an hour, then it travelled south. Ended up on Hill Lane in Countesthorpe, where it remained,' said Tom.

'And if the phone moved, it was taken there deliberately. Someone had it,' added Jane.

Katie pressed her lips into a thin line. 'Right. Tom, log every timestamp and pull the cell site data. Reeves, we need a car on Hill Lane quietly. If the phone's still on, we need to know where it is and who's carrying it, unless it's still in the car. Then it will be easy to find.'

Katie rapped on the frosted glass and stepped into Rook's office. He glanced up, brows drawn.

'Sir, we've got movement on Michael Blake's phone. It was active at eleven last night   at Helen Blake's address, Stonelea. Stayed there for an hour, then travelled to Hill Lane, Countesthorpe. That's where it's still showing.'

Rook sat forward, eyes sharp. 'Stonelea? You're telling me Michael Blake's missing phone was at his wife's house around the time she turns up dead?'

Katie nodded. 'Yes, sir. And whoever had it drove it south afterwards. It's still showing live in Countesthorpe. Whoever took it either killed him, as we know he had it, or has been to the scene and removed it.'

A few calls were made and a crew was sent to Hill Lane to see if they could locate the phone. It was likely to be in a blue BMW unless it had been tossed from the window. They were to look for the vehicle first. If it wasn't there, additional units would be called to help search the field where the phone had pinged. TDC Ilkley went with them so he could track the phone if it moved.

Katie left the office with a surge of adrenaline. Whoever carried Michael's phone had tied themselves directly to both murders, and now she had a thread she could finally pull.

CHAPTER 20

The January morning air was damp, the grass still slick with dew. Blue lights pulsed faintly on the country road where two patrol cars had pulled up. Beyond the hedgerow, in the middle of a rutted track cutting into the field, sat a dark blue BMW. Its windows were fogged; they had started to ice over, the front wheel stuck in a muddy hollow.

TDC Tom Ilkley trudged through the wet grass alongside two uniformed constables. The stillness of the car was eerie. He noted the registration straight away.

'ED19 PTR… that's Edward Blake's BMW.'

One of the PCs tried the door. It opened without resistance.

'Not even locked,' said the PC.

Ilkley leaned down, torch sweeping the interior. The car was very clean. Some hairs on the driver's seat were the only sign of use; otherwise it seemed immaculate. The ignition was cold. It was a cold morning, but the car had probably been there for a few hours. He opened the driver's side door fully and bent down.

There, in the side pocket, sat a mobile phone.

'Here we go.'

Ilkley pulled on gloves and carefully lifted it out. The screen was cracked but faintly glowing. A photograph of Michael and Ewan Blake smiled up from the lock screen.

'That's our victim's phone. Dumped in his brother's car,' he sighed.

One of the constables whistled low. 'Convenient, isn't it? Car reported stolen an hour or two ago, and now this.'

Ilkley bagged the phone, sealing it with methodical precision. 'Convenient's one word. Bloody suspicious is another.' He switched it off. It only had nine per cent battery left.

He stepped back, surveying the car. Whoever had driven it hadn't even bothered to conceal it. Ilkley reached for his radio.

Ilkley called in an update. 'Control, TDC Ilkley. We've located Edward Blake's BMW off Hill Lane, Countesthorpe. Vehicle unsecured, no driver present. Victim's phone was recovered from inside, driver's door pocket. Request SOCO attendance to lift prints, forensically recover the car and photograph the scene please.'

He looked at the constables, his jaw tight. 'Don't touch anything else. This just went from a stolen motor report to something a hell of a lot darker.'

Katie was halfway through scribbling notes onto the whiteboard when the door swung open. TDC Tom Ilkley came in, shoulders damp from the morning drizzle, his expression set hard. Reeves looked up from her laptop.

'Well? What've you got?'

Ilkley dropped a brown evidence bag onto the desk between them.

'Found in the driver's door pocket of Edward Blake's BMW. Car was dumped in a field off Hill Lane, Countesthorpe. Unlocked. No driver, no keys. Screen lock photo, Michael and Ewan.'

Katie straightened, the air in the room tightening. 'Edward's BMW? The one he reported stolen this morning?'

'That's the one. Uniform found it. Tyre tracks on a muddy bit that wasn't frozen and the car left in the field. Looks like someone ditched it in a hurry. Phone was sat right there, plain as day. Didn't even try to hide it.'

'That's too neat. If someone stole it, why leave the car unlocked and the phone right inside? It feels planted,' said Reeves.

Katie nodded. 'Agreed. Almost like someone wanted it found. And fast.'

Ilkley rubbed a hand over his jaw. 'SOCO's on the way to lift prints. But whoever dumped it wasn't bothered about it being found.'

Katie turned to the board, writing BMW + PHONE → STONELEA 23:00 in block letters. She tapped the pen against it, thinking aloud.

'Phone active at Helen Blake's address at eleven p.m. last night. Car reported stolen by Edward at eight thirty this morning. Both turn up together in Countesthorpe. If Edward's telling the truth, someone stole his car, kept Michael's phone, and moved them both. If he's lying...' Katie started.

'Then Edward planted it to shift suspicion off himself.'

Katie gave a short, humourless laugh. 'Either way, he's in the frame.'

Ilkley folded his arms. 'You want me to bring him in?'

Katie hesitated. 'We might have to.'

She glanced at Reeves. 'Get comms to check ANPR for the car between nine p.m. and when it was found. If it went past a camera, we'll know who was driving.'

Reeves nodded quickly, already typing.

Katie exhaled, eyes lingering on the phone. 'Someone's moving pieces on a board they think we can't see. But they've made a mistake. Leaving us this.'

Katie organised herself and Brenton to go and arrest Edward Blake. Before leaving the station they had given Edward a call to see where he was. He was at home; he was expecting an officer to call about his stolen car, so they didn't disillusion him at that stage in case he tried to hide any evidence. They were still short of a murder weapon, the knife.

Edward had to be informed of Helen's death as well as arrested for it.

Edward opened the door to Katie and Dean. 'Hello, I wasn't expecting the murder team to come and take a report of a car theft.'

Katie looked at him, weighing him up. 'Edward, love, is everything OK?' said an older lady who walked into the living room towards them. She was a lady Katie would put to be in her seventies, but her immaculate dress and makeup gave the impression she could have been in her fifties. Her neatly bobbed silvery-grey hair, brown tweed skirt, and crisp white blouse were very smart.

'This is my mum, officers. Mum, DS Katie Lounds and her colleague, they are investigating Michael's death.'

With that, she sat on the sofa and burst into tears, pulling out a small white floral handkerchief and sobbing into it loudly. 'Have you caught him yet, whoever killed my boy?'

'We're following some leads, Mrs Blake. We have some suspects, we just need to get a bit more evidence. We will get there.'

'I haven't seen Helen since. Is the boy alright, little Ewan? He can come and stay with us if Helen needs some time.'

'As far as I know, he's being looked after. Edward, if we could see you outside.'

Edward gave his mum a hug as she dabbed her eyes. They stepped outside.

'Edward, I don't like to do things like this, but I have some more bad news. Helen has been found this morning, deceased, suspicious, but we are having some things checked and a post-mortem done today.'

'Oh God, how bad can it get for this family? Where's Ewan? Is he okay?'

'He's with your wife. Helen dropped him off yesterday as she was upset about something.'

'I have to go and check on them both,' he said and started to walk towards where his car should be parked. 'Damn, I forgot. I'll have to get Dad's keys, hold on.'

Katie stepped in his way. He looked confused.

'I'm sorry, Edward, not now.'

'What do you mean?'

'Due to evidence that has come to light, I am arresting you on suspicion of the murders of Helen and Michael Blake.'

She cautioned him and explained the grounds for his arrest as he slid down his father's car and ended up sitting on the floor, sobbing.

'No, no, no,' he shouted.

Katie left Blake with Brenton to be booked in and returned to her desk to scribble a quick interview plan. She already knew what she wanted to put to him but wanted a plan to make sure she didn't miss anything.

His solicitor was called and, luckily, was in the car park about to leave from a prior job. They were ready for the interview very quickly. Blake was allowed a consultation with his solicitor, but after less than ten minutes he said he wanted to get on with it. He didn't need legal advice, he claimed, as he hadn't done anything.

The interview commenced.

CHAPTER 21

Katie opened the interview. 'For the record, Edward Blake, you've been arrested on suspicion of the murder of Michael Blake and Helen Blake. Do you understand?'

She went through the offence definition and reminded him of his rights. Everyone introduced themselves, and the interview began.

'Yes. I understand. But I haven't killed anyone.'

'Your car was seen and identified outside your sister-in-law's house around the time the coroner suspects she was killed.'

'I know how it looks, but it wasn't me. I wasn't driving it. It was stolen.'

'Yes. That's what you reported this morning. Where were you between ten p.m. and three a.m., Edward? Can you give us the names of any witnesses or anything to prove where you were?'

'At home, asleep. I went to bed around eleven p.m. My parents were in the house, but they didn't see me. They were in bed. I didn't get up until about eight a.m.'

'Is there any way to prove you didn't drive your car to Stonelea? Do your parents have CCTV, a Ring doorbell, or anything?' Reeves asked.

'They don't. Someone on the street might, but not us.'

DS Lounds continued, 'Does anyone else use your car? Are they insured to drive it or have keys?'

'No. No one has permission or keys.'

'No one has permission or keys. There were no signs of broken glass on the car, no break-in at the house to get the keys. How was your car taken and driven, Edward?'

'I don't know.'

'Have you left your vehicle with anyone recently, given keys to anyone?'

'The only other time I didn't have the keys on my person or in the house was when I was with you, at the police station in Leicester being interviewed.'

Katie remembered this. He had double-parked a works vehicle in the small car park, and the keys had been left behind the desk in case it needed to be moved. How would anyone know they were his keys or want to take them?

'Bear with me a minute, please.'

Katie took out her phone and messaged Owen. 'Rick, urgent. Check my notes of the time of the interview with Edward Blake and Mansfield House on Tuesday. Check the FEO CCTV, looking to see if anyone borrowed the keys or moved a blue BMW in the car park, please.'

The message was delivered and about ten seconds later, she received a thumbs-up emoji.

'Your car was then found on Hill Lane in Countesthorpe, in a field. That's on your way home?'

'Not really. I'd go up Countesthorpe Road and cross over Lutterworth Road. Hill Lane would be out of my way. What reason would I want to kill Helen? Helen was all Ewan had left.'

'Now that, Edward, is very interesting, because that's not the case, is it? You don't believe that?'

'I don't know what you mean,' he said, screwing up his face into a scowl.

Katie slid across the desk, the screenshots of the messages she had retrieved from Helen's phone in front of him. 'You think Ewan is yours?'

Edward turned pale and looked like he was about to throw up. He took a deep breath but remained silent.

'So, did you go and try and locate Michael, not to get your coat back, but to confront him about the paternity of Ewan? Did something kick off between you, and you hit him?'

'No, no, that didn't happen.'

'But you believe Ewan is yours. Maybe you wanted him because Pam and yourself couldn't have children?'

'That's not true. I am happy being Uncle Eddy. I get to see him all the time, but none of the responsibility or cost,' a lump forming in his throat.

'But he doesn't call you 'daddy', does he, Edward?' Katie said, trying to elicit some honest emotion. 'That must stick in your throat every time you heard him call the brother you thought was a useless, extravagant man.'

His face became angry. Angry was good, because sometimes angry led to a suspect blurting out all sorts, but Edward remained in control, just.

Composing himself, he said, 'Look, I was driving around town, yes. I admit that.'

DC Reeves asked, 'Driving where, exactly?'

'Near the Cathedral. Around the city centre. I was… looking for Michael.'

Lounds continued, 'Looking for him? At that time of night?'

'He had my coat. Stupid, I know, but I wanted it back. It had my wallet and cards in it. I thought he might still be about. I didn't know he was dead.'

'So you just happened to be circling the Cathedral in the middle of the night for a coat?'

'I know how it sounds, but it's the truth. I wanted to see if he was there. I thought maybe I'd run into him. My wallet and ID were in the coat too. I needed them.'

'And did you?'

'No. I didn't see him.'

'Yet CCTV shows your car parked up. So if you weren't with Michael, what were you doing?'

Edward hesitated, voice lowering. 'I… I went inside the Cathedral.'

'At three in the morning?' queried Reeves.

'Around that, yes. Maybe ten past. I went to put the ledgers back. I'd taken them from the meeting. I then realised I didn't know when I'd be going to the Cathedral to put them back, so thought I'd drop them in while I was nearby. I didn't want anyone thinking I'd stolen them.'

DS Lounds considered his answer. 'So you walked into a murder scene, replaced church ledgers, and left without seeing your brother lying dead?'

Blake was becoming more defensive. 'He wasn't there when I went in! I swear it. I saw nothing, nobody. I just put the books back and left. Straight back to the Airbnb.'

'If you were looking for him to get your coat back, why didn't you follow him from the meeting to swap with him?'

'I didn't know it was him that had taken it. As others had left, once I was away from the flat, I realised I didn't think Freddie or his wife, or Enoch or Derek had taken it.'

'You left the meeting around two a.m. What were you doing until three a.m., and why did you think Michael would still be in town and not off home?'

'He likes to go for a couple of pints when in town and gets his taxis from Jubilee Square.'

'What about Helen? Why was your car outside her house last night at ten?' Katie asked.

'I don't know. I wasn't there. Someone else must have taken it. I'm telling you, I didn't go near Stonelea.'

'Edward, you've now admitted to trying to locate Michael in town around the time he was killed. You parked up and by your own admission went to the Cathedral, where Michael was found dead. Your car is then seen outside Helen's at the time she died. When your car is recovered, in the side driver's pocket is Michael's phone, the phone he had with him at the time he was murdered. Explain that, please. That's a lot of co-incidences, Mr Blake.'

Edward snapped back at Lounds. 'Because someone's setting me up! Can't you see that? I went to put the ledgers back, yes, but I didn't kill Michael. I didn't touch Helen. Someone wants you to believe I did.'

'Who, Mr Blake? Who would want to do that?'

There was no response as Edward broke down and began to cry. 'It wasn't me, it really wasn't. I don't know what to say.'

(Silence. The solicitor shifts slightly, placing a steadying hand on Edward's arm.)

Mr Holt spoke up. 'My client has explained himself. Unless you can provide clear forensic evidence, I advise him to make no further comment.'

'Interview suspended at fifteen forty-four,' said Lounds as she ended the interview.

DC Reeves booked Blake back into custody, and Lounds went upstairs to see Owen and to make a call.

When she made her way back into the office, Rook and Keene were in their office. Neither looked very happy, as though they were exchanging words.

'Sarge, I've got it,' said Rick Owen, almost jogging over to her. 'You're not going to believe this.'

'Don't be so sure,' she said, raising an eyebrow. 'Try me.'

Rick set up the footage on his laptop. Alan Briggs was in the front office at Mansfield House when Edward arrived for his interview. Why? He waited for Katie to take Edward down the corridor, then walked outside. He came back about five minutes later, went up to the desk, spoke to Marilyn, and she handed him what looked like keys.

'Bloody hell,' said Katie. 'Why does he want those?'

Rick skipped the footage forward to show Briggs handing the keys back about fifteen minutes later.

'What was he doing?'

'I don't know,' said Rick. 'I couldn't get the car park footage to download, but I've watched it. He doesn't go to the BMW. He looks at it as he walks past, then leaves the car park and heads toward the centre of town.'

'Excellent work, Rick. Can you ping that over to me?'

'Yes, Sarge. Right away.'

What is going on, she thought to herself, sitting at her desk. One thing to try again before she speaks to Rook... 07966 553 433. If that links to Briggs, she will be in the inspector's office asking for a rare thing: a copper to be arrested.

She dialled the number and waited. It clicked in and started to ring. A vibration was heard from under one of the desks in the room. Katie went over to it. Alan Briggs' bag was beneath it. She cut it off, and tried again, not wanting it just to be a coincidence. The bag vibrated again, and stopped when she cut the call.

Reeves was watching from her desk.

'Which phone is that?'

'It's the number that was down as 'Dad' in Casey's phone, the same number which appears to have been in some kind of romantic liaison with Helen.'

'So that means Briggs was around town in the early hours when Michael was killed, looking for Edward, at the direction of Casey. To speak about a woman, he said, didn't he?'

'Yes, you can bet now that's Helen.'

'He could have got the phone from the murder scene too, first on scene for CID, and kept it.'

It was all whirring around in Katie's head. She was trying to make head or tails of it.

'Oh God, why didn't I think of it before? Alan told me he had a daughter called Amelia and a son Dom, Alex Dominic Casey, and what's the betting he goes by Dominic, but he also shortens it to 'Nick'.'

'From the ledger meeting, of course. That's how he knew who he thought Edward was and how he could give Briggs directions and know when he left. Shit. No wonder

Alan was trying to divert us away from Nick, saying he was just a handyman and nothing to do with anything.'

Katie made her way into the room where Rook and Keene were.

'Solved it yet, Missy?' sneered Keene.

'Getting there.'

Katie recounted the events of the morning: the stolen car, Alan taking the keys, Dominic, Dom and Nick, the mobile phone number, the messages and 'Dad'.

Keene took the bag from Katie, put on some gloves and fished about for the mobile phone.

'Ring it again so we know which it is.'

Katie dialled. The phone in Keene's hand vibrated. She hung up.

Both men stood there, shocked. Keene brushed away a flap of hair that had fallen across his face, looking pale.

'It doesn't mean he's killed either of them, but it's bloody suspicious.'

'We only need suspicion, Sir.'

Rook's phone started to buzz. He apologised and took the call.

'Hello. Yes, DI Rook. Oh hello. Okay, what have you got? I appreciate you rushing it through. Really? Anyone else's? Okay, yes, that's to be expected. I really appreciate the quick turnaround. Bye.'

'Katie, you went with Reeves, Briggs and a PC to Helen's this morning, didn't you?'

'Yes, PC Phillips, used his marked car.'

'Did you see any officer handle the mug and tablet box before Reeves seized them?'

'No, no-one from our team did. Think the paramedic did, but he was gloved up.'

'I don't say this lightly. Arresting one of our own is not what any officer wants to do,' Rook said, very concerned as he spoke. You could see the implications for the team and the force running through his mind the press releases, even more animosity towards police than usual.

'What was the call?' interrupted Keene.

'The mug, the blister packs and the medicine box all have Briggs' prints on them. Helen's and Briggs'.'

'What the hell has that man been up to? I hope you're right, Katie. He's a good thief taker. If he is clean, you've screwed up and you'll slide another step down, I will make sure of it.'

'No, Grahame, that's unfair. I'm on board with this. Whether he has killed either of them or not, he's involved, hiding evidence, diverting our investigation, he is personally involved with a murder victim, he's done in the job.'

Rook jumped in. 'I'll take this on my back if it goes wrong. Get Alan Briggs in. I think we need to bring him in, for both jobs. I'll try and get Beaumont opened. We need privacy for a serving officer to be interviewed, not so that every Tom, Dick and Harry is snooping. I'll make sure the incident for his arrest and the custody log are cloaked. At this stage, no-one outside this room, and Reeves, if you need her, Katie, to know he's in.'

Earlier in the day, at the hospital, the post mortem had taken place.

The cold air carried the metallic tang of disinfectant. The room was quiet, save for the occasional scrape of steel on porcelain and the soft rustle of gloves. Helen Blake's body lay beneath the stark overhead lights, pale against the white sheet.

Dr Imran Malik worked methodically, his notes clipped neatly to a board beside him. He removed stomach contents, carefully transferring samples into vials for toxicology. His brow furrowed as he dictated.

Dr Malik, dictating: 'Stomach contents show presence of zolpidem. Estimating ingested dose equivalent to four or five tablets, ten milligrams each. Not sufficient to cause death in an otherwise healthy adult female. Toxicology to confirm.'

He paused, leaning closer under the lamp. Fine pinpoint haemorrhages petechiae peppered the whites of Helen's eyes. He noted bruising beneath the skin at the base of her neck, just above the collarbone.

He gently inspected her nose and throat with a probe, the light catching faint redness inside the nasal passages.

Dr Malik, quietly to himself: 'Not consistent with overdose… consistent with obstruction of airways. Smothering.'

He stripped off his gloves, stepping back from the table. DS Lounds had been suspicious about it being an overdose and thought the scene had been staged. She may have been correct.

Katie stood at the window of the office, arms folded against the chill seeping through the glass. Below, in the car park, DI Rook and DI Keene walked side by side, their pace steady and purposeful. Between them was DC Alan Briggs, shoulders hunched, his usual swagger absent.

They stopped by the row of police vehicles. Katie couldn't hear their words, but she saw the flicker across Briggs' face, first surprise, then dawning realisation. His mouth opened as if to protest, but no sound carried up. He glanced between them, searching for a way out, but Keene's face was set and Rook's eyes were steady.

After a long pause, Briggs' shoulders sagged. He nodded once, slow, almost mechanical.

Rook laid a hand on his back not friendly, not dominant, just a quiet acknowledgment. A gesture that said, you know how it works. I don't want to do this, but it has to be done.

The three men walked towards a waiting police car. Briggs didn't resist, didn't make a scene. He slid into the back seat, closing the door himself. To anyone watching from a distance, it could have looked like colleagues heading to a job. But Katie knew better.

The car engine started, and the vehicle rolled smoothly out of the car park. Behind her, DC Jane Reeves' voice broke the silence.

'That looked… formal. Was he arrested? '

Katie turned from the glass, her expression firm.

'Yes. He has been. Doesn't matter if he's a cop - he's a suspect. He has to be treated the same as anyone else. '
Reeves nodded, biting her lip, the weight of it settling.

Katie looked back through the window, just in time to see the tail lights disappearing onto the road. She knew Rook had arranged it discreetly - Briggs wouldn't be paraded
through his own station cells. Beaumont Leys had been opened specially, away from familiar eyes.
The CID office carried on with its usual hum, but for Katie, the air felt heavier. A fellow officer led away like any other suspect.

Caution given at commencement of interview.

DI Rook took the lead. 'Alan, you understand you're here as part of our enquiries into the deaths of Helen Blake and Michael Blake? '
'Yes, and I'll repeat what I've said before. I had nothing to do with either death. It's a tragedy. That's all there is. '
A tragedy, yes, but one that wasn't what it first appeared to be.
'Ok, Helen, 'Rook continued. 'What can you tell me about you and her? '
(Briggs shifts in his chair, folding his arms.)
'I've not killed her. '

'You'll understand why we need to explore your connection to her. We've had conflicting accounts, Alan. At times, you've appeared protective of Helen. At other times, she seemed frightened of you. Can you explain that? '

'Helen was under a lot of strain. Her husband dead, Edward all over the place. People get emotional, scared, say things that don't always make sense. But I never threatened her, never harmed her. '

'Yet we have witnesses who describe her looking uncomfortable in your presence. Did you visit her address at Stonelea last night? '

'Why would I? '

'Because Michael Blake's phone was active at her address around eleven p.m. last night. It stayed there for over an hour, then travelled south and was later found in

Edward's BMW. That ties Helen's house directly into the timeline of both deaths. That phone disappeared from the crime scene, you were out looking for Edward where the murder took place and were one of the first officers on scene, plenty of time to take the evidence. So I'll ask again: did you go to Stonelea? '

(Briggs leans forward, voice sharper.)

'No, SIR. I did not. You're grasping at straws. '

'We're not grasping at straws. We're investigating and following every lead we get. You know how it works. Right now, Alan, you are part of a very small circle of people who were close to Helen. She trusted you at times and feared you at others. We believe her death was staged to look like suicide. Whoever did it wanted to silence her. You had both the access and the opportunity. '

Briggs snaps: 'You're out of line. I've worked alongside you, and you think I'd '(cuts off, shakes his head) 'No. No, I won't say anything more. '

'That's your right, Alan. For the record, you deny visiting Helen's address last night, deny any involvement in her death, and deny having any personal relationship beyond professional support? '

'Correct. '

'Interview terminated at sixteen nineteen hours... 'That's it?'

'No, I just want to make a couple of phone calls and then we will carry on '

A short time later the interview resumed.

Caution given at commencement of interview.

Again DI Rook took the interview 'Alan, I'm going to ask you directly: where were you at three-thirty am. On Thursday morning, the time Michael Blake was killed? '

'At home. Asleep. Like most people.' 'Anyone who can confirm that? 'Briggs shrugs 'No. I live alone. '

'See, Alan, that's a problem. Your son, Alex Dominic Casey, is in custody. He's told us he was out with you that night, showing you around town and helping you look for Edward Blake. He named you as his father. Do you want to explain that? '

Briggs scowled 'He's lying. He's trying to drag me down with him. '

DI Keene stepped in 'So you accept he is your son? Drag you down with him, what has he done then? 'Silence 'He says you were looking to speak to Edward about a woman. Was that woman Helen Blake? 'No reply came.

'Were you having an affair with Helen, Alan? Is that what this was about? Afraid Edward would tell Michael? '

'I wasn't having an affair. I'm not answering this rubbish. '

DI Room continued 'Let's move forward then. Last night between ten p.m. and five a.m. Where were you? '

'At home.' 'Alone again?' 'Yes. '

'What vehicle were you in?' 'None. I was at home. '

'But you went to Helen Blake's address. You drugged her. Tried to make it look like an overdose. Your fingerprints are on the medication, on the bedside table, next to where she lay dead. Posed. '

Briggs puffed out his red cheeks 'I didn't kill Helen. If my prints are there, then I must've touched them at some other point. Maybe when I'd been there before, maybe I touched it when we found her '

'You didn't, we have bodycam from the moment you all entered the room. You didn't touch the tablets or the mug. '

'You also signed out Edward Blake's BMW keys from the front desk at the station. Why?

What did you need them for? 'asked Keene 'I don't remember doing that. '

'You don't remember? 'Smirked Keene. 'It was only a few days ago. Not something you do every day. Alan, Edward reported that BMW stolen this morning. The car was found dumped in a field with Michael Blake's phone inside. You had the keys and the opportunity to get a copy cut. You're on FEO CCTV taking them and returning them about fifteen minutes later. Did you take the vehicle to Helen's to make it look like Edward killed her? '

'No. You've got this all wrong. '

DI Rook jumped in: 'Then explain it. Explain your prints. Explain the keys. Explain Alex putting you with him, looking for Edward, the night Michael died. You can't, can you? '

Briggs just sat staring at the table in silence. Shaking his head. Beaten.

DI Rook ended the interview 'For the record: you deny being at Stonelea, deny harming Helen Blake, deny stealing Edward's vehicle, and deny being present at the time of

Michael Blake's murder. Interview suspended at seventeen twenty-eight .'

CHAPTER 22

Katie was discussing what Briggs had said to DI Rook and Keene over the phone and how it linked to their case as a whole. They were all exasperated. Then a phone started to ring. It was hers.

'DS Lounds,' she said, swiping the screen to take the call. 'Ok, thank you, put her through.'

'It's Jennifer Barnes-Halford, sir. She is the local self-appointed "neighbourhood watch"' making air-quote gestures with her hand even though no one was there to see them 'in Helen's street.' She switched the phone onto speaker. 'I'll put it on speakerphone, hopefully you can hear it through this phone.'

'Hello, Jenny, how can I help you?' she asked.

'Ooh, DS Lounds, I saw him. I saw the man who was driving the blue BMW when it left Helen's this morning. I saw him, and it wasn't Edward.'

'Who was it, Jenny?'

'Ooh, I don't know his name, but he was stood outside the house with you. After you'd spoken to me, I went back to my house and Percy was on the windowsill, so I went to move him, and of course that meant I was looking out to where you were. I wasn't watching you.'

Katie was getting a little impatient, but she knew someone like Jenny could hold vital information.

'He was standing with you, talking to you, he got into the car with you. I thought you had arrested him.'

'Describe him, please, Jenny.'

'Ooh, I can do better than that, love. Hold on.'

Katie could hear Jenny handling the phone she was calling on, pressing keys and making beeps. 'Hold on, I'm not very good at this technology thing. I took a picture of him last night, and today with you, to check he was the same man. Slimy-looking chap. Percy didn't like him; he growled at him.'

A moment later, Katie received a notification that image files were being downloaded. She was only on mobile data, so it was taking a while. Her impatience grew until finally the images appeared on screen.

'Jenny, are you sure? This is very serious. I need to know you are sure.'

'Ooh, I am. It's him. Look, he had on that same jacket last night too. That's why I took the picture of him. Dodgy-looking bloke, isn't he? I wouldn't trust him as far as I could throw him. Well, you know what I mean; I don't think I could actually throw him.'

'Well, thank you so much, Jenny. We may have to come and take a statement from you later, and there is the potential of an ID parade. Is that okay with you?'

'Yes, that sounds fantastic. Just like *The Bill*.'

Katie hung up the call and immediately WhatsApped the images on her phone to Rook and Keene. The one from this morning was clear. The one from the night before was a little blurry, but she was right. Same man. Same brown tweed jacket, same height, build and hair just taken from the side last night but it was him. Definitely him.

'Ok, Grahame, come with me. Katie, you monitor if you've got time. We're having another interview with Alan.'

Just as they were about to leave the office, Katie's phone began to ring again. They were still on the line with her. The number she knew to be Dr Malik's. She took the call as she walked. 'Post-mortem update, boss. I'll take it.'

Katie sat at her desk, pen in hand, when her mobile buzzed. She checked the display and answered quickly, ready to take notes.

'Dr Malik. You've finished with Helen?'

'Yes. DS Lounds, you'll need to hear this. I found zolpidem in her system around four or five tablets. Enough to sedate, to render her drowsy or unconscious. But not enough to kill her.'

Katie straightened in her chair. 'So she didn't overdose.'

'No. Cause of death is not consistent with that. She had petechiae in her eyes, bruising across the collarbone, and reddening in the nasal passages and throat. Classic indicators of suffocation. She was smothered most likely while already unconscious from the sleeping tablets.'

Katie's hand tightened around her pen. 'So someone wanted it to look like a suicide, but made sure she couldn't wake up.'

'Precisely. The scene was staged. I'll complete the report once toxicology confirms, but I'm satisfied that Helen Blake's death was unlawful.'

Katie swallowed hard, her mind racing. 'Thank you, Doc. Keep me updated the moment those tox results are back, if you would please.'

She ended the call. Michael was murdered in a cathedral. Helen, smothered in her own bed, staged to look like despair. The same shadow hung over both deaths and Katie knew now it was no coincidence. She brought Keene and Rook up to date and knew what she had to do next: secure evidence from the scene.

Katie grabbed her radio and called Control. She was given the collar number of the officer who had taken over from PC Phillips at Helen's house. She point-to-pointed him.

'Hello, Sarge.'

'PC Raybould, are you still at Helen Blake's house?'

'Yes, we are. SOCO have finished, and we're about to carry out a final search.'

'Can you do a couple of things for me before you both leave, please?'

'Sure. What do you need, Sarge?'

'Could you seize the pillows from Helen's bed, and re-do some of the house-to-house on properties with CCTV or door cams? We're looking for a female on a pushbike around the same time the blue BMW was parked outside between ten and midnight.'

'Leave it with us.'

'I know it's getting late, but it's urgent. Thank you.'

Katie updated both Inspectors over the phone. Keene was less bullish and offensive than usual. She updated them with the information from Dr Malik and confirmed her conversation with PC Raybould.

DI Rook did the introductions and then started with the questioning.

'Alan, we're resuming the interview. Since we last spoke, further evidence has come to light. We now have your phone and a witness that places you at Helen's address at the time she was killed.'

His eyes were darting around. 'My phone? What about it? What witness? Some mad old bag?'

'The messages you sent Helen Blake. Ten fifteen p.m., you told her you needed to see her. At ten twenty-eight, you told her you were coming to her address. Do you deny sending those?'

'I… don't remember.'

'Last night, you don't remember last night?' (Leaning in) 'We also have an eyewitness. Someone who saw you in Edward Blake's BMW outside Helen's house that night. You said you hadn't been there. You said you didn't take the car. Both lies. Do you want to explain?'

His breathing was quickening, and beads of sweat appeared on his brow. 'No. They're mistaken.'

'Alan, this is your chance. The lies aren't working. Your phone, your messages, your presence in Edward's vehicle, and fingerprints on the medication it all puts you at Helen's. You need to start being honest. You were there, Alan. Helen was alive when you arrived. Tell us what happened.'

Briggs sat with his head in his hands, silent for what felt like an eternity. 'Alright! Alright!' He slammed a palm on the desk, then dropped his head into his hands again. 'I'll tell you everything. But I haven't killed anyone.'

'Good. Then you'd better start talking.'

Briggs took a breath. 'I'd been seeing Helen on and off for some time. She was working at the accountancy firm, doing some clerical work, when they reported a burglary. I took her statement, and that's how I got to know her. We only saw each other about once a week, usually when she knew Michael was away or definitely at work, and when Ewan was either at school or at Edward's.'

'You know you should have declared your interest in this case as soon as his body was found?'

'I know. I know this is the end of my career. Even though I haven't killed anyone, I've been stupid. Things had been getting a bit heated. She thought Edward had seen us together in a pub over in Narborough. She said he was threatening to tell Michael and ruin their marriage. He was bitter because he and Pam had split up after he'd been having an affair.'

'Go on.'

'I told her I would have a word with him. She called me on that Wednesday night to say he was at a meeting on

Queens Street. She said she would let me know where he was later, and I could go and find him and speak to him, somewhere away from the house. I didn't hear from her for hours. I knew Dom was at that meeting, so I asked him to let me know when Edward left. Told him Edward had the long grey woollen coat and Michael had the expensive "undertaker"-style black coat, as he was struggling to tell them apart. About two a.m., Dom said he had left, but he had lost him. Helen then called to say his phone ping had died; it had popped up again near St Martin's Square. Dom was out with his mate, so I asked him to have a look and let me know where he was.'

'Where were you all night?'

'I was nowhere until about two a.m., then I came into town. I sat in a bar and waited for an update. God knows what I was thinking in the middle of the night. Desperate to not get caught having an affair, maybe.'

'Killing Edward would stop him telling Michael, wouldn't it?'

'I've told you, I didn't. It got to about three-ten-ish; that's when Helen had told me his phone had pinged up in St Martin's, so I had a look around there. It was cold. The rowdy, stupid drunks reminded me of my uniformed days standing outside the rancid clubs, waiting for the drunk, puking idiots to go home. I'd had enough, so I went home without seeing Edward or Michael.'

'How would Helen know where Edward's phone pinged? Or is that just your cover story now Helen is dead? Or was she actually tracking you to Michael, and you knew Michael wouldn't be a problem to your relationship if Michael were dead?'

'I don't know. No, I didn't see either of them.'

'Did you take Michael's mobile phone from him when he was dying, or from the cathedral when we arrived? Be honest. You know this is the end of the road for your job and your pension. Just be honest.'

'No, I didn't. I haven't had his phone at all. Haven't seen it. You say you've got it, check it track it. It's never been in my possession, I promise you.'

'I take it this is why you denied finding any evidence of your son's car in town on the CCTV, even when we knew it was there?'

'Yes, I'm sorry. Obstruct police, pervert the course of justice, I know.'

'Tell me about the BMW car keys. We know you "borrowed" them?'

'Opportunity. I didn't know he would leave his keys at the front desk. I just wanted to listen to what he was saying to Katie. It just sprung into my mind. Helen was refusing to talk to me after I failed to speak to Edward about his threats to tell Michael. She was refusing to see me. She thought I'd killed Michael. I thought if I turned up at hers in his car and knocked, kept myself out of view, and she looked out and saw Edward's car, she'd open the door. So I took the key, made a copy and returned it. My plan was to pick it up, drop it back off without him knowing after I'd seen her.'

'So why didn't you take it back? Why did you dump it in a field? Would've been a much better set-up to leave it back, seemingly untouched at his house.'

'When I left, a woman walking her dog went by. As I got to the car, I had my back to her, and she said, "Evening, Edward. Sorry to hear about your brother. How's Helen doing?" I turned around, and when she saw it wasn't Edward, she said something like, "Who are you? This is Edward's car, isn't it?" She also mentioned someone on a bike looking into the car earlier when she'd gone for a walk. I panicked, dumped the car five minutes down the road, and called a cab.'

'What happened in the address?' asked Rook gently, leaning in.

'She didn't want to see me when I messaged. I turned up, knocked, she looked out, let me in, assumed she saw the BMW. When she opened the door, I just pushed in. She was in a right state. She said she was scared, scared of other people, scared of me. I tried to reassure her. She said she thought I might be involved with killing Michael, and that meant she was involved as she had led me to him. I tried to tell her I didn't find him, either of the brothers. She was hysterical. I told her to go to bed. She said she couldn't sleep. I told her I'd make her a hot chocolate and she could have some sleeping tablets. She said she didn't want tablets as she couldn't swallow them. I told her I'd help her take some. I know I shouldn't have, but she needed rest. I crushed two up and put them in the chocolate. I put the packet on the side with the mug. She said she couldn't take them whole, so I didn't think she would go and take more and overdose. I only put two in there, I swear. I waited until she fell asleep, half an hour or so, and I left. I couldn't find the key to lock the door. I just left.'

'She was asleep and alive when I left. I gave her two sleeping tablets that wouldn't have killed her. Outside, I saw a woman walking a dog, and a woman on a pushbike cycling up the road. I thought I'd seen her before but couldn't place her, only caught a glimpse.'

DI Keene stepped in. 'We think we know who the woman with the dog is. It may be nothing, irrelevant, but describe the lady on the bike. If you're innocent, Alan, you need to remember details to help us help you.'

'I only saw her for a few seconds. She looked at me, I looked at her, and then she cycled down an alley. The lady with the dog spoke to me, I panicked, and drove off. The woman on the bike was probably about forty, maybe European. She wasn't pure white. She was on a pink bike and didn't seem to be pedalling much, so I guess it was one of those electric ones. It was hard to tell her height while she was on the bike. She was wearing a black North Face puffer jacket and a black cycling helmet.'

As she listened through the monitor, something flickered in Katie's brain, something she'd seen a few days ago but couldn't remember. It was starting to niggle. She looked at Alan on the screen. For once, she thought he was probably being honest and straight up. Maybe not telling them everything, but what he had said was probably right. She started to feel a twinge of pity, but then snapped herself out of it.

'We will leave it there for now, Alan. If no one has anything else to say, I'll end the recording.'

'One last thing, Alan. DS Lounds had a voicemail go through to her work number in the early hours from Helen. She had been desperately trying to get hold of me. Did you listen to that and delete it?'

Briggs lowered his head. 'I was there when the call came through. I heard it as she recorded it. She was saying she needed to see Katie, but for her not to bring me, as she thought I was involved in some way. I knew I wasn't, so I deleted it. I didn't know she was going to die.'

'You do realise, if you had just let Lounds know the urgency of the message, she could have spoken to her. If you hadn't killed anyone, there wouldn't be any proof, so it wouldn't matter. But we could have taken steps to protect her. Move her from her home, and she may not be dead now. Ewan may at least have one of his parents left,' said Rook, looking terribly disappointed with his colleague.

'I have nothing I can say. I know the consequences now of everything that I did. I didn't think she would end up dead. I'm sorry. It's no consolation, but I am. I'll never be more sorry about anything. Don't you think I've played all this over and over in my head, my culpability, everything?'

'Interview ceased at nineteen forty-two.'

Briggs was taken back to the custody desk, looking forlorn, tired, his shoulders slumped. None of the confident, cocky Alan remained. He was booked back in and placed in a cell.

CHAPTER 23

Katie spoke with Rook again.

'I'd like to go back with Reeves, if I could, to do the second interview with Casey. Now we know what Alan says, see if he confirms.'

'You don't think it's him stalking you?'

'I know it's his car, but something isn't right. Look, I've had another message since he was locked up, so it can't be him.'

'Ok, if that's what you think, off you go. I trust your instincts; you've not let me down yet,' he said.

'I'm going to have someone come with me with a bodycam, and I'm going to go through Briggs' locker and get a warrant to search his address. There are a few outstanding enquiries we still don't have the murder weapon, the knife. We've got to dot the i's and cross the t's.'

'Right, boss. Long day, but we're getting close. Something is niggling me about that cyclist's description it'll come to me.'

Katie located Reeves sitting at his desk, going through statements and telephone messages. She updated him with what Briggs had said during his interview.

'We need to clarify a few things with Casey, see if he backs Alan up.'

'You think Alan is telling the truth that he didn't kill either of them?' queried Jane.

'I'm beginning to believe him. He's in the wrong, he's tried to mess up our investigation, but I don't think he actually killed either of them.'

Katie went to join DC Jane Reeves for the interview with Casey. She wanted to see his reaction, to find out whether he recognised her or if he was telling the truth about it being a friend who had asked him to follow the red Honda. Casey had already met with his solicitor. The recording equipment was set up, and all legal formalities were completed.

There had been no flicker of recognition towards Katie when she walked in, not one. Maybe he had been telling the truth. He didn't even give her a second glance; he surely wasn't that good.

Katie began, 'So Dominic, let's recap what you said last time.' She let 'Dominic' float, and he didn't react.

'So Dominic is the name you go by?' He nodded.

'Mum wanted to call me Alex, but Dad said it sounded like a girl's name, so everyone knows me as Dom, apart from Mum, who calls me Alex, and you lot, of course.'

'So, DomiNICK,' she said, deliberately stressing the last syllable. 'You're also known as, or give your name as, Nick to some people. Like the people at the cathedral. Why?'

'Don't want them knowing my business, do I?'

Katie pulled a still from the CCTV from Queens Quarter Apartments and slid it across the table.

'So this is you the person they all know as Nick. You were at the ledger meeting, and that is how you know Michael and Edward.'

'Yup.'

'But you didn't really know them, couldn't tell them apart other than by their coats, so when Michael left wearing Edward's coat, you thought it was Edward. Your dad wanted to speak to Edward, but it was Michael you found by mistake.' He remained silent, staring down at the photograph. 'Do you realise your mistake may well have cost Michael Blake his life?'

'I've not done anything. Dad wanted a word, that's all,' Reeves asked.

'About what?' she said.

'A woman,' he explained.

'I dunno. Knowing my dad, he was probably seeing some other bloke's wife.' Katie and Jane looked at each other.

'So are you going to tell us who your dad is now?'

'No comment.'

'Well, it doesn't matter, Dom, because we know,' said Katie, leaning in and making eye contact with him.

'No, you don't. You're trying to trick me, trying to pretend you know so I give you the name when you don't really know.'

'I'm not allowed to lie to you in interview, Dom. They might in American cop programmes, but here in England, we can't do that,' the sergeant said.

'No comment.'

'Ok, your dad has been arrested on suspicion of murder, and he is at another police station right now. He's being interviewed.'

'You're lying,' he said, starting to appear very panicky. Getting up from his seat, he punched the table.

'Sit down, Dominic,' she said, putting her hand gently on his arm. 'Getting irate isn't going to help.'

'I'm not high-rate,' he said, punching the wall but sitting back down. Why do so many youths think it's "high-rate," Katie thought to herself, smirking.

'Detective Constable Alan Briggs is your father. We know that. We have your phone; we have his, the one you were communicating with.'

Casey looked deflated. Tears started to run from his eyes into his cheeks.

'My dad hasn't killed anyone, Miss, I'm sure of it. He wouldn't do that. He's a bloody idiot when it comes to women, he's stubborn as hell, but he wouldn't kill anyone.'

'Did you speak to him after you directed him to the lane near the cathedral?'

'Yes, the next day.'

'What did he say?'

'He said he couldn't find him, assumed he must have got a cab, had a go at me for getting him out the house when I couldn't even do a simple thing like follow someone.'

'Has he ever said anything to you after that that made you think any different?'

'No, honestly, no.'

'Do you know where he was last night? Were you with him at all?'

'No, I was at mine with my girlfriend. We got a pizza and some beers, didn't even hear from him.'

As he was talking, Katie kept on. 'Has he ever borrowed your car?'

'No.'

'Have you ever given him a lift anywhere, let's say since that night at the meeting?'

'Yes. A couple of days later he asked me to take him to Countryforde or summat, something to do with picking something up. He went in, was about fifteen minutes, and then came out again.'

'Does Countesthorpe sound right?'

'Yeah. Come to think of it, it was one of those dead-end roads, some posh houses down there, a bit of money. A car came and parked right outside, and he came out the side door and got into the car and told me to drive.'

'Did your dad give you anything to look after, or anything to get rid of after the meeting night?'

'What do you mean?'

'Anything, did he give you anything?'

'No.'

'Ok, I think we are about done, Dom. Do you know me? Have you seen me before?' she asked, not expecting an affirmative answer given his reaction to her.

'No, I don't think so.' Katie looked at him and believed him. Maybe he was telling the truth that his passenger had just wanted him to follow her, and he had taken no notice, just doing what his friend asked.

'Just one other point to recap from your first interview, if I may. I know you won't give me a name, but you said your friend asked you to go to the village where the red Honda was for sale, and that you saw the car in town a few days ago and tried to follow it for him. Was the person who asked you to do that your dad?'

'No, a mate from a masonry course, not Dad, I promise.'

'Will you give me his name? I believe what you have told me today. I just want to clear everyone's name who isn't involved.'

'I can't, he'd kill me. He said he's killed someone before, but he's full of bullshit.' Even though he said that, he looked genuinely concerned.

'Do you know the person who was in that Honda, who it belongs to?'

'No idea. I never saw anyone, Miss, honestly. You do a favour for a mate and see what happens.'

'Talking of which, you did your mate a favour on Wednesday,' Katie said, looking at her notebook. 'What was in the duffel bag that you dropped off at the industrial estate in Oadby that evening?'

'I've no idea, nothing to do with me. He said he had to drop something off to a mate who had a car repair business there. Didn't ask out. Just drove, that's all he was just using me, I guess.'

'Ok, thank you. If there's nothing anyone else would like to say for the time being, I'll end the interview there.'

Katie nodded and returned to her desk, locking her papers away. Jane yawned from across the room.

'Long day, Sarge,' she said, glancing at her watch. They had been on duty for nearly fifteen hours, which wasn't unusual during a live murder enquiry. Both women looked and felt exhausted.

'You can say that again. Who'd have thought when we came in this morning that we'd be dealing with a second death, two arrests for murder, and one of them from our own team? It's been hectic, to say the least. You get off home, Jane. I won't be far behind.'

'See you tomorrow, Sarge,' Jane replied, spotting Keene at the door and straightening slightly, her tone a touch more formal.

Katie's stomach was rumbling. She had only eaten a pasta salad all day and was starving, but at the same time too tired to eat.

'Hungry, Lounds?' It was Keene walking across to her desk.

'Good call. I'm not patting you on the back just yet, though.'

'Understood,' she replied, but it was something that he had actually given her some praise rather than trying to belittle or undermine her.

'Sounds like you need this more than me,' he said, holding out a sausage roll in his hand.

'Take it, Lounds. It's not often I give my grub away.'

'Thanks, Sir,' she said, a little startled at his change in attitude. He walked away back to Rook.

She unwrapped the sausage roll as she walked down to the changing rooms. Night shift was on; Friday night would be busy in town, and they were all kitting out for the nighttime economy shift. There was a lot of chatter, noise, and grumbles as they got ready. Katie remembered back when she had to stand out in front of pubs and clubs while predictable drunks made the same stupid jokes about weeing in a policeman's hat and offers of 'arrest me' and 'can you take those handcuffs home with you,' splitting up scuffles and trying to avoid those throwing up. Being January and very cold, she bet that each one of them was hoping to get a nick in early so they could bring their prisoner in, into the warmth of the station and sit for a while to do some paperwork. She didn't envy them at all.

Katie drove home, thinking about the case, wondering what they had missed, what the final link would be to crack it. They had two in, but she wasn't sure that they had murdered Helen or Michael, or if they had acted alone or together, or if someone else was involved. The streets on the outskirts of town were busy as she drove home; it was dark, the street lights and snow kept it illuminated.

She pulled onto the drive of the farm and parked outside her barn conversion. Monty was sitting on the windowsill. Poor old Monty though she always left him two bowls of biscuits in the house, he still made her feel guilty when she was at work all day by running straight up to his bowl as though he was starving. He did just that as she went in she emptied a tin of tuna into his bowl.

She went and showered, got changed into her pyjamas, and collected Monty from downstairs along with a custard doughnut from the bread bin. She made her way to bed.

Her bed was most welcome. A heavy duvet made her warm very quickly as she finished the cake. Her bedroom had been plain cream walls when she moved in, but she had made it homely, with some pictures her brother had painted, some colourful throws, and some framed vinyl album sleeves. She liked her bedroom; despite the pressures of the job, it helped her feel more relaxed. Monty was washing himself before settling down.

Katie was trying to clear her head of the case to be able to sleep when her phone lit up. Her heart sank. 'I spy with my little eye,' and a photo of Katie's red Honda appeared. The back of her neck prickled; the shiver wasn't because of the cold. She couldn't tell where the photo had been taken; it was too close up.

It wasn't Briggs. It wasn't Casey. It had to be the passenger whoever that was. Eventually, she fell asleep.

CHAPTER 24

Back in the Office, they regrouped. Rook, Katie, Tom Ilkley, Jane Reeves, Rick Owen and Dean Brenton, all ready for potentially another long day.

From yesterday, they had a few confirmations and some additional information.

Edward's car had been recovered, immaculately clean other than lots of dog hairs on the driver's seat and Michael's phone being in the front pocket.

CCTV enquiries last night had yielded some footage from a couple of Helen's neighbours.

Brenton had made a tray of coffees and picked up some chocolate croissants from the supermarket on the way in, so they helped themselves to breakfast as Tom set up the laptop for them all to view the CCTV.

They watched the footage. It was as Alan had stated. Edward had turned up in his car; it was at a distance, but you could see it was him. Some time later, a person cycled by the house with the camera, which was a few doors down from Helen's. It showed someone, most likely a female, wearing a black puffer jacket, hip-length, with what looked like a green hoody, hood up but under a wonky black cycling helmet. The bike was pink and had a unit attached to make it electric-assisted. The rider didn't look directly at the camera; they cycled by Helen's house and the car a couple of times, just staring.

The bike cycled up to the BMW and stopped. The rider got off, laid the bike against a garden wall, and walked up to the car. She was then obscured by the car as the footage was from a house opposite and the rider behind the car, but you could see the driver's door opening and the rider sitting inside for a few moments. She then came out, picked up the bike and walked it off, down between the two houses. They didn't leave the street.

Five minutes later, Briggs comes out of Helen's address, gets into the BMW and drives off. They watched for a little longer, skipping the footage. Six minutes later, the cyclist emerges from down the side of the house and cycles out of the street.

Katie stood up. 'I need to ask Edward and Alan a question.'

'We'll have to arrange further interviews and get the solicitors here.'

'It's just a question. I want to know if Alan's dog sheds hair. It's an XL, so probably not much.'

'Okay,' said Rook, 'tell me.'

'Edward's car is immaculate. He wouldn't be driving around in a car full of dog hair. If it's not Alan's dog, and the photo shows long black and white hair, then I think we've got our suspect.'

'What are you thinking?'

'A female gets into the car, plants the phone, goes in and kills Helen, who had an issue with Edward and Helen?'

'Pam Blake,' she said, answering her own question. 'She'd want to frame him after finding out Ewan could be his, and after he lied to her about not being able to have children. She's got a bike in her flat, and she's got Clyde, that big St Bernard who sheds like mad. His hairs would've been left on the car seat when she sat in it to hide the phone.'

'Hell, you could be right. And doesn't she have the boy with her now?' asked Tom.

'I'll ring the Sergeant at Beaumont to go and ask Alan the question. You go to the cells and ask Edward,' said Rook.

'Will do,' said Katie. 'Tom, can you organise a couple of uniform with a van to be on standby? If I'm right, we need to go for Pam Blake straight away.'

Katie made her way down the stairs into the custody suite. She spoke to a sergeant behind the desk, explained what was happening, and was told Edward was in cell twenty-three. She walked around to desk two and down the corridor of cells, the smell the usual acrid stench of feet, sweat and vomit. Katie looked through the spy hole and could see Edward just lying on his bed, staring at the ceiling.

She opened the hatch, making him jump and sit up.

'Edward, it's DS Lounds. I just need to ask you a quick question.'

'Not unless my solicitor's here. No chance. You've already tried to fit me up.'

'Edward, this is urgent. It's a general question, not about the murder specifically. It's also about Ewan's safety.'

He stood up abruptly. 'What's happened to him? Is he okay?'

'The officers who recovered your car said it's pretty immaculate inside. Is that normal?'

'Yes, I have it valeted twice a week inside and out. Why?'

'When did you last have it done?'

'On the way home from work on Friday.'

'So, you didn't drive it between having it valeted and it being stolen?'

'That's right. You believe me, it's been stolen.'

'Had you been to see Pam, or seen Clyde since, maybe on your way home?'

'No. What's this about? What have Pam and Clyde got to do with this?'

'The car seat is covered in black and white long hairs. Do you think Pam would hurt Ewan, Edward?'

'No, no. Oh shit, I don't know, maybe to get back at me if she thinks he's mine. Oh shit, shit, please do something. You think she killed Michael instead of me, then killed Helen and framed me. It's all coming together. Find her, please. Save my boy.'

'Thank you, Edward.'

She left him, the metallic clunk as she slid the hatch back up echoing in the corridor. He was screaming and pacing back and forth.

She rushed back up to the offices. Rook had spoken with Alan via the custody phone. He was bemused at the question but said his dog wasn't shedding at present and it was brindle.

'Okay, team, we need to get over to Blaby. Pam needs bringing in, but be careful. The thirteen-year-old boy is also there; he's had enough trauma already,' Rook allocated jobs and who was to go with them. They made their way, arranging to meet the crew with the van in Enderby Road car park.

They congregated in the car park close to the stairs to the flats above the shops, just out of view of the window. The walkway outside Pamela Blake's flat was narrow, paint peeling from the walls. Katie glanced at DI Rook, who gave a small nod. Katie rapped firmly on the door.

'Pam, it's DS Lounds and DI Rook. We need to talk to you. Can you open the door, please?'

At first, silence. Then footsteps inside. A pause. The sound of a lock clicking back. The door opened a fraction. Pamela's face was pale and tight. She took four or five steps back, backwards into the living room.

'You shouldn't be here,' came a response.

'We need to come in, Pam. This isn't the way to deal with things.'

The door opened wider. Katie's heart dropped. Pamela had a knife in one hand and in the other arm, clutched close, was Ewan, wide-eyed and crying.

Pam's voice was high and trembling. 'You'll let me walk out of here, or I swear I'll hurt him. Don't think I won't.'

Katie raised her hands slowly, palms out.

'Pam, no one wants anyone hurt. Not you, not Ewan. Just take a breath. He's frightened. Let's put the knife down and talk.'

Pam pressed the knife closer to Ewan's neck. 'Don't you dare patronise me. You've ruined everything. All of you. He's all I've got left.'

Ewan whimpered, his hands gripping Pamela's jumper. Katie kept her gaze steady on Pam's face, her voice calm, deliberate.

'Look at him, Pam,' Katie pleaded. 'He's terrified. You don't want him remembering this, do you? You're his aunty. He needs to know you protected him not that you hurt him.'

Pam's eyes flickered, uncertain, her grip wavering for a second. Katie seized the moment. Clyde was barking near the kitchen door. For a big dog, he looked scared.

'Pam, look at me, not him. You want me, don't you? Not Ewan. You're angry at me, not your nephew.'

Pamela's focus shifted to Katie, rage twisting her features.

'Nephew? Nephew?'

As her arm loosened around Ewan, Rook lunged forward, yanking the boy free and pulling him back into the hall. Ewan sobbed into his chest as Rook shouted,

'Got him! Get uniform in here now!'

Pam shrieked and launched forward towards the door, knife waving around. Katie tried to sidestep but felt the blade slice across her bicep, hot pain blooming down her arm as she felt warmth and wetness flood her sleeve.

Through gritted teeth she said, 'Knife down, Pam! Now!'

Pamela swung wildly again, but Katie grabbed her wrist, twisting hard. The knife was still tight in Pam's grip. They crashed against the wall, Katie pinning Pam with all her strength as two officers thundered up the stairs, one with his taser drawn.

'Taser! Put the knife down!'

Pam tried to lunge towards the officer with the taser, and a scuffle broke out.

'We've got her, Sarge!' someone shouted as the knife clattered to the floor.

Together, Katie and the officers forced Pamela to the ground, cuffing her hands behind her back as she screamed incoherently.

Rook appeared again, Ewan safely behind him, his face streaked with tears. He bent down beside Katie and said quietly, 'You alright, mate?'

Katie glanced at the blood running down her sleeve, her breathing ragged. 'I'll live. Get her out of here before he sees anymore.'

Pam was dragged to her feet, still thrashing and shouting Edward's name, as Ewan buried his face against Rook's chest. Rook handed Ewan over to TDC Ilkley, instructing him to take the boy to one of the police cars. They would have to bring him to the station until a decision was made about whether Edward would be released, or if he could speak to Ewan or get him to his grandparents.

Then it occurred to Katie that Ewan may not yet have been told his mother was also dead. What a bloody mess, she thought. This poor boy, mum and dad murdered, possibly by his aunt who had been holding a knife to his throat. He would have some serious stuff to deal with in his head in the years to come.

'Boss, I'm not sure if he knows about his mum,' she sighed, looking quite upset and in a lot of pain.

'I think we will get a family liaison officer to contact Edward's parents. We have no idea of any other next of kin for Helen at this time. Speak to them, give them the news, and then see if they will take Ewan for the time being. Whether he is Edward's or Michael's son, they are still his grandparents.'

'I'll speak to the lads staying on scene, make sure they feed Clyde and leave him with some water. We'll see what we are doing with Edward. If he's released, he can collect the dog; otherwise, he may have to go to his parents for the time being too,' said Jane.

The car park echoed with Pamela's screams as the officers half-dragged, half-carried her down the flight of stairs. Ewan's sobs had quietened, muffled against TDC Ilkley as he kept the boy close, protected.

Katie followed, her sleeve sticking to her arm where the knife had cut her. The sting grew sharper with every step, but she kept her face composed. She couldn't let Pamela see weakness.

Pam was shrieking, 'Edward did this! He set me up! You're all blind, every one of you! You'll see, you'll see!'

Neighbours' doors cracked open as they passed, faces pale and curious. Uniformed officers demanded they stay back.

Out on the car park, the blue lights of the waiting van reflected off wet tarmac as it pulled around to be in front of the flats. Pamela fought the officers, legs kicking, face contorted with fury.

'Get her in before she takes someone's head off!' shouted one of the uniformed officers. She was shoved into the back of the van, still shouting.

Rook indicated to Katie to say the words. She had figured it out; it was her arrest:

'Pamela Blake, I'm arresting you on suspicion of the murders of Michael Blake and Helen Blake. You do not have to say anything, but it may harm your defence if you do not mention, when questioned, something you later rely on in court. Anything you do say may be given in evidence.'

Pamela spat in her direction. 'Rot in hell, all of you!'

'Thank you,' Katie said to the taser officer, walking the uniformed officer and TDC Tom Ilkley back up to the flat. 'Could you two remain here and do the search? I would like the knife seized, plus we need you to search for a few other things.'

She glanced around the flat, her eyes settling on the far end of the room where the clutter had gathered. The heraldic shield that had once held two crossed knives now held none. One used on me, maybe one used on Michael, she thought.

'Can you get that knife down to Dr Malik at the LRI? Ask him to see if it matches the wounds on Michael Blake. Let's find out if this knife, or its counterpart, could have been the murder weapon. I'll give him a call; he may be able to do it from photographs. Bring the shield as well.'

The PC nodded.

'We are also looking for a black Northface puffer coat, a green hoody and…' She stopped as she spotted it. That was what was niggling her about the description and the footage.

She walked over to the pile of clutter, moved a mirror and revealed it. 'We need this foldaway, pink electric bike taking back to the station too, please.' Again, the PC nodded.

'Continue with the search. Anything with blood on it, mobile phones, digital tablets you've had a read of the job anything relevant. Oh, and bodycam and photograph everything in situ before you take it, please. We need it tight.'

'Yes, Sarge,' said PC Phillips and Tom Ilkley in unison.

'Oh, can you give Clyde a quick walk so he can do his business and then leave him some food? He may have a long day without anyone here,' she added, stroking Clyde, who had bounded over to her for some fuss after all the chaos. She leant down and gave the huge mound of slobbering fluff a cuddle. 'It'll be alright, boy.'

The van jolted as it pulled away. Inside, Pamela rocked back and forth on the bench, cuffed, muttering Edward's name over and over like a curse. The two uniforms watching her from the rear of the van, through the cage, remained silent, letting her burn herself out.

In the unmarked car behind, Katie sat with a paramedic, her arm bandaged hastily. The sting throbbed under the gauze.

'That'll need a couple of stitches. You were lucky it didn't go deeper into the muscle.'

Katie gave a thin smile, glancing through the van's rear window at Pam's silhouette thrashing inside.

'Lucky isn't the word I'd use.'

Rook sat beside her, grim-faced, one hand rubbing his temple.

'Hell of a mess, Lounds. But you kept that lad alive. That's what matters.'

Katie looked out at the rain-streaked Leicester streets flashing past. 'We'll see if it's enough.'

The echo of iron doors and the buzz of fluorescent lights greeted them as Pamela was hauled to the custody desk, still wild-eyed, her voice hoarse from screaming. The custody sergeant raised an eyebrow at Katie's bandaged arm. They had brought her to Euston Street even though Edward was already ensconced in a cell, but she did not know that and hopefully would not find out.

'What've you brought me this time?' asked the custody sergeant.

'Pamela Blake. Two counts of murder. Violent on arrest, cut DS Lounds with a knife, still agitated. She'll be charged with GBH later. You'll want her on constant watch,' replied Rook.

Pamela spat again, straining against the cuffs.

'You've got the wrong Blake! It's Edward! He's the snake!'

The sergeant barely blinked, jotting down notes. Katie stood back, suddenly weary, her arm throbbing in time with her heartbeat, heavy when she tried to lift it.

Rook leaned close, speaking low enough for only her to hear.

'Get stitched up. Leave her to stew. When she's calmed, we'll go again.'

Katie gave a curt nod. But inside, her thoughts were racing. Would Pam crack, or would she still blame her husband?

Whilst Pam was booked in and taken to her cell to cool down, Rook went back up to the office. TDC Ilkley and PC Phillips continued with the search and later returned to the station with their bounty. Katie made the phone call to Dr Malik. The cut was very distinctive on Michael's body, so he could make an initial assessment from scale photographs on the knife from a few angles. She had forgotten it was the weekend and apologised profusely. She arranged for Tom to do that.

She slipped off to the walk-in centre; she couldn't bear the thought of six or seven hours at the LRI just waiting to be triaged. She was back within a couple of hours with some temporary strips, her arm cleaned up, and a warning that she needed to get stitches done as soon as possible. But she wasn't going to forgo the chance to interview Pam.

DS Lounds' voice cut through the stillness of the interview room. 'This is a formal interview under caution. It is being recorded both audio and visually, and is being monitored by others in another room. Pamela Blake, you have been arrested on suspicion of the murders of Michael Blake and Helen Blake.'

Pamela's eyes flickered, restless, but she said nothing.

'You do not have to say anything,' DS Lounds continued, her tone steady, 'but it may harm your defence if you fail to mention, when questioned, something you later rely on in court. Anything you do say may be given in evidence.'

The words hung in the air, heavy, almost suffocating. She paused, letting them sink in, then explained clearly what the caution meant.

Katie stepped in, her voice calm but firm, outlining Pamela's other rights and entitlements. The room felt colder now, smaller, as if the weight of the law itself pressed in from the walls.

'Yes.'

'For the record, can you confirm your full name and date of birth?'

'Pamela Jane Blake. Eighth July 1985.'

'Thank you. Also present in the interview room is your solicitor. Can you introduce yourself?' 'Yes, Paul Holt for Barr Brown Solicitors. I am representing Mrs Blake in this interview.'

'And DC Jane Reeves is here with me. Pamela, I'm going to begin by reminding you why you're here. Evidence has come to light connecting you to both Michael Blake's death inside Leicester Cathedral and to the death of Helen Blake, later found at her home address. You've been arrested on suspicion of their murders. Do you understand that?'

Pam lifted her head. 'I didn't kill them. Either of them.'

'You'll have every opportunity to tell us your side. We're going to go through the evidence step by step.'

'I want to start by asking about your relationship with your husband, Edward. How would you describe it?'

Pam looked at her solicitor, who nodded. 'We're… separated. Things broke down between us. He was difficult to live with. Controlling at times. I've kept my distance.'

'Did you ever suspect him of being unfaithful?'

'Yes. He liked attention. He always needed to be admired. I thought there were other women.'

'Anyone in particular?'

'Helen. Helen Blake. I… I thought something was going on between them.' She sighed.

'Why Helen?'

'She and Edward were close. Too close. Always in each other's company, always whispering about something. I confronted him once and he laughed it off. Said I was imagining things.'

'And were you, do you think?'

Pam sounded bitter with her response. 'No. A wife knows. There was something. Even if he denied it.'

'And how did you feel about Helen in all this?'

There was a long pause. She shifted in her seat, her fingers tightening in her lap. 'I resented her. She had a way of drawing sympathy from everyone Michael, Edward, even the congregation at the cathedral. People thought she was sweet. I saw through it. She meddled.'

Her eyes flicked briefly to the table, avoiding his gaze.

'Did you ever challenge her directly?' 'No. What would be the point? She'd only deny it, the same as Edward. I stayed out of it. Tried to move on.'

'So you suspected they were having an affair, but you never confronted her?'

'That's right.'

'Did you ever think Edward could have fathered Helen's child?' Holt interjected. 'Pamela, you don't have to answer.'

'I wondered. Of course I did. When you're lied to enough, your mind fills in the blanks. But no, I never had proof.'

'Thank you, Pamela. We'll come back to Edward later.'

'Ok,' said Katie. 'I need to ask about your movements on the nights Michael Blake and Helen Blake died. Let's start with the evening Michael was killed, Thursday night into Friday morning. Where were you?'

'At home. I was in bed early. Around ten, maybe.'

Pam came back with, 'Can anyone confirm that?'

'No. I live on my own now.'

'So no visitors, no phone calls, no one to say you were there?'
'No.'

'Did you leave the house at any point that night, take Clyde out for a walk maybe?'
'No. I stayed in.'

'You're aware Michael was attacked at the Cathedral. Can you think of any reason your name might come up in connection with that night?'
'No. I don't go there, not anymore. My life isn't tied up in Edward's business. I've not been there since I told you, when I got the ledger for him a few weeks ago.'

DS Lounds changed tack. 'Alright. Now moving on to Helen Blake's death, Tuesday night. Where were you between nine p.m. and six a.m.?'
'Same as before. At home.'

'Again, no witnesses to confirm that I take it?' She said, the solicitor raising his eyebrow at the implied sarcasm. 'No.'

'Pamela, Helen died at her home address. Do you have any reason to visit her that evening?'

'No. I had no reason to see her. I had Ewan with me. She said she had things to do.'

'Well, you did, you thought your husband was sleeping with her. So you didn't go to Stonelea. You didn't see Helen?'
'No, I'd separated from him, not interested in what he does anymore.'
'We'll come back to that, Pamela.'

Katie pulled out a sheaf of paperwork. 'We've examined your phone. It shows you were using an app to track Edward's location on the night of Michael's murder. So you knew exactly where he was at the time Michael was killed, didn't you?'

Pam's eyes widened. 'I… I looked once or twice, yes. Edward can't be trusted. I wanted to know where he went, who he was with. That's not a crime. But that was Edward.'

'So you went to where the phone was tracking, saw Edward's grey coat and killed the wearer?'

Her voice pitch rising. 'No, no. Because he lies! He always lied to me. I wanted to know the truth. But I didn't kill anyone.'

'Pamela, we also have CCTV footage. It shows you cycling past Helen Blake's house on Friday night. And not just that the footage shows you interfering with Edward's car, parked outside. Do you want to explain what you were doing?'

Pam was flustered, looking at her solicitor, who looked stoney-faced. 'That's nonsense. You can't even see properly on those cameras.'

'It's clear enough. A woman matching your build, your bike, your coat. Why were you at Helen's house, Pamela?'

'I wasn't. I don't know what you think you've seen, but it wasn't me.'

Have you been in Helen's bedroom?

'I... I've never been in her bedroom. I never touched anything in that house.'

Katie pushed a photo across the table, showing a pillow with a small brown blotch. 'Then you have nothing to worry about. But if your DNA comes back on that pillow, Pamela, it will place you at the scene the moment she died. Are you sure that is the line you want to stick with? Oh yes, the pillow. You know we are treating Helen Blake's death as murder, not suicide. The post-mortem shows she was suffocated. The pillow we believe was used has been seized for the lab. You should understand how thorough forensic testing is these days: skin cells, sweat, trace DNA. If you handled it, we will know.'

'I didn't kill her. I don't care what you think you'll find. I wasn't there.'

'So, Pam, you tracked Edward's movements the night Michael was killed, and you were seen near Helen's house the night she died. That puts you close to both murders. But you continue to deny involvement.'

'Because I didn't do it! You're chasing the wrong person. 'DC Reeves asked, 'Then who should we be looking at? 'Edward. He's capable of it. You think I don't know the man I was married to? He hated Michael. They fought constantly over the cathedral. And Helen...' She stopped herself, then pressed on. 'She was a complication for him. If anyone had reason to silence them, it was Edward.' 'Edward Blake? Your husband?' said Reeves.

'We're separated. And yes, him. He's manipulative. Charming on the outside, but underneath... cold. He's ruined me, he could've ruined them too.' 'That's quite an accusation, Pamela. Can you back it up?'

She was so angry she was shaking. 'He used me. He lied to me. He controlled everything, the money, the house, even my movements. And he was obsessed with Helen. Obsessed. If anyone killed her, it was him.'

'So you're saying Edward killed Michael, and then killed Helen?' confirmed Reeves.

'I'm saying you should stop wasting your time on me and look properly at him.'

Holt interjected again. 'For the record, my client maintains her innocence and is offering her perspective on other possible suspects. She is not confessing to any involvement.'

Lounds made a note. 'Understood. Pamela, we'll be testing your account against all the evidence. We are going to take a short break there, while we speak to the rest of the team who have been checking lines of enquiry.'

Pamela Blake was returned to her cell where she was given an all-day breakfast microwave meal and a cup of orange squash. Katie and Jane made their way back into the incident room.

'Do you believe any of that?' Jane asked. 'No, I think it's her, we just need to firm up a few things, but I think we've got her. Why would she behave like she did at the flat if she didn't know we were closing in on her?'

Once in the office they found Rook and the rest of the team in a huddle looking at additional information. Dr Malik had confirmed that the knife images he was shown would tie up with the distinctive wound that killed Michael, though he would do a physical match-up with the knife and the injury photos if required.

Some of the dog hairs from the car seat were examined. Even to an untrained eye, it was obvious they did not belong to a short-haired brindle bully, but to a long-haired black and white dog. Tom had carefully compared them against all the hairs he had collected from Pam's flat, as well as those picked up while playing with Clyde.

'So, Pam was in the car, most likely planting the phone that she took when she killed Michael. Same make, model and colour as his brother's. It was probably only when she got home and opened the phone she realised she had the wrong phone and potentially the wrong brother.'

'Sarge, we also recovered the black puffer jacket and a green hooded top from Pam's, which potentially looks like a bit of blood on the front of the coat. It's being sent off for testing. Photos taken, I've emailed them over to you,' said Tom.

'Thanks, guys, it's all coming together.'

'We have her phone, we have the conversation about Ewan's paternity on her phone. It looks like she took a photo of it from Edward's phone and saved it,' said Brenton.

Rook took charge. 'Ok, we are going to get Briggs charged with theft of motor vehicle, pervert the course of justice, administering a noxious substance and misconduct in public office, and let him out. Keene is going to go across and do that now.'

They looked forlorn. For all that they weren't great fans of Alan, it would have an impact on them and how the public would be treating them until it blew over with another scandal.

'Edward, I want to hold him a little longer to make sure he and Pam weren't in it together, so let's hold off on him for now. Right, you lot, get some food while Pam has her break and meal. Jane, Katie, you can go back and carry on and see what she comes up with now we have fresh evidence.' The officers nodded, exchanging quick glances before moving   off.
'Boss.'

After everyone had eaten and got a new interview plan ready, they went back into the interview room with Pam and her solicitor.

DS Lounds again opened the interview and confirmed the introductions.

'Pam, can you tell me the last time you saw Edward and when was the last time he came to your flat, or have you met up with him when taking Clyde out?'

'He hasn't been since that day I had the ledgers for him. He's not seen Clyde.'

'Specifically, has he been to your flat either Friday or yesterday, or could he have been, does he have a key?' 'No, he hasn't been, he hasn't got a key. I've been in, so he couldn't have been there. I moved to get away from him, I wouldn't let him have a key would I? I'm glad to see you are finally taking me seriously and looking at him. Thank you.' Pamela grinned and nodded and made a small fist pump of excitement. It was to be short lived.

Katie leaned forward, ready to pile on the pressure. 'Pamela, I need to make you aware of further evidence. Your flat has been searched. The heraldic shield I saw earlier displayed two knives. When it was recovered, there were none. Dr Malik has confirmed that the injury Michael sustained is consistent with the missing blade. Where is it? Not the one you used to stab me.'

Pam's eyes narrowed. Virtually spitting, she said, 'Oh for God's sake. You're twisting everything! Anyone could have taken that knife. Anyone. Edward probably came and took it, to frame me!'

'You've just said he hadn't been since the ledgers night which was weeks ago. That he doesn't have a key. We'll verify that. But there's more.' She paused to let the thoughts settle. 'The bicycle we saw on CCTV near Helen's house, and the one the witness describes, on the night she died, has been recovered. It was at your address. Exactly the same make, model and colour, with the electric bike conversion kit on it.'

Slamming her hand on the table, she shouted, 'That's a bloody lie! A filthy, stinking lie! You think some stranger knows me better than I know myself? They didn't see me, they saw...' She stopped abruptly, breathing hard. 'They saw you, Pamela. How do you explain that?'

'Edward! Edward set this all up! He's been after me for years, you don't understand. He's always been cleverer, sneakier, always twisting things to make me look like the fool. He wanted Michael gone, he wanted Helen gone, and now he wants me in here rotting while he plays the victim!'

DC Reeves leaned in. 'So you're saying Edward planted the bike at your flat, a bike I saw days before Helen was killed? That he removed the knife from your shield? That he staged CCTV?'

Pam began hysterically laughing, realising most likely her story wasn't going down as well as she hoped. 'Yes! Yes, don't you get it?! He's capable of anything. He makes people believe whatever story he wants. And you lot, you lap it up like children at story time!'

'You're becoming very agitated, Pamela. Are you sure there isn't something you want to tell us now, before more evidence comes in?'

Sneering, she replied, 'You think you've got me cornered? You think I'm stupid? He ruined my marriage, he ruined my life, and now he's laughing while you all sit here and accuse me! You don't know what it's like living in his shadow, always second best, always the spare!'

'Pamela, stop. I'm instructing my client not to answer any further questions at this time,' interjected Holt. Ignoring him and almost shouting, she said, 'Edward did this! Edward killed them both, and you're all too blind to see it!'

'For the record, the suspect is shouting and appears extremely distressed. We'll pause the interview here.'

CHAPTER 25

They had a short fifteen-minute break where they got a drink for Pamela and allowed her time to talk to her brief before resuming.

'Ok, preliminaries out of the way. I have reminded you that you are still under caution and of your legal rights and entitlements. Are you ready to proceed?'

Pam looked beaten, resigned. Katie hoped that she had pushed herself to the edge, realised her lies weren't stacking up, and was going to tell them what happened.

'I just want to check, Pam, that you feel ok to continue. No illnesses we need to know about, no mental health problems, fit and well to proceed?'

'I'm fine, no issues, thank you.'

'Anything you want to add before we carry on?'

'No.' She sat with her head bowed.

'We have recovered your black puffer jacket that you were wearing at Helen's. It appears to have blood on the front. Is that Michael's?'

'No comment.'

'The black coat and the green hoody that you wore on the footage have both been recovered from your address. Do you have anything to say about that?'

'No comment.'

'Earlier in the interview you said Edward hadn't been to your flat or seen Clyde for a couple of weeks. His car has been valeted, but when it was recovered the driver's seat was covered in long black and white dog hairs, just like the trousers you had on when arrested. When did you go in his car?'

'No comment.'

'You also previously said that there was no evidence that made you feel Ewan was Edward's, but that's not true, is it?'

'No comment.'

Katie pulled some paperwork from her folder, turned it around to face Pam, and pushed it towards her. She made no effort to look up or look at the paperwork.

'Can you have a look at this, Pam, and tell me if you recognise it?' Nothing. Not a sound or movement.

'This is a screenshot of some messages between Edward and Helen. This was on your phone.'

Still no response.

'Ok, for the benefit of the tape, I'm going to read the messages, Pam.'

DS Lounds began to read the thread.

'The first message is from Edward. 'Come on, H, be about right, he's mine, isn't he? 'We've got to stop, we shouldn't have started it up again.' 'You said that years ago.

But here we are, something good has come out of it. Ewan. 'Don't deny it, you know he's mine. M couldn't have made a good, strong, intelligent lad like him.' 'Leave it, Ed. ''

' 'I can't leave it. I'll get a DNA test, a paternity test done if need be. You know M was away for that whole month when you fell pregnant.' 'Why ruin both our lives? Pam will never forgive you. ''

' 'She's so naive, she doesn't need to know. I just need to know. ''

'Ok, ok, enough, stop. I don't need to hear it. Do you know how many times I've read over those bloody messages, seeing if I could interpret it a different way? I can't. My husband was having an affair with his brother's wife and fathered her child. I thought I was his aunty and I'm really his step-mum.'

'Tell us what happened, from the start,' Katie asked, sensing she was about to crack.

'It was me. I killed both of them. I didn't want to hurt Michael; it should have been Edward. It was dark. He had his coat on.'

'Take it slowly.'

'I was tracking Edward in town, like I told you. I got an Uber into Leicester at about three in the morning. It took around twenty minutes. I started the iPhone tracking again and saw where it was flashing. I looked down a side street and saw Edward, well, the grey coat he loved so much. Edward must have been close, or his phone would not have led me there. I followed him. He was moving slowly, seemed dazed. It was dark. I had Ewan's ski mask that he left at ours, so I put it on. I picked up a bit of brick or rock from where some work was being done. I do not know why. I already had the knife with me. He was loitering. I crept up behind him. He must have heard something because he started to turn, but before he had fully turned I hit him with the rock. He stumbled and fell. I panicked and ran round the corner. A few minutes later I peeked back into the alley to check, but he was gone.'

Pam stopped and took a drink from her polystyrene cup that she had been chewing.

'You will make sure someone looks after Clyde, won't you?'

'Of course.'

'I panicked. What if he had seen me? So I walked down the alley which led out onto the front of the Cathedral. The door was ajar, keys in it, so I walked in. He was in there, holding his head, still stood up, his back to me, alive. I took off my shoes as they had noisy heels. It was dark. I walked up behind him and stabbed him once in the back, and he fell on the flagstones in the nave. He must have had his phone in his hand because it dropped onto the stones. I walked around him to pick it up. He groaned and it made me jump; he wasn't dead. I jumped back and knocked a ledger off the shelf onto the floor.' Her brow furrowed.

'I don't know why they were on there. I picked up one of the candlesticks and hit him on the head again, then dropped it. My hands were shaking. I put my shoes on and ran out. I locked the door, but then I heard voices echoing down the street, so I left the other one unlocked and ran back up some side streets, across an underground car park. The cold air stung my face. I sat there, heart hammering, just in shock, for maybe half an hour. Then I hailed a black cab and went home. I don't remember what I did with the keys, maybe the same as the knife.'

She paused, tears streaming down her cheeks, shoulders trembling. Neither officer moved or spoke, the silence pressing down like the night itself.

'It was only when I got home and looked at the phone, I saw a picture of Michael and Ewan on the screen. I thought that was odd; I couldn't get into it. I looked at my phone and tracked Edward. His phone was still showing in Leicester, near High Street. Edward must've been around the Cathedral too, as that's where he tracked. I didn't realise at that point. I thought maybe they'd picked up the wrong phones at the meeting. I couldn't get hold of Edward even the next day; I tried. Then you found the body. Helen contacted me to say Edward was dead, and that confused me even more.' Tears were rolling down her face. 'Why did Edward have Michael's phone?'

Reeves asked, 'Do you want to take a break? I know this is hard for you.'

'No, I need to get it out. Edward eventually turns up, and it's obvious I've killed Michael.'

She continued wiping her eyes.

'What did you do with the rock and the knife, Pam?'

'I threw them both in one of those industrial skips before I got the taxi. It was full; I assumed it would be taken away quickly. I've had to comfort Helen and Ewan knowing what I'd done.'

DS Lounds encouraged her on. 'Go on, what happened next?'

'You interviewed me, but it didn't sound like you were even considering me a suspect, so I tried to just carry on, behave as normal as I could.'

'What happened with Helen?'

'She brought Ewan round to me, asked me to look after him. Whilst I love the boy as my nephew, I loathed the fact he was my husband's son, and Helen knew that and she was letting me look after him, like she was taking the mick and rubbing it in my face that she was still seeing my husband. I was angry. I wanted her gone and Edward gone. I decided to go and see Helen. If she denied the affair, I'd show her the messages you've got. The night Edward came to see the ledgers, I sneaked his phone away. His nose was in the books; I read what I needed to, took pictures of them, and put it back. He hadn't changed his password since we split up: date of birth, easy.' She paused to wipe her face on her sleeve.

'I went to Helen's. I went on my pink e-bike, as you saw. I don't drive and don't have a car. I took the phone with me. I was going to leave it at hers somewhere, then somehow let you know that Helen had it, maybe try and divert your attention onto her. But when I rode into the street, I saw Edward's car was there. My blood boiled. I cycled up to it, and for some reason it was unlocked. I got into the driver's seat and just sat there, trying to decide what to do. I thought about waiting for him, confronting him. But then I remembered the phone. I hid it in his car and turned it on. I suppose your lot were probably already tracking it.'

'Ok, that confirms how long dog hairs ended up all over the driver's seat.'

'Yes, it gets everywhere, as you know, Katie. Edward would have hoovered it if he saw any hairs. Well, then I heard someone coming, so I cycled down the side of the house. I saw the car drive away. I went into Helen's. The front door was unlocked, but I knocked. No answer. I opened the door and called her. It wasn't late; she is usually up until at least midnight. No answer, so I went in. I figured Edward just left; I'd try the bedroom.'

'The door was wide open. I looked in, and she just looked asleep, but laid out all proper, dainty like. I saw the tablets on the table. I felt her pulse was slow. Then something in my head told me to finish her off, that it would look like an overdose. So I used a pillow, pushed it down on her for a short while. There was a weird noise coming from her. I removed the pillow. For some reason I went and washed my hands. I came back, and she wasn't breathing, no pulse. I put the pillow back. Sat her up a bit straighter, like she just fell asleep, and I left. I cycled home. It only took about ten or fifteen minutes at most on the bike. When I got back, Ewan was still sleeping.'

'It wasn't Edward at Helen's house, Pam. His car had been stolen. We have proven that he wasn't there.'

'Oh God, I thought that was the last betrayal, that she had given me Ewan so she could have Edward round.'

'Did you leave Ewan on his own?'

'Yes, he was fine. He's almost fourteen, plenty old enough. Clyde was there. He wasn't in any danger. I went home; he was asleep.'

'We are extremely grateful to you for being honest. There's one more thing we have to do, as you know there was a bit of a kerfuffle when you were arrested, holding a knife.'

'Yes, I know. I'm sorry, Katie. I panicked. I knew it would be my last day of freedom if I let you take me,' she said, looking directly and honestly at Lounds.

Reeves did the official arrest. 'Pam, I'm further arresting you on suspicion of grievous bodily harm against DS Lounds. You remain under caution. Do you understand?'

'I do. As I say, I was scared. Thought I could get out past you, Katie, and escape. I didn't think anyone would tackle me when I had the boy with me. I launched at you to get by you, and the knife cut your arm. I didn't do it on purpose. I didn't want to stab you; I just wanted to get away, but I accept I cut you. I hope it's not too serious and doesn't leave any lasting problems.'

She seemed genuine and remorseful, so they did not bother to question her any further. She was admitting cutting Katie; an ABH or section-twenty wounding wasn't going to add much when she had admitted two murders.

Pam was returned to her cell to await the charging confirmation from the Crown Prosecution Service.

The custody desk was quiet, the air heavy with the smell of disinfectant and tired officers finishing reports. Edward Blake stood at the counter, pale, dark circles under his eyes. He rubbed his hands together nervously as Katie approached, file tucked under her arm.

The Custody Sergeant spoke. 'Mr Blake, you're being released without charge.'

Edward looked up sharply, eyes flicking from the sergeant to Katie. 'Released? That's it? What about… what about Pam? And Ewan?'

Katie drew a slow breath. She'd done this before delivered hard truths but this time there was no satisfaction in it.

'Edward, Ewan's been taken to your parents for now. An officer will take you to Pamela's flat to collect Clyde. Make sure the dog is cared for too.'

Edward frowned, confused.

'Why? Where's Pam? What's happened?' Katie met his gaze.

'Pamela has confessed. She found out about your affair, about the paternity of Ewan. She followed who she thought was you into the Cathedral and killed Michael by mistake. Later, she went to Helen's, saw your car outside, and killed her. Pamela will be charged and remanded to court.'

The colour drained from Edward's face. His lips parted, but no words came at first. When they did, his voice cracked.

'She was hoping to kill me?' He looked stunned.

'No… no, this is this is my fault. If I hadn't… if I hadn't been with Helen, none of this would've happened. Michael would still be alive. Helen would still…' He broke off, swallowing hard, his eyes sad. 'I've killed them as surely as she has.'

Katie stepped closer, her tone steady but softer.

'No, Edward. Pamela made those choices. Not you. You made your own. How she reacted to those, that's her doing. What you need to think about now is Ewan. He's lost both his parents. He's going to need stability, patience… love. That's what will matter to him.'

Edward's shoulders sagged, his voice a whisper.

'How am I supposed to tell him? What do I even say?'

'You don't tell him everything. Not now. And not about… not about what you think regarding his paternity. Right now, you just make sure he knows he's safe. That he's cared for. The rest… the rest can wait.'

Edward nodded faintly, staring at the floor, as though the weight of the world pressed down on his back.

'We'll have an officer drive you to the flat. Collect Clyde. Then go to your mother's. Ewan will need you.'

Edward finally lifted his eyes, gratitude and devastation tangled together. 'Thank you, DS Lounds.'

Katie gave a small nod, but as she watched him walk away with the desk sergeant, she couldn't shake the thought: no matter what the law said, Edward would carry this burden forever.

The incident room buzzed with the sound of keyboards, phones, and tired officers. Stacks of files were piled on desks, takeaway coffee cups balanced precariously between folders. The whiteboards, once covered in speculation, now had neat ticks and notes across them.

Tom Ilkley and Dean Brenton sat side by side, eyes red-rimmed, fingers flying over the keyboards as they cross-referenced notes into the case file.

Brenton eased into a chair. 'That's it then. Confession on record, timeline checked, exhibits logged. Should be with the CPS in the next half hour.'

Ilkley stretched, rubbing his temples. 'Feels weird. We've been chasing leads for days, and now it's just paper.'

Dean exhaled slowly, glancing at the neatly typed pages. The weight of the investigation still lingered in the room, despite the paperwork making it feel sterile and final.

Jane Reeves glanced over her monitor with a tired smile.

'Paper is evidence; that's what makes it stick, Tom. Without it, none of the running around means a thing.'

At that moment, DI Keene stepped out of his office. His expression was its usual mix of irritation and weariness, but there was a different note beneath it. Something almost like pride.

'Right. You lot. I've just had it confirmed Pamela Blake's confession we're happy with. We've got her on the two murders. CPS should rubber-stamp the charges before long.'

There was a ripple across the room. Relief. Fatigue. The collective exhale of a team that had carried the weight of two deaths for some time.

Keene looked over towards Katie. 'And I'll say this, Lounds, you've done well. You've worked with the team, kept your head, and pulled your weight. First murder enquiry's a tough ask. You didn't drop it.'

Katie blinked, caught off-guard by the compliment, and then gave a small smile. 'It wasn't just me. This was a team effort.'

Rook spoke up. 'True. But it was you who put the pieces together the bike, the CCTV, the shield. Without that, we'd still be second-guessing.'

A murmur of agreement spread across the team. Katie shifted, slightly uncomfortable at the attention.

'Alright, enough back-patting,' said Keene gruffly. 'You've done your jobs; that's what you're paid for. But I suppose a pint won't hurt. Meet me at The Horse at eight-thirty sharp. First round's on me.'

'You heard him, a free pint off the governor. That's rarer than a confession in an interview,' said Tom, grinning.

Laughter rippled around the room, shoulders relaxing and tension easing.

'I'll hold the phone. We'll go and have that pint. Grahame doesn't put his hand in his pocket often. I'll take the call and be around to do the formalities with Pam once they've authorised the charges,' added Rook, giving a small shrug.

'It's a shame we had to lose one of the team before we got the result,' said Jane, shaking her head.

'All his own doing. He made his own bed, so to speak,' Katie responded. The group let out a rumble of laughter.

'It was someone else's bed which was his problem,' one of the lads added, and more laughter followed, heads nodding and eyes crinkling at the edges.

The room relaxed. Paper still shuffled, phones still rang, but the cloud over them had lifted. For the first time in a while, the team felt like they could breathe.

The snug was warm, noisy, and full of the kind of rough laughter that came only when the pressure finally lifted. Katie stood back a little, glass in hand, watching her team. Brenton was doing a poor impression of Keene, which had Reeves nearly spilling her drink, while Ilkley rolled his eyes with exaggerated despair. Even Keene allowed a thin smile to creep across his face.

Katie felt a tightness in her chest, but for once it wasn't anxiety. It was belonging. She'd doubted herself when she joined the murder investigation team, doubted her authority, doubted whether she could ever really fit. But looking at them now, the banter, the trust forged in long nights and difficult truths she was glad she'd made the move.

Setting her empty glass down, Katie slipped her coat from the back of her chair. She pulled it on, turning the collar up against the night.

'Home,' she said softly to herself.

She gave her team one last look, a flicker of affection in her green eyes, then slipped out into the cool Leicester evening. The air carried the scent of rain. Her car waited under the streetlamp, and for the first time in weeks, she thought of something other than murder. Monty, her adoring boy, would be stretched out on the sofa, tail twitching in mock indignation at her lateness. She smiled. A quiet night with him was all she wanted.

Katie unlocked the car, slid behind the wheel, and started the engine. The sound of the pub faded behind her. For the first time in days, the weight on her shoulders felt just a little lighter.

Katie pulled into her yard, the rain easing to a fine mist. The thought of Monty waiting for her softened the hard edges of the day.

She killed the engine and sat for a moment, breathing out slowly. The case was done. The team had pulled together. She'd proved herself.

Her phone buzzed.

She picked it up, expecting a message from Reeves or Ilkley still ribbing each other from the pub. Instead, the screen lit with a photograph. Katie froze.

It was her, caught mid-step at the pub doorway only minutes earlier, coat collar turned up, walking towards her car. The shot was close, far too close, as though the photographer had been standing right there on the pavement, their presence almost breathing down her neck.

Beneath it, a line of text.

'See you soon, Katie.'

A shiver traced down her spine. She stared at the screen, the silence of the car pressing in around her.

The murders might be solved. But someone was still out there. Watching. Waiting for their moment.

AUTHOR BIO

Marie Goodacre lives in Leicestershire, where her crime novels are set. Having spent her working life in the criminal justice system, she brings authenticity and real-world insight to her writing. When not at her desk, she enjoys reading, comedy gigs, and live music. Marie is currently working on further cases featuring DS Lounds.

www.ingramcontent.com/pod-product-compliance
Lightning Source LLC
Chambersburg PA
CBHW050546190726
48283CB00007B/2024